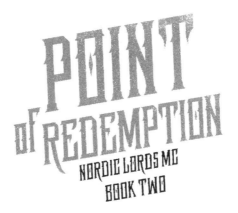

POINT of REDEMPTION

NORDIC LORDS MC
BOOK TWO

STACEY LYNN

Editing provided by: Taylor K's Editing Services

Cover design provided by: Cover It Designs

Internal formatting provided by: Fictional Formats

POINT of REDEMPTION

PROLOGUE

Ryker

Five years earlier

Faith wrung her hands together nervously as we sat in my Ford pickup. Spring was just hitting, which meant the days were still cold as shit, and even though heat was blasting through the vents, Faith shivered in her seat while clutching and unclutching her hands around the shoulder strap of her seatbelt for something to do.

"This is going to be bad, Ryker," she finally said, her eyes watching me hesitantly. "This is going to kill my mom."

"I'll talk to my dad, baby." I reached out and ran my hands down her jet black hair. So beautiful. My fiancé was gorgeous. And kind. She was sweet and tough at the same time, and she had eyes like diamonds that could pierce you with just one look. I'd loved her since the moment I turned sixteen. I wanted to marry her for two years, and two weeks ago, she finally agreed. I couldn't be fucking happier. I had everything I wanted—everything I needed—sitting right next to me in my pickup.

What I couldn't sit back and do was let the club turn on Faith and her mom, Roxy, because they had to take out her dad. It wasn't their fault he had become so nervous and jittery and willing to turn his back on the club for something he didn't do. But any show of disloyalty had consequences in our world, and Danny Winston faced his earlier in the night with a bullet to the head.

With my hands at the bottom of her long locks, I yanked lightly at the end until she brought her eyes to mine. I cupped her cheek with my other hand and pulled her forward, pressing my lips to her soft and silky ones before I rested my forehead against hers.

"I'm sorry, honey, but you know it had to happen. The club will still have your back though, babe. I'll make sure of it."

Fuck Faith's mom. I didn't give a shit if she was left to rot. Her drug addiction made her bitchy, insane, and a completely loose cannon. I would have been thrilled if the club had taken her out as well if it hadn't meant that all of Faith's family would have been gone.

She shook her head against mine. "You need to patch in, Ryke. They won't listen to you otherwise, and your dad won't do shit. It's the only way my mom will survive." She paused and swallowed slowly. The pain and sadness in her words hit me in the chest. I hated seeing her upset. My hand moved to her neck. I could practically feel the lump inside of her throat. Her pain and fear saturated the small space between us. "Knowing she's still connected to the club in some way, it's the only way…"

"I won't, Faith." It wasn't the first time we'd had this argument. My brother, Daemon, and I wanted nothing to do with our old man's motorcycle club, The Nordic Lords. We wanted our women, we wanted our lives, and we didn't want the chains that came with the darkness that shrouded the lives of the men we'd seen growing up.

She blew out a shaky breath and pulled away from me, staring out the window. When she closed her eyes slowly and then opened them, I could see the distance she was putting between us. I never understood why she wanted the club life so bad, except for the reason that it was the only thing she'd ever known.

"Go inside, babe." I reached across her lap, opened the door to her side of the truck, and pressed another kiss on her cheek. "I'll go talk to my old man and see what he can do to protect your mom now."

A tear rolled slowly down her cheek, taking some of her black mascara with it. More tears welled in her eyes. Her voice was emotionless when she spoke. "My dad's dead, Ryker. He turned on the club, and there's not a damn thing anyone can do about it. There is no way the club will watch out for us now." She shook her head, looking lost as she climbed out of my truck. She faced me once her feet hit the ground, one hand on the door and one on the side of the truck.

"I love you, Faith. I'll be back soon."

She pressed her lips together and nodded jerkily. Then she slammed the door, rocking the cab of my Ford. I stayed in the driveway in front of her small, bungalow-style house and watched my fiancée walk to the stairs, shoulders curled forward and head down, completely defeated.

Fuck. I ran a hand through my black hair before slamming it against the steering wheel. The horn blared through the quiet air, making Faith jump at the doorway. Her head whipped around to mine and I saw everything she was feeling.

I waved my hand in apology for scaring her before I put my truck in reverse and made the short trek across town to talk to the Nordic Lords' Vice President—my dad.

For her, I'd patch in and join the club. I'd give her anything she fucking wanted in life if it would erase the sadness in her crystal clear blue eyes.

1

Ryker

Present Day

I looked across the deck of the oil rig. This rig was where I found my solace from the noise in my head that still hadn't faded after five years. Every two weeks, a knot tightened in my gut when we boarded the helicopter and headed back to the mainland of New Orleans for another two weeks where I'd drown my memories before they ate me alive. The rig used to feel like a reprieve from all my bullshit. Lately, it had felt like a prison sentence.

"Heli's loaded and ready to fly." Our rig captain, Tucker, clasped a hand onto my shoulder and gave me a small shove as he hustled by me on his way to the helipad. The sound of the whirring blades almost drowned out his shouts when he yelled at the other men who had been waiting for the final preparations to be made. Gear had been weighed, along with the men. Heli checks were completed, and we were ready to fly.

I followed the rest of the men into the helicopter and felt a forceful breath leave my chest once I buckled into my seat and put my headset on. We were three miles from the rig, still twenty minutes from land, when Tucker's voice came through my ear piece.

"You coming out tonight or are you headed back to your ball and chain?" He was almost old enough to be my dad, and even though there were eight other men on the bird with us, I knew he was talking to me. A few snickers came through the headset following his question.

"You doing anything different tonight besides pissing and moaning about how much your lives suck while you get drunk?" I asked in order to avoid any questions about Meg.

From across the small aisle, my friend, Pete, caught my gaze and shrugged, giving me the silent answer that he was up for whatever. Besides Pete, no one knew the arrangement I had with Meg. Pete had been friends with Meg's husband, Byron, long before I met Byron. I showed up in New Orleans with nowhere else to go and got to know Byron well before he landed me a job on his deep sea oil rig along with Pete. Before Byron died, I made promises to him that I could never walk away from.

I had done that once, and I wouldn't do it again.

Faith.

Bile rose in my stomach like it always did when I thought about her. Five years later and I still wasn't over the betrayal or the sting of her deception I had witnessed with my own eyes.

Taking care of Meg was easy. It came with no expectations from either of us except for financial support and friendship. Other than that, we were free to pursue whatever we wanted.

Mostly, it was me doing the pursuing. It didn't matter how often I encouraged Meg to get back out there and find a man who could truly love her again. She always insisted she was fine.

Until the day came that she changed her mind, she was my responsibility. It was the wish of a man who had come to mean almost as much to me as my own brother, Daemon. And since Byron's death was also due to my incompetence, I would honor my promise to take care of Meg and their little boy, Brayden.

Tucker threw back a laugh, breaking me out of whatever the hell my mind was starting to think about. He was a big guy with a full, closely cropped beard. He had a beer gut the size of Alabama and was as rough as any guy could be. When he laughed, his shaking stomach reminded me of the Santa Claus that Daemon and I used to see at the shopping mall when we were kids.

"You're such a shit, Ryker. Someday your heart is going to explode from all the stress you carry around with you."

My lungs began to restrict and my teeth ground against one another at the sounds of the men laughing through their headsets. They had no idea the shit I kept buried inside where no one could reach.

"Sort of like your gut." I poked my finger toward the old man's stomach. More laughter rang in my ears, along with the jeering for me to join them before they headed home for their stay.

I narrowed my eyes at the rest of the men. I had only been working on the rig for four years, but we were tight. Spending twenty-four hours a day for two weeks straight with the same, small group of men had turned them into my pseudo-family. Men who worked on oil rigs in the middle of the Gulf of Mexico had a tendency to scatter as soon as we hit the mainland. The men I worked with had wives and families all over the States. I was surprised by the looks on their faces; it seemed like this was a planned invitation and party.

"What?" I asked slowly. A muscle tightened in my jaw as I forced out the one word question.

Pete looked around the helicopter apprehensively while some of the men grinned wildly.

"Bachelor party time, Ryker."

My lips curled into a sneer in Hunter's direction. Dumbass men. No matter how many times I told them it wasn't like that with Meg and me, they never gave up.

"We're not getting married."

My shoulders shook when a hand from the seat next to me grabbed it and shoved me back and forth. I speared Hunter with a look that should have had him scared as hell, but he was too crazy to be afraid of me.

Hunter laughed with the rest of the men, except for Pete, whose face went ashen white and his hands curled into fists. "You've been banging that woman for two years, Ryker. It's only a matter of time. Besides, Tucker needs some strippers to keep him company tonight."

A small laugh escaped my throat before I could stop it. Tucker and his hookers. The man was insane and also recently divorced—probably due to the hookers he couldn't keep his hands off of.

I shook my head anyway and saw Pete relax. He understood why I took care of Meg, but he wasn't always happy with the fact that Byron told me, instead of him, to take care of her. They'd all been friends since they were kids; however, Byron understood my past. The asshole probably knew before he died that I would never be able to leave another woman alone again. Byron also understood that Pete had a life to live, whereas my life was solely wrapped up in whatever weekend pussy I could find on our "home weeks" and working on the rig.

"You guys enjoy your own hookers. I'm not interested." I clipped it out and they knew from the tight expression on my face that I wouldn't change my mind. The men gave me shit and then went on to discussing sports and something else I started ignoring while the memories that were always on the fringe of my mind fought to become forefront in my head.

I had smelled the blood outside my dad's house before I hit the front door. The metallic smell had filled the night air, and I'd reached for my gun, holding it firmly in my right hand like my dad had taught me to every day since I was six years old. *Our life makes this skill necessary, son, but never shoot unless you mean to kill. There's almost always another way before it turns to death.*

He had been wrong. Because that night, when I had gone to my dad's in order to convince the club to take care of Faith and her mom, there had been no other way.

When I'd walked up to the house, I saw Cherry, Liv's mom, lying on the couch, her brains blown all over the place. My dad was on the ground, blood drying from a wound in his head, silently struggling to stand up. Then there was a man with his back turned to me, aiming a gun directly at my brother's girlfriend, Liv.

There had been no other option in that moment. I had opened the screen door, my gun cocked and loaded. The quick squeak of the hinges on the door immediately alerted the man to my presence.

He turned and aimed his gun at me. We fired simultaneously— but also at the same time, my dad jumped to his feet to save me. Both of our bullets pierced his torso. Distracted over the fact I had just shot my dad, I let the man run toward the back door. He fired one more shot at me, missed, and then took off.

And I had let him go. I had fucked up. I had frozen and stood there while my dad bled out in front of me due to a bullet I had given him. I'd stared at the scene in front of me: Cherry dead on the couch and Liv's head hanging limply on her shoulder, completely passed out with vomit dripping from her chin and blood draining from her leg. And after Daemon and the other men in the club showed up, they told me to get the hell out of there and let them clean up the mess.

A stronger man would've gotten his shit together and cleaned up the mess himself.

Instead, I had gone to Faith. I ran to my fiancée, the woman I needed, the woman I loved, in shock and desperate for her to remove the blood and guilt from my hands, only to find her locked in a kiss with a man wearing a Black Death cut. His hands pressed into her cheeks and her fists gripped his leather cut. They made out like they were lovers while I stared at them from the driver seat of my truck, watching my fiancée making out with a man from a motorcycle club that was an enemy to my dad's club.

I did the only thing I could think of to escape the guilt, the anger, and the hatred for a woman who would so quickly turn on me. I left town and drove my truck until I hit the coast. Besides my infrequent talks with Daemon whenever he would call, I never looked back.

"Hey, fucker, what the hell's wrong with you?" The jostling of my shoulders snapped me back to reality. I wiped the sweat from my forehead and blew out a breath, staring at Pete's face as he bent over, inches from my eyes. "Where were you?"

I shook my head and noticed the helicopter was empty except for us.

"Nowhere, man," I told him, removing my headset and unbuckling my safety harness. "I need a fucking drink."

Pete grinned. He took a step back from me so I could stand up and then followed me out of the helicopter. "Let's go find some women, then."

Not exactly what I originally had in mind, but I'd take it. Easy women always quieted the nightmares in the darkness of nightfall. That and whiskey. Lots of whiskey.

"Aw man, check her out."

I almost didn't look, but Pete's eyes turned glassy as he checked out someone behind me, and I knew it wasn't from the alcohol. His lust-filled expression made it too tempting to not take a peek.

Hot damn. Long blonde hair assaulted my vision the second I turned around. It fell down her back to a tiny waist. It was a waist that made men want to dig their fingers into it. Then there were her legs. Legs that seemed to go on forever, even though she wasn't very tall.

Men fantasized about women like this. They jerked off to visions of women with her Barbie-doll shape, and I wasn't any different. She was the perfect distraction.

My lip curled, and I took a large sip of my whiskey, the ice rattling against the glass.

"Told you you'd like that," Pete said, leaning over next to me.

The bar we were at was a dump. It was a few streets over from Canal Street—just far enough away from where the majority of New Orleans tourists wouldn't typically venture. It was where Pete and I hung out for a night or two to unwind from the constant stress of not killing ourselves in the middle of the Gulf. There was a jazz musician on the stage playing his saxophone, and while I hated jazz music—never understood it—he sounded good. "Those legs… those tits… damn. She's the hottest chick I've ever seen."

I watched my buddy drool over the woman at the end of the bar as she sat nursing a glass of red wine all by herself. She looked like she could be waiting for someone, probably a man, and I wasn't in the mood for a bar fight. Not tonight.

I wanted to drown myself in my liquor, call a cab, and then head to Meg's house so I could be there before Brayden woke up the next morning.

"You can have her." I stared at Pete and watched his eyes practically go cross-eyed as he took another peek at the beautiful distraction.

"Nah, man." He tipped his beer bottle to his lips and took a slow swallow. "Looks like it's you she's interested in. What the fuck is it with women wanting tall, dark assholes like you in their bed?"

I grinned and laughed despite myself. Fuck it. If he didn't want her, I'd take her. I slapped him on the shoulder and uncurled from the barstool, rising to my full height, just over six feet. "Because women know pretty boys with their preppy haircuts and girly blue eyes are shit in bed."

"Fuck you, man." But Pete was laughing as he said it. It was the same shit we always gave each other. Pete looked like he belonged on a billboard modeling Calvin Klein underwear in Times Square, not working on a rig with a bunch of broody, overweight, and bearded men. He turned his back to the bar and surveyed the rest of the decent-sized crowd while I slowly sauntered over to the woman with the wine glass.

I caught her looking at me out of the corner of her eye before I reached her. I knew that look. It was the look that said a woman wanted you but wanted to pretend she wasn't easy, either.

As I hit the barstool next to her, her eyes darted away from me and down to her almost empty glass. A hint of a smile ghosted the edges of her lips.

"Ryker." I extended my hand.

She looked for a second, her grin growing slightly larger, but she didn't take it. I shrugged and put it back in my front pocket. It didn't matter. I didn't need to know her name. She was beautiful, and I'd gladly take her to bed for one fun-filled night. A night that included more whiskey and wine, very little sleep, and even less talking.

She looked at me, interested yet hesitant, over the top of her wine glass before finishing it off. "Your mother not like you?"

I grinned wickedly. "Take me to bed or lose me forever."

Her eyes melted into soft pools of lust right before she choked on her last drink of wine. "Pardon?"

"I'm sorry." I flashed her a lopsided grin and shrugged. I wasn't sorry. "I thought we were randomly quoting *Top Gun*."

"Funny."

"And smart." I looked down at my chest and her eyes followed. "And sexy. At least that's what the ladies tell me."

She looked at me like I was trouble. She wasn't wrong, but still, she smiled. "Arrogant, too."

"I prefer confident and charming." I splayed my hands flat on the bar in front of me, slapping it once to get the bartender's attention, and then turned to her. "Now that we have my positive attributes out of the way, let me buy you a drink."

"Another for the lady, please." I raised my almost empty highball glass. "And another whiskey for myself. Two fingers."

"Elizabeth," she said slowly, and that hint of a smile returned to her lips. "My name is Elizabeth." I caught the faint tease of an accent that sounded a bit too familiar. A bit too northern for her to be local. I blinked and nodded toward the bartender.

From the corner of my eyes, I watched Elizabeth's eyes drop to my glass… and my fingers. A pale pink hit her cheeks as she swallowed slowly.

This was going to be easier than I imagined.

I thought about starting basic conversation while the bartender refilled our drinks but stopped myself. I didn't need this woman getting thoughts in her head that I actually cared about her. That always made the next morning more of a headache than necessary.

I slipped the bartender a twenty when he slid the drinks in front of us and turned to Elizabeth. Beautiful name for a beautiful girl. She truly was. She wasn't dressed like she was seeking attention in skinny jeans and a grey shirt that draped off one of her shoulders. Her eyes stayed fixed on her drink as if she really *didn't* pick up men in bars often.

I sighed. Maybe I should give her to Pete. She almost seemed too innocent, too kind, to be mixed up with me, but I really needed to forget the memories that were still too close to the front of my mind from earlier.

"So," I started to say, but was interrupted almost immediately by the buzzing of my phone. "Sorry." I apologized and watched her take a deep breath. Gaining courage or relieved she had a break from me? Whatever. I shrugged my shoulders and pulled my phone out of my back pocket where it was vibrating away.

I expected Meg. She almost always called to see if our helicopter landed safely.

I didn't expect it to be Daemon. It'd only been a few weeks since I talked to him, but I knew he was freaking the fuck out now that his ex-girlfriend, Olivia, was back in town and knocked up by a cop they had all been friends with years ago.

Sighing, I knew I had to take it. He'd hound me until I picked up.

"What's up, brother?" I asked as soon as he growled my name. Instantly, I knew something was wrong, but I smiled at Elizabeth anyway. She watched me with nerves written all over her face and a slight trembling of her hands while she clutched her wine glass with her long, slender fingers and perfectly manicured nails. Damn, she was really gorgeous. If Daemon fucked this up for me, I'd strangle the asshole.

"I need you, Ryke."

My heart skipped a beat. *No.*

I quickly took a swig of my whiskey, draining the entire glass. Something was wrong. Daemon's voice sounded full of pain and desperation. That was the only way he'd need me anyway—if he were desperate.

I looked at Elizabeth. Her brows were pulled together, concerned about whatever was showing on my face. "I'll be back in a few minutes, yeah sweetie?" I smiled, trying to make it sound friendly and genuine. Based on her frown, I failed miserably.

Blackness... pressure was pushing down on me and stealing the breath from my lungs. Whatever Daemon had to say to me was going to fuck with my head. I knew it.

I told him to hold on before I pushed through the doors to the jazz bar. The summer humidity in New Orleans slammed against my chest, making it hard to breathe while I began pacing the sidewalk.

"What's up, D?"

His voice was shaky as it came through the phone. Shit. My brother was losing it. "I need you, Ryke. I need you here."

No. Fucking. Way.

My feet froze on the cement and I collapsed against a brick wall. The cement dug into my back through my thin black t-shirt. Back to Jasper Bay? The man was fucked outside his head if he thought that was going to happen.

"What the fuck, Daemon?"

"Liv's been shot." *Blood poured down her legs as vomit dripped from her lips, Cherry's brains splattered all over the couch.* I gasped for breath as the night almost five years ago flashed in my mind.

My dad jumped. Guns went off. Two bullets fired right before my dad collapsed to his knees, sinking to the floor.

My free hand gripped my hair before I smacked my head against the cement to get the pictures out of my head. *Blood. All that damn blood.*

"She okay?" I asked. Maybe? Something came out of my mouth, but it felt filled with cotton, so I couldn't be sure. Olivia shot? Again?

"No, Ryke. She's not. I need you, man. I've never asked you for a single fuckin' thing. But this? I need you. Shit isn't good." Daemon was impatient, angry even. I could tell he was tense and scared. Shit…

I had left him alone to deal with this once before.

But still… I couldn't.

"I can't, Daemon. You know I can't go back there." I couldn't stop the memories. Bullets. Blood. Black Death MC Member with his lips on Faith's. *Fuck!*

He growled at me, using the name brother in a way that meant something deeper between us than just our blood. Damn it. "My girl's been shot and she's lost her kid. And we have problems in the club that are bigger than any shit we've ever seen. I need you."

No way. There was no way I could do what he was asking. I had Meg to take care of now. Another promise made to a woman who lost her man, another death on my hands.

Jasper Bay was my past. One I couldn't return to.

New Orleans… Meg… Brayden… those were my priorities now.

But I couldn't stop remembering. Olivia, eighteen years old and tied to a chair with blood everywhere. It seeped from her legs and trailed down her cheeks. She reeked like piss and vomit, and her head was flopped to the side, unconscious.

I was so screwed.

I inhaled a deep breath, my eyes closed, and the heat beat down on me in the New Orleans night. My hand ran through my hair again, and I scratched the back of my neck until I hurt.

Finally… slowly… I breathed out my acquiescence. It was going to kill me to go back, but shit, Daemon was right. I had left him alone to deal with the fallout from the shooting five years ago.

I could never forgive myself if I let it happen again.

"All right, brother. I'll get there as soon as I can." Daemon breathed heavily through the phone, as if my willingness to return home allowed him to dispel the weight on his shoulders. "I'm not stayin', though. One week, that's it. I can't be there for longer than that."

I ended the call, snapped the phone closed, and slipped it back into my pocket before he was done talking again.

This wouldn't end well.

2

Faith

There was always a moment when I was working where the shame over what my life had become inevitably rushed to the surface. I hated that moment. It was the hardest part of my job… my life. I had become so well trained that my body no longer faked the physical reaction I wished I could hide.

"Come on, Diamond." James moved against me. His hands were by my head, and I turned my face and closed my eyes so I didn't have to see him. Not that James was bad to look at. As far as clients went, he was one of the better looking and nicer ones I had.

My hips rocked involuntarily, my body shook, and my arms tightened around his lower back. He released immediately after me.

It was over, and it wasn't so bad that time. The shame I felt at my inability to control my orgasm surfaced like a small ripple instead of the vast wave that normally hit me. I would not cry in front of James. I would save it for later, if I allowed the emotions to come at all.

We dressed in silence, and once I'd fixed my hair, James turned to me. He pushed his light brown hair back with one hand, his other hand loosely held his black framed glasses at his side.

"Forgive me for asking, but I've always been curious," he spoke slowly, as if he was afraid of hurting me. Ironic, yes?

I raised one eyebrow, waiting for him to finish.

"How did a nice, beautiful girl like you end up as one of Penny's girls?"

I wanted to say that my mom sold me to pay for her drug habit, but I didn't. And it was only partly true. The rest was too painful to think about—the life I had before my dad turned on the Nordic Lords. The night before my ex-fiancé, Ryker, killed his dad and took off and out of town without a word to me. One text, dismissing our relationship, was all I got. A relationship where I'd loved him since before I knew what love was. I no longer allowed myself to think about that part of my life.

The truth was... sometimes life gave people lemons, and they made lemonade.

Life gave me a handful of rinds, seeds, and pulp, and I made the most of the crap hand I was dealt.

I shrugged in answer.

"How'd a nice guy like you end up calling for one of Penny's girls?"

I had never asked a client this question, but James made me wonder. He seemed genuinely nice. He had a preppy haircut and he looked intelligent and handsome with his plastic framed glasses and the fancy suits he always wore when he called on me. He drove from five hours away just for two hours with me.

He blinked once, then twice, debating whether or not to answer.

"My wife had an affair with my best friend and I can't bring myself to touch her."

His honesty stunned me. So did the lack of emotion in his voice. "So an eye for an eye sort of thing?" He smiled, but his eyes were sad. I knew that look. It was the same look I saw when I looked at myself in the mirror. "Why don't you leave her then?"

He was silent for a bit, then turned away as he tucked his tie into his pocket and shrugged on his suit jacket. "I care about my wife and I won't divorce her. I just... can't forgive her either."

I understood how that felt. It felt strange to connect with someone whose life was so different than mine, yet full of similar pain.

"I can find someone else," he said, turning back to me, "next time."

I shook my head and smiled. It may have actually been genuine. He was nice and didn't hurt me. As far as clients went, I could spend time with worse. "It's okay. You're not so bad."

He laughed once. It was deep and rich and full of a lightness that told me even though he was going through a hard time, he had an easy life. I envied him instantly.

"You might not be so good for my ego." His eyes flickered to me and then to his wallet. He'd already paid one thousand dollars for my two hours. I was a whore, but I didn't come cheap. He handed me a generous tip with an almost sheepish look on his face. I couldn't tell if he was ashamed of what he was doing or if it was pity for me.

"So, can I ask what you do after this?"

"Shower." I regretted the quick response when his already hesitant smile flattened. I could almost see the guilt over what he'd done to me. I didn't see it on a client's face very often, and for some reason I didn't want him to feel so bad. It wasn't his fault I had the life I did.

He nodded.

I watched James walk down the hallway of the hotel and away from me. He had only come to see me a handful of times, but there was something about him—the lost look in his eyes when he mentioned his wife, the way his shoulders curved inward as he walked away, that told me how defeated he felt. It made me call out his name before he reached the stairwell and disappeared from me. I had a suspicion I wasn't going to be seeing him again anyway.

"Go home to your wife," I told him, resting a hip against the doorway, my arms crossed in front of me. I let them fall to my sides. "Figure out how to make it work."

His lips pursed together like he was thinking of saying something, but he changed his mind. He raised his chin and lifted his hand in a half-hearted wave. "Good-bye, Diamond."

Diamond.

I blinked away the memories of the dark eyes that used to croon the name into my ears as he made love to me. Stupid me for choosing that as my working name in the first place. It pierced straight to my chest every time. As if my punishment wasn't bad enough.

"Bye, James," I returned with an understanding smile before he vanished into the doorway. I watched the empty hallway, unashamed that someone could walk out of their rooms and see me in my satin robe and negligee with my hair looking freshly fucked. Everyone in Jasper Bay knew who I was—knew who I'd become. There was no point in hiding it anymore.

Turning back to the room, I clicked the lock in place before stripping back out of my clothes and stepping into the hotel's scalding hot water. I always showered before I left, needing to wash the feel of a man's hands off me immediately.

I replayed the conversation with James in my head as I dried off from the shower and re-dressed in my skinny jeans, silver ballet flats, and a loose-fitted black top that hid my figure. It was the first friendly, and potentially honest, conversation I'd had in almost five years.

I hit the back stairway intent on leaving Penny's for a night at home with my drugged out mom. I'd watch mindless television, maybe knit a scarf. If I started now, in July, I might have it done by the time winter hit in northern Minnesota. I scoffed at the idea. Screw that. Wine and ice cream seemed like a much better plan.

I was mentally creating a quick grocery list as I walked down the back hallway in Penny's. It was lined with private rooms where clients could request blowjobs and quickies. The room upstairs where I had been with James were used for the "longer term" requests and the rest were rented out by the week. Reputable men like James were rare finds as far as clients went. Most of the clients and boarders were bikers from the Black Death Motorcycle Clubs other charters passing through town for the week.

Surprisingly, the main room in Penny's was tastefully decorated. I took in the red couches and the women who sat around and tried to catch attention from the men who perused the room. They smiled, they swayed their hips, and they licked their lips. They took every good thing God had given to women and used it for evil and sinfulness, all while keeping a fake smile of interest plastered on their faces.

We were wicked women. Unforgiveable. It made absolutely no difference that I was forced into this life. It didn't matter that my mother's life and safety were held over my head in return for willingly and happily spreading my legs.

I was no different than the women who chose this life.

We all did what we needed to in order to survive.

"Diamond." The deep, greasy voice rang in my ear and snapped me back to the present. I twisted around and looked at Mills. He was gross. The worst Black Death member when it came to what he wanted physically. He actually preferred it when I acted like I didn't enjoy it. He was sick. Demented.

And I was his favorite whore.

I tasted vomit deep in my throat, but smiled pleasantly. "Yes, Mills?"

His eyes roamed my body, making me wish I could go back upstairs and take another shower. Thankfully, I was off duty for the next few days. Mills would have to wait.

He finished his slow and slick perusal of my intentionally, well-covered frame and nodded his head toward the door.

"Someone's looking for a room."

"And?" I asked, cocking a hand to my hip. "I'm off duty." The only benefit to being as good as I was at pleasing men was that I had earned the respect of several Black Death members. They let me quit working the main floor two years ago and I started working in their office handling all their accounts… at least the legal ones. Booking rooms for boarders was part of my job description. My other job description was taking appointment only clients, like James. I was, after all, the best whore in northern Minnesota.

"The client's in a hurry and Hammer's on a run." I rolled my eyes. Of course he was. The president of Black Death was almost always on a run of some sort.

"Fine," I said as I rolled my eyes.

Mills grinned. A full set of yellowed teeth appeared. By the way the light bounced off of them, they looked rotten. Like his soul.

I spun around, needing to get away from Mills, and I was in such a hurry that I quit paying attention to the people in the room until I met another Black Death Member, Slick, standing with his back to me. His leather cut stretched across his back and I knew his arms were crossed over his chest. His feet were firmly planted as he refused to let our visitor walk around him.

And when I finally saw him, I wished Slick would have kicked the man out the door, directly onto his ass.

Ryker. Fiancé.

The vomit taste was back in my throat as I skipped over his face, my brain not allowing me to focus on the man I had wished for years would come back and save me.

Stupid idiot, I scolded myself. He wasn't that anymore. He had taken off and left me alone to deal with the fallout of my dad turning on his own motorcycle club. The only opportunity to keep my mom alive was aligning with Death. Literally.

My eyes dropped to the floor and I saw his boots. I saw the jeans that fit him perfectly. I saw the wrinkly black t-shirt that stretched across his chest and biceps. I saw the black duffel bag in one hand, and his other hand rolling into a fist and releasing.

"Faith?" I couldn't keep from looking at him when he said my name. I looked up and saw him blink several times, as if he thought I was an apparition.

His jaw dropped in shock.

I wanted to reach out and slap the shit out of him while at the same time throw myself into his arms and beg him to save me, to take me away from my hell. But it was too late. The Faith he knew was gone forever.

"You work here?"

I cocked my head to the side, trying to understand how he didn't already know this. Had Daemon never told him what I had become? That thought was followed quickly by what in the hell was Ryker doing here?

The question was answered as it slipped through my mind. Olivia had been shot. Daemon probably called him. Black Death had put me on lockdown since I could be connected to her. It was the one freedom they'd given me weeks ago—allowing me to reconnect with my old friend.

Now, they wouldn't let me visit her in the hospital or talk to her. Everywhere I went was accompanied by two Black Death members tracking my every move.

I blinked quickly several times as I remembered the night Ryker had promised to fix everything. And then instead of doing that, he had left me; he'd left my life a thousand times more screwed up than it already had been.

I was here, and it was *his* fault.

My lips curved into a smile. My back straightened. I would not fall back into his trap. He wouldn't be here long, anyway. I knew he wouldn't. There was no way in hell Ryker was sticking around town.

"I'm the best they have." I watched him wince with a sick smile of satisfaction ghosting across my lips. "And you need to leave. Nordic Lords aren't welcome here anymore."

"I'm not a part of Nordic Lords." I watched his hand curl into a fist again. His shoulders were tense and his eyes scanned the room like he was prepared to take out every man in the place. He looked like he wanted to throw me over his shoulder, haul my ass out of there, take me back to his rig off the coast of New Orleans, where I'd heard he was working and living, and never let me leave. My stomach flip-flopped at the thought.

Crap.

I leveled my eyes at him, hoping my expression was close to ambivalence in order to mask the pain searing through me.

"I'm not a part of Nordic Lords," he repeated more firmly.

I shrugged. Close enough. I was about to tell him that when a warm hand came out and clasped me at the back of my neck. I moved closer to Slick, as if I enjoyed him touching me.

One side of Ryker's lips twitched as he glared at the man pretending to be my guard. In a sense, I supposed he was, considering they owned my ass.

"You need go to. Like Diamond said, we don't have a room for you." Slick stressed the "we", but we weren't and never would be a "we". I didn't bother to correct him. The less Ryker knew of me, the better.

"It looks like a lot has changed around here." Ryker still hadn't taken his eyes off Slick's hand on me. I wondered if it was jealousy. And then I wondered why I cared anymore. Ryker had been the one to leave me. If he was jealous, it was his own damn fault.

I smiled. It wasn't genuine, and I saw a flash of rage in his eyes. "That can happen in five years."

Ryker's head dropped, and he took a deep breath before drawing his eyes slowly back to mine. He didn't check me out, not the way most men did, but I still felt his gaze on every inch of my skin. It prickled with interest.

Shit.

"I supposed I shouldn't be surprised," he said, his lips twisting into a wicked grin. "You always did seem to prefer Black Death."

I scowled. What in the hell did that mean?

He left without another word. Slick dropped his hand from my neck when Ryker was gone. I turned to him and glared.

"While that pissing match of yours was fun to watch, next time, do it without your hands on me." I turned and stalked to the back office without waiting for his response. I wouldn't get one anyway.

3

Ryker

I climbed behind the wheel of the black SUV rental and exhaled a deep breath. What the fuck just happened? What in the hell had I seen? Faith? A prostitute at Penny's, which was run by Black Death?

I growled and slammed my hand against the wheel. The back of my head pressed against the headrest, and I stared at the roof of the vehicle as if inspecting the grey fabric would calm the assault on my mind.

Faith was a whore. I shook my head back and forth repeatedly, probably looking insane to the people on the sidewalk who passed by me, but I didn't give a shit.

Faith worked at Penny's Boarding House. My head dropped toward my lap. My fiancée was a whore.

Ex-fiancée.

Did distinguishing the difference matter? She made that choice when she sucked face with a member of Black Death. She didn't bother waiting for me to talk to my dad before she threw herself into the arms of another man for another club. And this was where she ended up?

Disgust over what her life had become and the life she had

chosen over me combined with a slow boil of rage I felt building inside me.

She had chosen a life with her dad's enemies over a life with me. If she wanted to earn their protection by spreading her legs, why should I give a shit about what happened to her?

I threw the SUV in reverse and hauled my ass to the hospital where I knew Daemon was waiting with Olivia. I had no desire to see Olivia sitting in a hospital bed. I pictured the eighteen-year-old tied to a kitchen chair with blood falling from her leg and resisted the urge to hurl my lunch all over the rental as I headed out of town.

Coming back was going to be a mistake.

It was going to fuck everything up.

The shrill sound of my ringing phone snapped me back to reality like a rubber band.

"Hey, Meg," I answered, one hand on the wheel, elbow propped up on the side of the door, and the phone in my other hand.

"You weren't here when Brayden woke up," she started, and I caught the nervous hitch in her voice. I cursed myself silently.

"Shit, Meg… I'm sorry. I had to get out of town in a hurry." I could picture the boy. The boy who still cried every night for his dad, even after two years. The boy who panicked when I didn't show up within an hour of me telling him I would. I had been so fucked up after talking to Daemon that I had forgotten where my priorities were.

"It's okay," she said through the phone. Some of the pressure left me. Meg was sweet. Her voice floated through the phone like she didn't have a care in the world. Like she didn't miss the man she had always called her soul mate. She actually believed in all that girly shit like fate, destiny, soul mates, and claimed she had been blessed to find hers young in life despite the abrupt and way too soon ending.

I pulled off the highway exit for the hospital and slowed my rented Tahoe on the dirt shoulder, throwing it into park. "Let me talk to him."

"I know you're busy. I don't want to waste your time."

"Meg," I scolded her teasingly. It was our way. Somehow our friendship eased the pain in my chest. "Put Brayden on the phone."

It was silent for a beat while I heard murmuring on the line and then the excited ear-piercing squeal of the four-year-old. "Rykie!"

I smiled. I couldn't help it. That boy's high-pitched voice helped calm the storm raging inside me. "Hey, little man. Sorry I wasn't there when you woke up."

"You said you'd be here." I could practically see his little chin wobble as he fought back tears. The little kid was messed up after his dad promised he'd be home after his two week stint on the rig but never made it.

"I know," I told him soothingly, wishing I was fucking back in New Orleans teaching the kid how to build a *Minecraft* world on the computer. "I had something come up that I really needed to go do, but I'll be home in a week. I promise I'll see you before I head back to the rig."

"Where are you?" He was still pouting, but hesitant. Sometimes I wondered if my voice soothed his fears as much as his voice soothed mine. I swore that taking care of Meg and Brayden helped me more than them sometimes.

I looked out the window to the never-ending evergreen pines lining the highway. *Home.* That wasn't right. I tripped over my answer, so unsure of what I was feeling.

How did I explain it to a four-year-old?

"I'm in Minnesota, little man," I finally answered.

I heard a smile in his voice. "Will you bring me something home with you?"

Chuckling, I asked, "What do you want?"

"Milk duds. A huge box."

I laughed, my earlier rage melting away. "You got it, Brayden. I'll bring you the largest box of Milk Duds I can find."

I flinched when I heard his loud shout followed by another, equally loud, clunking sound.

"Sorry. He dropped the phone." Meg's voice came through the line and she was calmer, happier, than she had been only minutes before.

"No problem, Meg. I'll see you guys in a week, okay?"

"Okay, thanks again… I know this is a lot for you."

My hand tightened on the steering wheel. "It's not a problem," I gritted out. I wasn't annoyed with her, but she always felt like an inconvenience, when in reality, if it wasn't for Meg and Brayden, I might have jumped over the edge of the rig in the Gulf one night.

The guilt of knowing you're responsible for taking innocent lives was a burden I wished on no one.

I promised her I'd call and check in on Brayden everyday while I was gone, knowing it would soothe his little mind.

By the time I reached the hospital, the calmness I had felt while talking to Brayden and Meg had evaporated. I walked the halls of the hospital, searching for Olivia's room, trying to do everything I could think of to forget my run-in with Faith.

I found Olivia's room, and from a small window next to her door, I spied Daemon standing over her bed, one hand on her cheek.

It'd been almost five years since I'd seen him. Or Olivia.

It felt like I was transported back in time to five years ago. Had I not left, I would have seen Olivia in a bed exactly like this.

Daemon spoke to her, and suddenly, something my mind had blanked on earlier rushed to the front of my mind.

Diamond. Those assholes called her Diamond. My nickname for Faith. Had she fucking chosen that as some sort of stage name?

Rage burst forth through my chest in a way I'd never experienced or felt before. My veins felt like they were going to explode as it coursed through my body, and before I knew what I was doing, I slammed open the door to Olivia's hospital room and grabbed a handful of Daemon's shirt.

My fist connected with his jaw right before he flew back into the wall.

It did nothing to stop the beast inside of me. I was panting. Noise rang in my ears like someone had pulled the fire alarms.

I heard shouting. I saw Daemon fling himself around.

I saw guns pointed at me.

Daemon screamed at me while I stood with my arms and feet braced for a return blow.

And then time stopped.

His jaw dropped. Olivia gasped. Daemon blinked, and slowly his gun disappeared behind his back while the one to my left slowly lowered, too.

"You're such a son of a bitch, Daemon. How in the hell could you not tell me that Faith was working at Penny's?" I was still panting, my rage not yet quenched. Daemon was thicker than me now, but I had four years in age on my shithead little brother. I could still take him.

He flinched and braced himself for another hit. "You never asked. Not once did you ask about her."

My hands squeezed into fists. Every muscle in my arms trembled. Was he fucking kidding me? Why would I? What was left to say after watching Faith cheat on me?

Diamond. I closed my eyes. It fucking hurt. Her betrayal. The use of that damn name I had started calling her when we were young teenagers, long before I ever knew I was actually in love with her. How could she use that name? Did the men she fucked call her that? *Why* would she do that?

I shook my head and looked at my feet. My hands settled on my hips as I gasped for calming breaths that were taking too damn long to start working.

"Ryker?" The soft voice cut through. I raised my head and saw the fear and sadness plastered on Olivia's pale face like a beacon of light. I blinked, my pain momentarily gone, and closed the space between us.

I had missed her. Olivia embodied goodness and had been like my little sister when we were growing up. Family. At one point, we had been family.

"How you doin', baby girl? I heard you got yourself into some trouble again." I smiled despite myself, and as I bent over her, Olivia's head dropped against my shoulder. My arms went around her, holding her tightly.

She had been shot shortly after finding out she'd lost her baby. When Daemon had called me to come home, he had only told me that she and the cop, Travis, had broken up right after finding out she was pregnant, but I still didn't know why they were together the day she ended up with bullet wounds grazing her shoulder and abdomen and he ended up bleeding out next to her.

Sounding annoyed, Daemon snapped, "We need to get out of here."

I pulled away from Olivia, but kept one arm around her. If it was bugging the fuck out of my brother that I was touching his girl, I was going to keep doing it to mess with him. That's what big brothers were for. Not that they were officially together yet, but I knew that's what Daemon wanted. I also knew that since he'd lost her once, he wasn't going to let it happen again.

"We aren't done with our talk," I said, watching his eyes slowly move from my hand on Olivia's back to my glaring eyes.

He sighed and blew out a breath. "Thanks for coming." He ran his hands through his light brown hair that hung to his shoulders. His goatee was a mess, and his eyes had purple circles under them. A bruise was forming on his cheek and under the other eye. Hadn't I only hit him once?

The thought of Daemon getting his ass kicked made me smile. I'd deal with the rest of all the bullshit later, but damn it all if it didn't feel good to be standing so close to my brother again after so many years away.

From the corner of my eye, I caught the man who had pulled a gun on me. He was almost as pretty as Pete, but he watched me with guarded caution.

"Ryker Knight," I told him, taking in the Nordic Lord cut and the inked alligator down his forearm. The fucking thing looked real with the scales, blue glowing eyes, and bright red tongue.

"Finn, mate. Nice to meet ya'."

His accent surprised me, but I couldn't place it. There were Nordic Lords Charters all over the world, but the club rarely had contact with international ones. I flipped through my old memories of the club.

"English?" I asked, knowing there was a charter in Manchester.

"Australian." Nordic Lords didn't have a charter in Australia, at least not that I knew of. I nodded at him and killed my own curiosity. Wherever this guy came from, it wasn't any of my business. I was only here for a week to help Daemon out.

I heard a soft sigh come from behind me and spun around, catching the eye of someone else who looked vaguely familiar. "Shit, J? You're still here?"

I blinked again, taking in her tanned skin and sun-bleached blonde hair. Last I had heard, after her boyfriend Scratch died, Jules had taken off to Arizona

She started to shake her head like she was going to correct me, but then raised her hand and waved. Her voice and fingers shook a little bit. "Hey, Ryke."

I glanced around the room. Besides Finn, the four of us had grown up together. Friends for a long time. It had never bothered me much to hang around Daemon or Liv. Even Faith was younger than me. They had all been my family, and they all looked the same and yet different at the same time.

I had to get out of the enclosed room before the weight of the past reared its vicious head again. Who knew what in the hell I'd do.

"We need to get out here," Olivia said. "I hate being in hospitals."

"Let's go then, woman." I smiled, thankful for the interruption. Then I grabbed a bag I saw lying on the floor in an effort to get everyone else moving.

4

Ryker

The Mustang was one hell of a beautiful car. I couldn't believe Daemon had actually finished the damn thing. I ran my hand slowly along the black paint job with its two white racing stripes and smiled. I remembered the shit our old man had given Daemon for hauling such a piece of crap out of the Club's salvage yard. One wheel was missing, the underbelly looked like a giant pile of rust, and the engine was missing eighty percent of it.

This car, the one in his garage, was amazing.

The Mustang was something I'd asked about days ago. But between caring for Olivia, taking her to her ex-boyfriend's funeral, and Club business Daemon had needed to take care of, this was the first time we'd been able to spend just hanging out.

"You did good, brother," I said, turning to Daemon and Jaden, also a club member and Daemon's long-time best friend. They had their asses resting up against Daemon's work shelf that ran along the back edge of the garage. Tools were hung everywhere in an organized order. Daemon hadn't touched a damn thing or moved anything from where our dad had insisted it be placed.

He raised his chin to me in acknowledgement before he pushed off the counter and walked toward me.

"There's something I need to tell you." He ran a hand down his face until he smoothed out his goatee.

I spun around, resting my ass against the hood of his car, and crossed my arms. Jaden stayed silent against the back wall, drinking his beer, his eyes narrowed on us, apparently knowing the conversation that was about to happen.

"Why do I have a feeling I'm not going to like what you have to say?"

Daemon sighed and his hands fell to his hips. "It's about Faith."

Faith. For the last several days, I had tried to pretend I hadn't seen her working at a whorehouse. I hadn't yet reconciled whether or not I cared, which said more than it didn't. I vacillated between wanting to tear her away and kidnapping her to New Orleans to start a new life away from all this bull shit versus thinking she had gotten what she deserved for turning her back on me.

Which meant, as I stood there in front of Daemon watching him nervously take me in, I wasn't going to like whatever he had to say.

My nose twitched. "Okay." I blinked, preparing myself for the worst. "And?"

Daemon looked over his shoulder and back at Jaden, who shrugged and gave him a what-fucking-ever look, before Daemon again ran his hand through his hair.

"Look, man," he started and then stopped.

His ability to draw shit out started eating a whole in my gut. "Just tell me, D."

He sighed again. "They own her. Black Death fuckin' bought her."

The words scrambled in my head until they didn't make sense. Bought her? What the fuck did that mean? I was about to ask, but Daemon kept talking. Rambling like a fucking teenage girl.

"Fuck. I knew she went to work at Penny's about a year after you left, but I thought she did it because she needed the money for her mom or some shit. I never knew she was sold to them."

"Sold?" I choked out. What. The. Fuck. My eyes widened. My body chilled as the blood drained from my face.

Daemon took a step away from me. Smart man. It felt like the garage spun in circles around me. My hands curled into fists until I felt pain burn in my knuckles. What in the hell did that mean?

"Yeah." Daemon exhaled a deep breath. "Her mom sold her to them in exchange for their protection after her dad was killed. Apparently Mills made the offer the night…" He stopped. Everything flashed in my head. "The night everything happened with dad… and Liv."

"Fuck." Had I gotten it wrong? I scrubbed my face with my hands, hoping to wash away the insanity that pulsed in my veins. It didn't work. With my eyes closed, red filled my vision until I felt uncontrollable. I spun around and punched the hood on Daemon's car. "Fuck!"

Pain shot up my arm at the same time Daemon cursed my name.

"You knew?" I shouted at him, facing him, ready to charge.

Jaden stepped forward. "We just found out."

"When?" I growled. I might have been foaming at the fucking mouth I was so pissed. "When?" I repeated, feral eyes glancing between the two men who were watching me like I needed a straitjacket. "What the hell?"

"The other night at the meet, Ryker." Daemon took a step toward me. Swear to God, I snarled at him when he moved closer. What the hell was happening to me? He raised his hands, palms out, like he was cautiously approaching a rabid animal. I fucking felt like one as my adrenaline pulsed through my body. My skin itched, my muscles shook, and my teeth ground together painfully hard until my jaw hurt.

I needed a damn drink. Or a case.

I pushed off his car and stomped out of the garage, headed toward his house—not mine—I hadn't yet let myself think of it that way, even though it was the home we'd grown up in. Gravel crunched beneath the footsteps following me until I was almost at the front door. I grabbed the handle with one hand and then let go. When I turned around, Daemon and Jaden both eyed me warily.

Pussies. What the fuck was I going to do? Go off on a one-man killing spree, shooting all the Black Death Members in town? What the fuck good would that do?

The vision of Faith with her hands clenching onto Mills' leather cut, his lips and hands all over her, pulsed in my head. She had cheated on me. Hadn't she? She had run to them when she doubted my ability to care for her. Why else would that dick have been there that night?

Unless Daemon was right. If what he said was true, then I had fucked up. I had completely fucked up the best thing that had ever happened to me.

Shit.

"How could you not fucking tell me that they own her?" I shouted before throwing the door open and letting it slam shut behind me.

Daemon followed right behind me, his entrance into the house coupled with another slam of the door. "I just did!" He threw his arms in the air.

I shouted something back at him, but I was way too messed up to think clearly. My rage fought to rush him, tackle him directly into the wall behind him like we did when we were young, and pummel the ever loving shit out of him.

But then a small little voice spoke and my breath caught.

"Mama, it too youd!"

My eyes snapped to Daemon at the same time he frowned. Who in the hell would bring a kid here? He looked like he was holding his breath at the same time he looked at Jaden.

What the hell was I missing?

And then I remembered Brayden. The sensitive little boy who used to cover his ears and rock in a corner when noises scared him. And even though nothing that happened in the last ten minutes made any damn sense in my head, I didn't want another kid scared.

With slow feet, I turned on my heels and saw her. Shit. I blinked rapidly several times at the little girl who was cowering behind Jules' legs as if it was her safe haven. One of Jules' hands was wrapped behind her, gently and calmly running her hand through the little girl's blonde hair. She peeked her eyes out around Jules' legs and bit her bottom lip. Then she ducked back into her hiding spot.

I crouched down in front of Jules after I saw her shakily smile at me, silently giving me permission to approach the little girl I assumed was her daughter. She looked like her anyway. When did Jules have a kid?

"Hey there," I said slowly. I plastered on a friendly smile, willing the rushing blood in my body to calm down. It worked minutely. "Who are you?" The little girl peeked out and disappeared again.

"To-fee. I two." I laughed softly at the muffled reply.

Jules corrected her, still smiling at me yet nervously biting her lip just like the little girl when she looked back at Jaden and Daemon behind me. "Sophie."

I nodded once and picked up a block. "I'm Ryker. Do you want to play blocks with me?" I eyed the multi-colored tower and focused. This would help calm me down. Kids did that for some reason. Get down and play at their level and it felt like all the hard shit in life evaporated. I needed it now if I was ever going to figure out what to do with Faith.

I shook her out of my head and focused on the blocks. The tower. The little girl, Sophie, who was still hiding from me. I planted my ass on the floor and grabbed the zipped bag of blocks nearby. Screw it. I'd build a tower by myself and pretend shit around me wasn't falling apart like a poorly built Lego house.

It took seconds for Sophie to peek her little blue eyes out from around Jules' leg again. She smiled slowly and, almost as nervous as a mouse, approached the tower I was starting to build. Behind me I could hear harsh breathing coming from Jaden. I hoped like he hell he would calm the hell down or get out. Based on the nervous glint in Sophie's eyes, I didn't think she was used to a bunch of large men screaming around her.

Jules sighed heavily right as Sophie and I began working on the tower. The shocked silence that had filled the room almost as soon as Sophie shouted earlier disappeared.

"You knew about this?" Jaden clipped at Daemon behind me. It sounded more like a growl, and Sophie flinched.

"Here," I whispered to her, bringing her back to focus. I handed her a blue, square block. "Where does this go?"

I tried like hell to ignore the tension between the men behind me, but I couldn't. Especially after Jaden let the term bastard fly out of his mouth. It reminded me too close to the day Meg's parents had said the same thing to her when Byron died. They had never wanted their sweet and innocent daughter tied to a blue collar man working on an oil rig.

My eyes snapped to Jules when I saw her hands curl into fists in front of me. "Scratch's kid," she snapped. I glanced back at Daemon. He didn't look surprised as his eyes darted from Olivia, where she'd been lying on the couch, to Sophie. "And don't you ever call my kid a bastard."

My mouth dropped open while I tried to hide my shock. Scratch, Jaden's brother, had died just over two years ago in a motorcycle accident. Jules and Scratch had dated forever, but due to shit going on with her dad, who was the mayor of Jasper Bay, and how differently she'd been raised than the rest of us, Jaden had never trusted her. From what I'd heard from Daemon, Scratch died the night after he and Jules had some epic fight, which sealed Jaden's hatred of Jules forever. All I knew was that within weeks of Scratch's funeral, Jules had taken off to head to college in Arizona. Her returning to Jasper Bay when Olivia had been shot was a shock to everyone.

A quick glance at Sophie told me she was definitely Scratch's kid.

Based on the growl that escaped Jaden's mouth, he wasn't happy about this news.

Jules' strength impressed the hell out of me, and I couldn't help but lean back and watch Sophie build the tower while I kept an eye on everyone in the room. Jaden sounded about ready to boil over, but there was no way in hell I was going to let him bitch out Jules in front of her daughter. I had seen enough of it with Meg's parents. That shit stayed with Brayden for days after her parents showed up and demanded she move back in with them. Jules was quieter than Meg, but just as brave as she faced Jaden, defending her daughter to him. She wiped her wet eyes and looked directly into Jaden's angry ones. "She's Scratch's little girl... I told him that night."

That night... I assumed she was talking about the night he died. All I had heard was that he had laid down his bike on a stretch of highway filled with tight curves.

"You're fuckin' kidding me!" Jaden yelled at her. Sophie flinched again, and I saw her chin do that damn quiver thing Brayden's did when he was about to cry. I had heard enough.

"Little ears! Shit Jaden, watch it." From next to me, I heard Olivia snort. The irony of my swearing while yelling at Jaden wasn't lost on me, but fuck it. Then I leaned back toward Sophie, whispering in her ear, "You keep goin', sweetie. You're doing great."

Her eyes widened at me, and for the first time, her smile wasn't scared. Something hit my chest as I looked at her. It reminded me of Faith when we were kids— the innocence and the excitement that she carried in her light blue eyes. It reminded me of Brayden and Meg and my promise to never leave them.

And everything rushed my chest at the same time I heard Jaden let out another curse in the distance right before the front door slammed closed.

I had to get out of that room with Sophie and the girls and the reminder that if maybe, just maybe, I hadn't fucked everything up five years ago, that little girl staring at me could have been mine and

Faith's. That we would've gotten married like we'd planned, started our family, gotten the fuck out of Jasper Bay, and been together like we'd always talked about.

How was I supposed to make right on any of it when there was no doubt in my head, from the way Faith's eyes had turned cold as ice when she saw me, that she hated me? Absolutely fuckin' hated me. And what good would it do to ask her forgiveness—especially now that I had priorities back in New Orleans? Meg and Brayden. I had promises to make good on in a place that was a world away from Jasper Bay.

I was fucked. Either way, I had thrown away every damn good thing in my life, and from what Daemon had told me, it could have all been some huge fuckin' misunderstanding that I hadn't been man enough to deal with at the time.

The doubt, the rage, the reality that I abandoned Faith when she needed me the most, and the fact that it was my fault—my *fault*—that she was now where she was, doing what she was doing… it exploded in my chest.

I had to get out of the room and away from the innocence of a child who had just started trusting me. I needed to get away from the murmurs of apologies to Jules and away from the damn anger boiling inside me that I would take out on the wrong damn person if any of them so much as looked at me.

I left the room, grabbed a beer from the fridge, and didn't give a shit that I heard every condiment and beer bottle rattle inside the fridge as I slammed the door shut. I was already outside, gasping for breath. My hands curled tightly into fists; I was surprised the glass in my hand didn't shatter.

I poured the cool beer down my throat, not tasting it. I didn't taste a damn thing. I didn't feel a damn thing. Instead, I stared out at the backyard, feeling nothing and yet full of memories that I couldn't escape.

Faith, her damn long black hair had always been done into braids that fell down her back. When I was twelve, I yanked on them and ran away from her as she screamed at me, trying to throw worms at my head. When I was fifteen and she was just starting to grow the first hint of tits, my showers started lasting twenty minutes, even though I was too young to understand what she did to me. When I was seventeen, the showers lasted twice as long. By then I was fully aware of the lust that hit my chest when she'd turn those light blue eyes on me.

And when she turned sixteen? Two years younger than me, but I felt like she was finally able to be with me. And I had taken it. That first time I had felt her hands on my arms and her warm skin brushed against mine in a way that didn't feel platonic? The first time it didn't feel like she was looking at me like I was her big brother? I was done for. I had smashed my lips to hers in a way that probably hurt her and all she did was take it. She had threaded her fingers through my hair and gave back to me just as badly as I gave to her. That was the night we became inseparable. That was the night I promised I would always take care of her.

Damn it. Faith had been so strong. She had never acted like it bothered her that her mom spent more time drugged out on prescription pills than she did being a mom. Faith had practically lived at our house or Olivia's, taking solace from the shit that was her life. But she never complained.

"Fuck!" I heaved my beer bottle across the yard. I felt caged in the open air. My skin itched to haul ass back as quickly as I could to the rig, where life was so fucking simple that my head could shut down and I didn't have to think about the possibility that I had broken my promise to Faith.

I had left her. I'd been the one to betray her. Maybe it hadn't been the other way around, the way I'd always thought it was. Maybe my head had been too fucked up the night I took off to see anything clearly.

Shit.

My fingers curled around the edge of the deck right as I heard the screen door bang shut behind me. I wanted to break the damn wood in my hands and then beat myself over the head with it.

From my peripheral, I saw Daemon walk closer to me, two beer bottles in one of his hands and an unlit cigarette in the other.

"That was fucking interesting," he said, handing me the beer and taking a few steps until he was leaning against the railing. I heard the distinct sound of a lighter on paper and then the buzz as the paper burned when Daemon inhaled.

I popped the top off the beer, flicked the cap into the grass, and swallowed half the beer in one gulp.

I assumed he was talking about Jaden and Jules, but I couldn't stop thinking about Faith. It was one thing to think she'd become an escort because she wanted to. Or hell, even if it was because she needed the money.

But to know she hadn't been given a choice? That her druggie, fucked up, loser of a mom had *sold* her daughter to the hands of men who were ten times more evil than the club my dad had started and served? Muscles tightened all over my body and I heard my blood pulse in my ears.

"I don't know what to do for her." I didn't look at Daemon. He knew who the fuck I was talking about and it wasn't Jules or Sophie or even Olivia. Damn it. Had all the men I'd known grown up to be the assholes we'd always claimed we'd never become?

Smoke blew through the air as Daemon smoked his cigarette.

"Free her." Two words. Easy as fuckin' pie. I squeezed my eyes closed while he kept talking. "We get this shit done the way Black Death wants and they let her go."

I turned my head and glared at him. Since Olivia had gotten out of the hospital, Daemon and Bull, Liv's dad and President of the Nordic Lords, had met with Black Death. Black Death wanted to work together to prevent the Sporelli's, a mob family from Chicago, from bringing drugs into Jasper Bay through the ports. In exchange for the

Nordic Lords help, Black Death had promised to let Faith go.

"And what happens to Faith if it gets fucked up?" And when the Nordic Lords had their meeting with Black Death to overrun Sporelli, my ass would be back on the rig, away from everything going down here. I wouldn't hear if they got Faith back until it was all over.

"We don't fuck up."

I snorted. Daemon. Ever the damn cocky bastard he always was. All sorts of shit could get fucked up with that. All sorts of shit was fucked up no matter which way I turned. I couldn't leave Meg and Brayden to take care of Faith. Hell, I didn't know if Faith even gave a shit if I did anything to step in and help her. Did I want to put my ass back on the line like that with her?

Daemon pressed his lips together and shrugged. "It's not that fuckin' hard, Ryker. Get your ass back here, join the club, and do what needs to be done." He took a long pull from his beer while I gritted my teeth.

"It's not that simple, man." I shook my head. This was why I avoided him when he called most of the time. Five years hadn't done anything to stop him from trying to get me home.

But fuck if he didn't have a point this time. My head was so screwed up I had no idea what was right or wrong anymore or where my priorities were. My anger built until I kicked the railing on his deck so hard I heard wood crack.

Daemon's sarcastic laugh rang in my ears. "You break my deck and you're fucking fixin' it."

I laughed but it sounded weak. My little brother was a dickhead.

"She has to hate me."

He inhaled from his cigarette and threw the butt toward a dirt patch just off the deck. "Probably does," he agreed. "Does it really change the fact she shouldn't be doing that shit in the first place?"

Asswipe.

"Fuck," I said and raked my hands through my hair. "I can't... I don't... shit, I can't think about this. Everything's such a damn huge mess right now." Meg. The rig. Jasper Bay. Home. Faith. Olivia. All the shit with the club that wasn't my business, but I didn't know if I could walk away from it all again. This damn town had a pull on me that I had never been able to completely shake, even when I tried to ignore it.

Daemon rested his ass against the deck and took a long pull from his beer. "Yep. Welcome to our life. It's always been this way, but you're the only one who can fix it."

My head snapped to him and I glared at him. The earlier rage began a slow simmer. Why was all this shit my problem to deal with? The fight I'd been wanting with Daemon for hiding this from me in the first place began boiling in my veins again. I watched him clock my stance. He set his bottle on the edge of the railing and widened his legs, his fighter instinct kicking into play.

"How could you let her do this?" It was an irrational blame, and I knew it. She had been my responsibility to take care of, not Daemon's. But it was someone's fucking fault and I wasn't ready to point my damn finger at myself yet. Even though I knew it was, and Daemon knew it, too.

He laughed once, loudly. "Cut the shit, man. We all had to do shit to survive after that night. You think she wanted this? You have no idea the hell she went through, and if you wanted her taken care of, you should have been man enough to step up. Instead, you ran off, so ashamed of shit when it was a fucking accident in the first place, and left the rest of us to clean up the damn mess."

My hands balled into fists. His did, too. And I waited, both of us breathing heavily. Fuck Daemon. He had no fucking clue what it was like to know that, accident or not, I was the one responsible for killing my dad. But not only that… the responsibility of knowing had I showed up minutes, maybe seconds, earlier I could have saved Olivia and Cherry. My nostrils flared and my jaw clenched, ready to take the first swing and brawl all my rage out on my family's deck. But I couldn't. Something stopped me. I looked away from Daemon, grabbed my beer bottle, and flung it out into the yard. It smashed into the grass and shattered into pieces right next to the one I'd thrown earlier.

I was panting. An angry fucked up mess full of regret and shoulda-coulda-woulda's. From behind me, Daemon laughed.

"You're cleanin' that shit up, you know."

I laughed. And damn it, it felt good to do it, too. For a split second I was able to let all of it go. I let my rage evaporate into the air as I stared at the evergreen forest, knowing that Daemon had my back. Literally. He was younger and he was an asshole, but he would always be there for me. It helped me take a deep breath and, for a moment, chill the hell out and enjoy hanging out in the sun while standing on the deck and having a beer with my brother.

It only lasted a moment though before Faith's cold eyes flashed in my memory. I sighed. "I don't know if she'd want my help." Turning around, I rested my ass against the deck railing to see Daemon turn toward the house and hit the door frame.

A wicked smile threatened at the corner of Daemon's lips, like he had me caught in a trap. "This is Faith."

Three simple words. They slammed into my chest almost knocking me off the deck. What the fuck was I thinking? Damn it. Meg would understand. Hell, Meg was always the one telling me I had to move on and how she hated that she felt like I got trapped by Byron's forced promise. It was just one more trip to help the club get Faith out from underneath Black Death. Then she could do whatever she wanted.

I sighed and looked out to the forest of evergreens that surrounded the property. Free Faith. Head back to New Orleans. Take care of Meg. I could keep all my promises.

What a fantasy. I blinked and reality returned. "Faith hates me."

Daemon laughed off to my side. I wanted to punch him in the mouth for finding anything funny about this. He didn't know. "Probably, but there's only one way to find out."

My eyes snapped to him and I arched a brow, waiting.

He grinned and pushed off the railing, closing the gap between us. "Make an appointment, and go talk to her."

Was he fucking mad? Or stupid? Make an appointment to see my ex-fiancée, the whore? Those two words rattled in my brain until I knew I only had one choice.

I had to free Faith.

"Make an appointment." It came out as a whisper as it passed my lips. I shook my head, still disbelieving how much everything could change so quickly. And I knew as soon as that happened I would crave more. I would need revenge and justice for the men who had taken Faith in the first place. "You need help for that Sporelli bullshit in a few weeks?"

"Yup. You want in?"

I licked my lips and pressed them together in between my teeth. Simply asking the question changed everything. The answer was already obvious. "Yeah, brother. I'll be here."

I followed Daemon into the house. As I passed him, he slapped his hand on my shoulder, shaking me. "Welcome home, man."

I snorted and went to the fridge for another beer. "One big happy fuckin' family."

5

Faith

Days after seeing Ryker and my head was still clouded by the recent memory of him. Why did he have to look so freaking good? His short black hair that brushed over the top of his ears, his muscular chest that had filled out over the years, and his dark black eyes that I still saw when I closed my eyes.

Damn him. Damn him for coming back to town. I wanted him gone.

He was messing with my head all over again, even though besides that one run-in, we hadn't spoken. Not like I expected him to hunt me down and apologize for running out on me.

Or maybe I did. And the fact that he hadn't? That he hadn't tried to contact me despite the fact it'd be virtually impossible with Black Death watching my every move these days, it stung. It hurt.

I truly meant nothing to him. For years I hung onto the idea that Ryker would realize the mistake he made by running away. That he'd come back from the South, he'd beg for my forgiveness, and after being a bitch and giving him shit for leaving in the first place, I'd forgive him. We'd finish our happily ever after.

Now I was faced with the truth.

He didn't love me.

Maybe he never had.

Emotions that had been so easy to keep buried were at the forefront of my mind since seeing Ryker's scowl in the very entrance of Penny's last week. I stared at the doorway, squinted my eyes, and pretended I could still see him standing there. Wishing I could ask the one question I had always wanted to ask.

Why did you leave me?

I remembered the night. The night I cried about my dad, my fear of my mom's already shaky mental stability. The night he promised he'd do whatever he could to help my family despite my dad's screw ups. And then I had heard nothing from him. Despite sending him hundreds of texts and voicemails over the course of the next few days, I heard no response.

Until one week later when I got the simple message: *Not coming home. It's over.*

That was it. I could see the words stamped in my memory as if I was still staring at the screen on my phone. It's over. It's. Over.

And now, he was so close, yet still so far away. I couldn't do anything except ask the questions over and over again in my head. What had I done wrong? Why wasn't I enough? Why did he leave?

I slumped over the bar, thinking that pounding my head against the woodened bar sounded like a great idea. Shaking my head, I closed my eyes and fought against the memories, the loss, and the sadness that had crept into me and filled me so completely I hadn't felt like I could survive. But my mom had needed me. She went practically catatonic after the Nordic Lords killed my dad. It was his own fault for even considering ratting out the club to the F.B.I. when the charges against him were false. He had caved.

My mother and I had paid the price. And then she had turned to Black Death for protection and to support her drug habit. In doing so, she had promised them the only thing Cain wanted.

Me.

She handed me to their club's Vice President like I was her

dowry. In return for my willingness to do whatever they wanted, they'd protect her. They'd supply her with drugs.

I should have hated her. I *did* hate her. But she was my mom, and under the hate was the realization that she was completely fucked in the head. Always had been, probably. She was also the only family I had left. I had no skills outside club life. No college education. No money. Nowhere to go.

So when she handed me to Cain, I went, even as much as I hated her for it. And when he chained me to a chair in his office at Penny's, screwed me and licked me and finger-fucked me until my body finally began responding despite my best intentions to fight it, I wished my mom was dead.

I caved. With no options, I slowly began accepting my life and my place in it. It was never going to be good from the moment Ryker broke my heart. The most I had left was my own survival.

"Diamond."

I slowly raised my head from my hands and glanced to the side. I sighed, seeing Cain at the end of the bar with a victorious look on his face. He knew this was killing me and he was excited that once again I was reminded about my place in the world.

"What is it, Cain?" I asked, pushing off the bar and facing him directly. He was a large man with broad shoulders, a butch haircut, and hazel eyes that never showed emotion. He had scars on his face and arms. The white lines stood out against the black ink on his forearms that I knew he'd had done during his multiple stints in the state prison.

He was big. He was mean. And he owned my ass until the day he decided I was worthless to him. By the look on his face, that day had not yet come.

"My office. We need to talk."

I swallowed slowly. Sweat broke out against the back of my neck before I was out from behind the bar as I followed him. His office. A place where he'd kept me for weeks, for months, after he'd taken me. I hadn't followed him into his office in years. There had been no need.

Whatever he had to tell me wouldn't be good.

The first, cold tremors of fear hit me as I followed him down the dark and dreary back hallway. Pleasured moans of clients receiving some lunch hour benefits filled the thick and smoke-scented air.

"Sit." He pointed to a plain metal chair in the corner as soon as we'd both entered the room. No way was I sitting in that chair with the handcuffs wrapped around the bottom chair legs. I knew exactly what waited for me in the chair.

I didn't look at it. Instead, I kept my eyes on Cain's, searching for anything that made sense about this. This was where he brought the new girls to see if they were any good. I had already proven that years ago.

My nose began to burn. "I'll stand." I cleared my throat, but it felt thick and dry. I tried swallowing, but I couldn't get past the rock in my throat.

Cain arched an eyebrow. "You need a reminder on what happens when you disobey me?"

I didn't. I remembered vividly and still had scars from his belt on my back. They began to sting at the very thought of them.

But screw him. Punishment would be worth it. I was so damn tired of submitting to these animals. Tired of getting pleasure from it when I wanted to bash their heads in.

I crossed my arms over my chest defiantly. "What do you want, Cain?"

His eyes glinted with pleasure. As if the thought of beating me—whipping me—filled him with ecstasy. Finally, he blinked and tossed me an envelope.

My hands flew out and caught it before it smacked me in the chest.

I scowled at it, wondering what was in it.

"You have an appointment tonight, near the casino."

"Who?" I asked as I peeked inside the envelope. My finger

fanned across the stack of money. Someone had paid for me up front—and paid well.

"Ryker."

My heart fell to my feet. He paid for a night with me? I shook the question out of my head. "I…"

"You'll go," he stated and stepped behind his desk. Once he was seated, he propped his elbows on the desk top and tapped his fingers together. "Say your good-byes and get him out of town. I don't need him back here distracting you." He paused, and his standard, greasy smile appeared as his eyes roamed my body. "Consider this a gift. A thank you for all your hard work."

The lump in my throat grew to epic proportions. Ryker treating me like the whore I was. Some gift.

He waved me off, but as my hand hit the doorknob to leave, Cain's sick voice stilled every muscle in my body. Looking over my shoulder, I flinched at his warning glare.

"Don't forget what happens if you don't follow through."

I nodded as I stepped into the darkened hallway. The warning was clear—I disobey and my mother dies.

6
Faith

I arrived at The Pavilion Court thirty minutes early for my appointment, just like I always did. I may not have always been able to control what my clients did to my body, but if I arrived first, I felt a small sense of control at welcoming them onto my turf instead of walking onto theirs. It was all a façade, a ruse I played with myself to mentally prepare, but it was necessary. And knowing that I was going to spend an evening with Ryker made my façade more essential than necessary.

The clerk at the front desk didn't give me a second look as he watched me carry my bags to the room. Not that he had any reason to. I wasn't dressed like a casual whore. With my jet black hair pulled back into a sleek ponytail at the nape of my neck and my navy blue wrap dress and red heels, I looked like any other guest at their hotel.

I ignored my wildly beating heart as much as I possibly could as the elevator rose to the sixth floor. Entering the suite I'd been provided for the night's activities, I fought back the itchy, scratchy feeling that lined every inch of my skin.

In front of me was a small living area with a grey, leather couch, a simple black coffee table, and a small writing desk. To my left, I saw the doorway for the bathroom and directly passed it, a kitchenette area. Based on the instructions Cain had delivered to me in the envelope, I knew it was fully stocked. Through a doorway to the right, I caught a glimpse of an enormous king-sized bed with a bright white covering that was so bright and so fluffy it made me wonder if the hotel had recently renovated their bed furnishings.

This wasn't the dump of a room where I typically entertained clients at Penny's Boarding House. And even though it was nicer than any place I'd entertained clients before, discomfort cloaked me. All I could think of was that it was the type of place Ryker and I would have gone for a romantic weekend getaway had we ever left Jasper Bay.

I shut down the thought immediately.

If Ryker wanted a night with a whore, I'd give him the best damn show possible. I'd make it worth every dollar he spent for me.

I hoped like hell in doing so he'd leave town as fast as he'd shown up. And I hoped with even more force that my heart wouldn't be shredded in the process.

One night with Ryker. I would take it. I would use it. I would wrap the memory of it into a steel encased memory box so that on the nights when the darkness and despair over what my life had turned into crept into my mind, I could peel open the box and have one damn good memory. Ryker's hands on me all over again. The only man who had ever touched me in a way I wanted.

After I changed into lingerie more appropriate for my job, I fidgeted with a small glass of wine. My feet tapped the carpet while I nervously alternated between sitting on the arm rest of the couch and pacing the slowly shrinking room.

I would have done anything for Ryker. I would have gone anywhere with him as long as it meant we were together. And this could potentially be my last chance to ever see him again. To ask him why he left me all those years ago. To show him what that loss had done to me.

I was prepared. I was ready.

When I heard the soft click of the door opening, my teeth found my bottom lip and gently bit down. I pushed down the flutters in my stomach and nervously fidgeted with my black lace lingerie.

Reality smacked me directly in the face as soon as he hit the entry way.

I was the world's biggest liar.

I wasn't ready to see him at all. I wasn't ready to be alone with him. I wanted to run and throw myself into the hotel closet and slam the door until I was fully covered. This was Ryker.

His eyes caught mine and I froze, my teeth still biting into my lower lip—although harder than I'd been biting before.

He still had one hand on the door, not fully entered into the room. He was wearing simple black denim jeans, black dress shoes, and a short-sleeve, white Henley top. I drank him in as if I hadn't already tapped into a bottle of wine that had been stocked for us.

His black hair was almost as dark as mine. It hung almost to his ears, longer than it'd been before. Black scruff lined his jaw and cheeks. His eyes stared at me and froze me to the worn carpeted floor. His body was stronger, buffer than he was before, but still lean and athletic. He was mouth-wateringly delicious.

I wanted to smack him across the face and scream at him for leaving me, for forcing me to turn into the whore he saw in front of him. And then I wanted to throw myself into his arms, wrap my legs around him, and beg him to never let me go again.

The quiet click of the door finally shutting behind him snapped me back to reality.

I had one job to do tonight. Get Ryker to leave town forever. But first, I'd make sure he'd give me a memory to last a lifetime because I knew it was the last good one I'd ever have.

"Faith." My name rolled off his full, pink lips with a quiet surprise. It snapped me back to reality and away from my reverence of his body. With one word—using my real name—something no one did anymore besides the few times I'd been able to see Olivia over the last couple of weeks—Ryker made me feel sixteen years old all over again.

My palms began sweating, my heartbeat increased, and my thighs wobbled. I felt wrapped up in him all over again. It was a dangerous place to be, and I couldn't let him have the control. I refused to give it to Ryker Knight ever again.

My shoulders rolled back, the emotions I felt coursing through me disappeared from my face. I smiled my perfected seductive grin that was way too plastic to be genuine, but men never cared.

He flinched as I took the first, slow step toward him. A perverse thrill flowed through me at seeing Ryker standing so close to me, looking so uncomfortable.

"What can I do for you tonight?" I hoped like hell he couldn't see how my finger shook as I reached out and slowly ran a perfectly manicured fingertip across his jaw. I lightly dragged it down his chest, stopping at the waistband of jeans.

His head jerked back and he blinked once, then twice, as if clearing his mind. Then his hand reached out and grabbed mine that was still fidgeting, running lightly back and forth across his shirt, over the waistband of his denim jeans.

"Stop it, Faith." His voice was scratchy, and I froze at the sound of my name, again, rolling off his lips.

Something inside me snapped. How dare this man who I loved, who left me to this life, have any emotion toward me at all. I was here because of him, doing what he paid me to do, and he had the nerve to stop me?

Anger replaced my nerves and trepidation. How stupid of me to think I could seduce Ryker and leave unscathed by the night.

I pulled my eyes from his hand that held mine and looked directly at him. I didn't know what he saw when he looked at me, but he flinched when I spoke.

"Diamond," I snapped.

"I can't." He cleared his throat and shook his head. He looked uncomfortable, uncertain. I almost felt like a bitch. Ryker had given me that nickname. He said when I was sixteen that my eyes shined so bright and clear they sparkled like diamonds. "I can't call you that."

I tilted my head to the side and examined him. Regret flashed in his eyes, unasked questions were on his lips. I didn't want to hear them, and I certainly didn't want to answer anything he had to ask me.

"Tell me, Ryker," I said quietly, my own voice shaking again with nerves. My free hand went up and lightly scratched the skin at the back of his neck. I saw him shiver beneath my touch before he stiffened, reached up, and grabbed my other hand, too. "Tell me what you want me to do tonight."

He looked pained. His eyes snapped closed tightly, and he threw my hands away from him before he took two steps away from me. We were still in the entryway, and the move put his back to the door. His hands flew to his hair, tugging on the back of it before he spun around, putting his back to me.

Disappointment hit me at the realization that he had denied me. I was here, in a room he wanted, fully paid for, and Ryker was still turning me away. A pain I hadn't felt since the night I got his damn text smacked me in the chest with such force that I wobbled in my high-heeled shoes and took two steps backward.

I stood there, watching Ryker's shoulders heave and fall under deep breaths, and hated him. Screw him for denying me again. If I couldn't give him my body, I had nothing left for him.

When he turned around, his eyes fell on every place in the room, refusing to land on me. The feeling that I was nothing to him caused the backs of my eyes to burn with unshed tears. I wouldn't allow him to see the pain he had caused me.

I looked at my platform, high-heeled shoes and blinked rapidly until the burn dissipated. When I finally pulled my eyes back to him, I caught Ryker watching me intently before he looked away again.

Then he pushed past me, walking fully into the room, and headed straight for the bathroom. When he came out, he held a bathrobe in his hands and pushed it to my chest.

"Cover up. We need to talk."

His voice was so cold I shivered underneath his angry glare. I caught a flash of it before he walked to the kitchenette and grabbed a beer from the small fridge.

It left me in the entryway to the hotel room, completely rejected, holding onto a white, terry cloth bathrobe that would cover every inch of my skin. I slowly pulled it on, resigned to the fact that I still had to stay because if he left too early, if Cain found out he left too soon without me doing my job, there would be consequences I would need to pay.

With the robe on and the belt tightened around my waist, I still felt completely naked. I was short enough that the large robe tickled the floor as I met Ryker in the kitchenette and grabbed my own glass of wine.

Thick, palpable silence filled the room. Neither of us spoke, and from the corner of my eye I watched Ryker down his drink before he reached for another.

Right as he tipped it to his lips, with his eyes on the windows and not on me, he said, "I didn't come here tonight for this."

I heard his teeth grind together right before his lips wrapped around the edge of the thin glass and he took another large swallow. The wine glass shook in my hands.

Then why the hell was he here? And why in the hell was I?

I took a deep breath. I didn't trust myself to speak, but it was best to get the night over with. "Then why are you here?"

7

Ryker

I was a fucking pervert. I stood in the hotel room that I had requested for Faith to give us space and time to talk, to figure out what the hell went wrong. Except all I wanted to do as soon as her finger singed my skin was throw her on the huge ass bed and taste every inch of her creamy, white skin.

I had to get myself, my adrenaline, and my damn hard dick under control before I could talk to her.

Not even then would I be able to touch her the way I wanted to—not when I was too fucking terrified she would think the only reason I was touching her was because I paid for her. That wasn't it at all. It was simply the only way I knew to get her alone and out from underneath the eyes of Black Death.

Her owners. Fury boiled inside of me at the damn thought.

"Ryker."

I set down my beer and turned around, facing Faith. Her shoulders were pulled back as she watched me. She looked confident. She looked sexy as fuck. The robe fell past her fingertips and puddled on the floor around her feet, but it couldn't erase my memory of her in lace. Black fucking lace. God, she was beautiful.

"Why am I here?"

"I wanted to talk to you…" I stopped, ran a hand through my hair, and took a deep breath. "I wanted to explain why I left."

She scoffed. The blood rushed from her cheeks and her hands gripped the knot on the belt around her waist. "A little late, don't you think?"

It was. It was way too fucking late and I wasn't looking for absolution. Not from Faith. If what I'd figured out was true, I didn't deserve it.

It didn't stop me from walking toward her, though. For five years I'd lived with the anger that she had cheated on me the first chance she got, if not before. I had left thinking she had never loved me. But now, as I saw the pain and fear and nerves dance across her eyes, I knew without certainty that I had to be the biggest prick in the entire fucking world.

This was Faith.

The girl who'd loved me for as long as I could remember.

There was no way she could have done what I saw that night.

Not willingly, anyway.

"I think I fucked up," I admitted quietly when I stopped a few short feet from her. I could take one large step, reach out, and have her in my arms all over again. I'd be able to feel her fingertips dragging lightly down my skin, play with my hair, and have her lips on my skin.

Faith leaned back, rested her ass against a countertop, and crossed her arms over her chest.

"I'm pretty certain you fucked up."

I winced, and then I nodded.

I might have, but she also had no idea how fucked up my head was that night.

"I saw you that night," I gritted out. Her eyebrows pulled together.

"I don't know what you mean."

Her voice was quiet, mousy. I believed her instantly.

I needed another drink before I relived it with her, too. "Want some wine?" I asked and moved to the counter where the bottle was now half empty. I didn't wait for her to answer as I poured her a glass. She took it slowly from my hands, careful to avoid our fingers touching.

When I could no longer stand the silence or the memories beating down on me, I pulled my eyes directly to Faith. And then I had to blink because she was so damn beautiful with her light blue eyes and black hair and fuck... that black lace shit I could still see, even though it wasn't visible through the robe.

"When I left you that night, I went to my dad to patch in."

Faith gasped. I said the words as evenly and calmly as I would have spoken to her five years ago. This time, I watched her eyes widen in surprise.

My voice lowered. "I would have done anything for you, you know. I would have patched into the fucking club that I wanted nothing to do with just to make you happy." Memories. My cold truck. Her shivering hands. Her tears. They assaulted my vision until I felt the need to sit down.

I turned my back to Faith and moved to the small couch in the living area of the hotel room. It wasn't comfortable, but my legs were starting to shake and I had to sit. Better an uncomfortable couch than collapsing to the floor like a pussy.

I rolled the beer bottle between my palms and watched her. She stared out the window with emotionless eyes. I wanted to ask if she was remembering that night like I was, but she gave away nothing with her vacant expression.

"I went to my dad's house and saw... I saw everything, Faith. Fuck, I can still see it. I can still smell the blood when I'm on the oil rig twenty miles off the coast. I can see Cherry's blood, and I can see Olivia passed out in the chair. I can still hear the bullets going off and I can definitely see the way I fucked it all up by letting that bastard get out of the house before I got my shit together and started moving again."

My head dropped. I set the beer down before I scrubbed my fingers through my hair and across the back of my neck. It was pointless. I had done that move a million times over the years, and no matter how hard I scrubbed, I couldn't erase what I had seen or what I had done.

I heard Faith's soft footsteps padding toward me on the carpet, but I didn't look up at her. Instead, my elbows went to my knees and I held my head in my hands while I memorized the strands in the carpet. Grey carpet speckled with dots of red.

Red like blood.

I blinked and looked up.

Faith was mere feet from me again, looking uncertain and unwary. No longer looking pissed and dejected, though, so that was good. Better.

I almost smiled.

And then I kept remembering.

"Daemon showed up, the men kicked me out, and do you know what I did?"

I licked the front of my teeth, trying to hold in the anger that always hit me at that point in the memory.

"No." Faith cleared her throat and shook her head. "But I'm sorry you saw all that."

I blinked away the look of compassion on her face.

"I saw you," I growled. Faith flinched, and I pulled in a shaky breath. I had to calm the hell down again. But like always, I could feel my anger, the betrayal of seeing another man's hands on her, build deep in my blood. "With Cain. His hands all over you."

She frowned and then stopped breathing on a sharp inhale.

I rolled my tongue in my mouth. I could see it like it was yesterday. I could see it like it happened a minute ago.

"You were all over that asshole from Black Death."

We stared at each other for what felt like hours. Finally, she exhaled and collapsed into a chair. "That wasn't—" She looked dazed as she stopped talking and shook her head.

I felt like a gigantic ass. I always should have known.

"I know. I know that now, Faith. But that night… it was all so fucking scary and ugly and I couldn't think. I didn't know what the fuck Black Death was doing at your house that night, but at the same time, I thought…"

She shook her head. "You have to be kidding me." She shook her head again, and the dazed look in her eyes cleared. Before I knew it, they flashed anger. She jumped out of her seat. "Are you fucking kidding me, Ryker?"

I fell against the back of the couch.

"Faith."

"No," she snapped and pointed a finger at me. "You don't get to explain this shit. Holy shit!" She spun on her heels, running her hands through her black hair. I could hear her breathing heavily right before she spun around again and faced me. "You are an asshole."

My eyes widened. "An asshole? I had just killed my dad and came back to you, needing you, and you were all over the club's enemy."

"I wasn't all over him!"

"I know that now!"

"You should have known it then!"

I squeezed my eyes shut and balled my hands into fists. She was right; I should have.

"Jesus, Faith. I had just killed my dad. I wasn't exactly thinking clearly."

She blinked once and then twice. I heard her sniff before she pulled her eyes back to the window. "You are such an asshole. You have no idea what happened to me that night."

"I know." I cleared my throat, feeling the dryness and the lump in it. "I know that now."

Silence filled the room, and for the first time in years, Faith was so close to me. All I wanted to do was wrap my arms around her and feel her. I wanted to go back to the way it used to be so she could make me forget. Forget everything that had happened that night.

"Faith," I called quietly, standing up and closing the space between us. "You have to cut me some slack that maybe I wasn't thinking straight that night."

She scoffed and raised a hand to stop me. She bit her bottom lip and her chin shook slightly. "I don't have to do shit. Not now." She shook her head. Then she opened her mouth before snapping it shut again. "God, that night…"

"Tell me."

She shook her head. "You're a dick."

"I know," I said, taking a small step forward. I couldn't stop myself. I wanted to be with her, to make all this shit right again. That probably made me an asshole because regardless of what happened between Faith and me, I'd still leave again.

"Cain was there the night you dropped me off. He was talking to my mom about making a deal."

I nodded because now I knew that. I knew what the deal was. Except hearing it from Daemon felt completely different than hearing it fall from Faith's lips. I wanted to rip the man's head off with my bare hands as Faith stood in the center of the room, in a robe three sizes too large for her, looking timid, terrified, and fucking broken.

Her eyes cut to mine, slicing through the already broken areas in my heart. They were as cold as ice when she narrowed them directly at me. "Do you know what they did, Ryker?"

"I know they own you," I said quietly. Bile rose in my throat as the words left my lips.

Faith scoffed. It was cold and emotionless and so unlike the Faith I knew. I hated it. I hated hearing her sound like that. She shook her head and looked away.

"You have no idea what that means." Her eyes glazed over.

"Then tell me," I said, walking toward her. I hoped like hell she wouldn't back away. I had done this to her. Another innocent victim with their pain on my conscience. Fuck. Would I ever stop screwing over everyone I cared for? My brain told me to stop and back the fuck away from her.

My feet kept moving, unable to stop until I stood directly in front of her. "Tell me what they did to you so I know who to kill first."

She frowned when she looked at me. "Kill?" I watched her swallow slowly.

I nodded equally as slow. It'd be the first kill I did willingly. I'd probably smile and feel good doing it, too. "Daemon made a deal with Black Death, Faith. In a few weeks they're working together and in exchange Black Death is setting you free."

"What?" Faith's jaw dropped and her eyebrows shot up her forehead in shock. I couldn't stop myself. My hand went to her shoulder and I squeezed it firmly. I could barely feel her through the thick white robe. She froze under my hand.

She shook her head. "That's never going to happen. Daemon and the rest of the club are idiots if they think Cain will stay good on his word. He'll never let me go."

Her voice made my blood run cold. A small burn started boiling inside me. I wanted revenge on everyone who had fucked me and my family over. If Cain so much as thought of backing down on this deal, his head would be mine.

"Faith," I warned, but she shook her head and backed away from me.

"Cain won't ever let me go, Ryker. He'd kill me first, and I don't even want to think about what he'd do to my mom."

"Your mom? She fucking gave you to him."

"Sold," Faith snapped, and her lips pressed together. "I wasn't given. I was sold for drugs."

I knew that. It didn't make me feel any calmer as Faith snapped it at me like she didn't give a shit. Although maybe she didn't.

"And it doesn't mean I want her dead. She's the only family I have."

Was she fucking serious? I wanted her mom's head on a platter.

Any willingness I had to protect that woman five years ago was long gone. Roxy Winston had been a drain on their family for Faith's entire life.

"He backs down on his deal, on this agreement, and his ass is mine." I bent down and growled it inches from her face so she could see how serious I was. Then I pulled back. There was so much I wanted to apologize to her for. So much shit I wanted to get off my chest. "Faith-"

"Don't you get it, Ryker?" She stepped away from me and slowly turned around. Before I could process what she was doing, her back faced me as she lowered her robe. With her arms bent at the sides, the robe fell down her back and draped across the back of her waist. She reached up with one hand and pulled her hair over her shoulder so I could see the black lace.

I wanted to run my hands over her skin and feel the lace beneath my fingers. But I stopped myself. My eyebrows pulled in, confused as to what she was trying to show me.

"Look," she said. "Look closer."

I did. I moved in and bent down and watched her shiver beneath my hooded gaze. And then I felt the need to hit something because I could finally see what she wanted me to see.

"Faith," I said as I lightly reached out and began tracing the scars with the tip of my thumb. My teeth ground together and my jaw radiated in pain from trying not to scream at her. I could barely see them under the lace, but they were there. White scars, some still pink. I moved the robe down, wishing the lace was gone so I could see the maze of angry slashes and scars that decorated her fucking gorgeous skin.

"What is this?" I growled. The back of the robe fisted in my hands and I pulled it off. I didn't see the beauty in front of me, the woman who could always make my dick hard in seconds. Now I saw the broken and marred skin and all of it was my own damn fucking fault for not taking a minute five years ago to stop and think for one damn second.

Faith looked at me from over her shoulder. I dragged my eyes, reluctantly pulling them off her skin and scars, and saw the deadness in her eyes. "Disobedience has its consequences."

She shrugged her shoulders and moved away from me, but I stopped her. One hand went to her waist, and I tightened my grip on her hip before she could walk away. I stared at my hand on her skin, wishing I was touching her for a different reason.

"I'm so fucking sorry."

Her eyes grew wet before she looked away from me to the floor. My fingers twitched on her hip, and I felt her jump slightly.

"Faith," I said, my throat raw with pain and regret. "We'll free you from them. I fucking swear it."

She spun around, and my hand fell from her skin down to my side. She reached out, grabbed the robe from my other hand, and shrugged it on, knotting the belt tightly around her waist.

"What you don't understand," she said quietly, "is that I'll never be free again."

"Faith."

She shook her head and pointed at the door to the bedroom. "Is there anything else you need from me tonight or can I go?"

Was she kidding? There was no way I was fucking letting her go now.

"I want to talk, to figure out what to do now."

She smiled sadly. It didn't reach her eyes, and I could tell she was still fighting to not lose it in front of me, but I didn't want her to go. I didn't want to say good-bye.

"There's nothing you can do. My fate was sealed the moment Cain showed up at my house that night."

I shook my head. It wasn't.

She took another step toward the door to the bedroom and looked back at me. "I think... I'm going to go to bed, then."

I opened my mouth to speak, to tell her that I didn't want her to, but I let her go. I could at least give her one night where she felt safe and was able to sleep alone, knowing no one was going to hurt her.

"I get it, you know," she said softly as she reached the doorway. "I get why you were messed up and why you left. You don't owe me that apology. But for years I waited for you to show up and save me." A tear fell down her cheek before she wiped it away. "There's nothing left to save, Ryker."

She disappeared through the doorway, shutting and locking the bedroom door before I could stop her. Before I could swear that I would save her and free her and I'd do whatever the fuck she needed me to do, to be whoever she needed to be. But I didn't.

Because even that would be a lie.

Just like she felt she'd never be free, I would never be the Ryker she knew.

I collapsed back on the couch, listening to the sounds of the running water, and staring at the light coming from the bedroom door, hoping Faith would come back out so we could talk. So we could figure out how to fix everything.

But she never did. And when the light went out underneath her door and the noises stopped, I kept staring and wishing I could have been the man she needed me to be way back when I was still capable of being that man.

8
Faith

I was awake before the sun rose. I wasn't sure I'd slept at all. The memories of my night with Ryker assaulted my mind, twisting and turning and tumbling in my head with such ferocity that sleep had been impossible.

Ryker was in the other room, only feet away from me for the first time in years, and all I wanted to do was go to him. I wanted to know what his arms would feel like if I slid next to him on the small pull-out couch. I wanted to feel, just one more time, what it would be like to be loved by him.

Fear of failure, fear of Black Death, and fear of allowing myself to get close to him only to lose him again kept me hidden under the fluffy white comforter. I was in a bed that was more comfortable than anything I'd ever slept in, and yet it felt too large, too empty, and too cold. The one person in my entire life that I'd ever wanted to share a bed with was too close and too far away at the same time.

But I knew Cain would expect a report and he would be waiting impatiently until I arrived at Penny's to give it to him—to tell him I'd done my job and that Ryker would be leaving and never coming back again.

The thought of Ryker's words from the previous night, the deal with Black Death and them freeing me… it was too impossible to accept. It would never happen. Cain had made it clear that he would never let me go.

Fools. The Nordic Lords, Ryker included, were fools if they thought Cain was a man of integrity. If he was, I wouldn't have spent months tied to a chair, forced to perform, and then beaten until I did it perfectly.

Cain had managed to beat all my hopes and dreams out of me with the lashes from his belt and his whip.

Which made Ryker dangerous. His dark, deep eyes that had showed so much emotion last night when he spoke and watched me reminded me of dreams that would never come to fruition.

I would never have a good life.

I would never have a life at all.

It was time I finally accepted that, and it was time to do the job Cain required of me.

I had to get Ryker out of town, despite everything inside of me screaming to hold on to him and never let him go.

With a resolve blossoming in my painfully tight chest, I found the courage to climb out of bed and somehow say my final good-byes to Ryker. It was for the best. It would protect not only my heart, but my life, as well as my mother's.

Even though Ryker had been right the night before; she had never been any sort of mother any daughter should want to protect.

I quietly dressed in a pair of black jeans, red ballet flats, and a plain white T-shirt. Then I threw my long, barely brushed hair into a ponytail high on top of my head. A quick glance in the mirror showed a pale-faced, beaten woman with no hope left.

It was how I always felt. I was so fucking tired of it.

But it was my life, and it was time I remembered it.

Slowly, so I didn't wake him if he was still sleeping, I pulled down on the levered door handle and pried the door open a few inches. It was then that the muffled voice I heard coming through the door sliced a wound through my chest that would never be repaired.

"I know, kiddo… your daddy misses you, too…"

Ryker's voice. Tears of pain immediately swelled in my eyes and I was too stunned, too shocked. I didn't know what I felt, but it prevented me from moving. I should have closed the door or made my presence known immediately.

Instead, I stood with my hand burning against the door handle and listened to every word he spoke into the phone like the masochist I had become. A lover of pain.

Each word he spoke cut deep and wide into my chest until I was sweating. But still, I kept listening.

"I'll be home soon… love you, too… can you put your mom on the phone for me?"

Love you. Your daddy misses you… your mom…

He had a kid. The only man I had ever loved, the only man I had ever willingly touched or ever cared for… I'd been replaced.

He'd moved on.

My nose stung and my eyes burned. The door handle I was staring at became a blurry ball of silver in my hand.

And still, I continued listening.

"I know, Meg… I'm so sorry… I'll be home soon. Two days. Tell Brayden I'll see him then… you too, sweetheart."

Though his voice was muffled through the door, I heard his kindness and reverence as he spoke to the woman. He talked to her like I used to relish him talking to me. Like a man in love.

I hated Meg. I didn't know her and I would never see her, but it didn't stop feelings of hatred from rising up from somewhere deep inside my soul.

I had to get out of there. It was clear that any hope I ever had with Ryker—even when I denied myself having that hope—was worthless.

He was gone. Then what the fuck was last night? A chance to absolve himself from his responsibility or his regret he had in leaving me behind? What difference did it make?

He had a family.

Family.

The shock drained the blood from my face as I stood, wild-eyed and feral feeling, and I scanned every surface in my hotel room. I was cornered with no way out. The room was too high to jump out the window and leave without seeing him again. There was no option.

I had to get out of there. And Ryker had to go. I never wanted to see him again.

Prying my burning fingertips from the door handle, I grabbed my suitcase, lifted the handle, and entered the living area.

Ryker noticed me immediately and was on his feet, walking toward me. I pushed the small suitcase in between us, putting something—even as small as it was—in between us. A buffer. My black, worn out overnight bag was my damn protector.

Family. I love you, too. Your daddy misses you.

I squeezed my eyes shut, tuning out the voice in my head and the pounding pain in my chest. I was trained to be better than this. I rolled my shoulders as Ryker pressed his hands into his jeans pockets and I forced myself to recall every whip and lash, I had received by Cain when he wanted me to behave a certain way.

Fucking love it, Diamond. Suck his cock like you love it. Smile like he's your goddamn hero.

I remembered all of it. It was the only way to leave here without any more lashes hitting a direct target on my beaten heart.

"Are we done?" I asked.

A frown line appeared between Ryker's eyes. "Done with what?"

"Your night? You obviously didn't hire me last night to fuck me. I wanted to make sure you didn't need anything else before I go."

"Fuck...?" He shook his head and ran a hand through his hair. His eyes danced to the empty bedroom and back to me. I watched his jaw tighten and my fingers curled tighter around the suitcase handle. "What the hell is wrong with you today?"

"Your payment, Ryker. You paid for a night, not the next day. And I have other appointments, so…"

"What the hell, Faith?" His eyes widened. I wished I didn't care, but being a bitch was the only way I was getting out that room.

"Listen." I waved my hand, dismissing him. "Last night was fun, the whole walk down memory lane, but you're leaving so there's no point in talking about anything. You want to go against Black Death? Go for it. But we both know you've got more important shit going on back home than worrying about me. So if you wouldn't mind—"

My words were cut off immediately when Ryker was suddenly in front of me. My suitcase was the only thing separating us as he leaned down until his face was inches from mine.

"Shut up."

My mouth dropped open and then snapped close. He was so close I could smell him. I could see the scruff on his cheeks and my reflection in his dark, beautiful eyes. Dark, long lashes that had always made me jealous. A jawline that screamed sexy masculinity.

And his hand was on my chin, forcing me to face him. He examined me slowly, our breath the only sound in the room as they mingled together. My knuckles ached in pain from the death grip I had on my suitcase.

"You heard me on the phone." His eyes volleyed back and forth between mine. His lips turned up slightly at the edges. "It's not what you think."

I ripped my chin out of his warm grasp and immediately felt cold. I hated him.

I wanted to hate him.

I couldn't though, and I hated that more.

"I don't know what you're talking about. Can I go now?"

I took a step back and pulled the suitcase with me, but Ryker's hand came down and tightened over my fist on the handle, stopping me.

Slowly, his fingers uncurled every one of mine and the suitcase was pushed away before it thumped to the floor. The small sound didn't break the stare between us. Nothing could pull my eyes away from Ryker as he moved forward again, forcing me to take another step back.

Amusement lit in his eyes, and I felt my pulse increase.

When my back hit the wall, Ryker moved closer until only a breath of space separated us. His hand reached out and gently ran down my jaw before he cupped my cheek in his large, firm, and calloused hand. It felt divine. Against my better judgment, I leaned in.

Home. He felt perfect, precisely like I remembered. Exactly like the man I'd always wanted and loved. All hard lines. Intimidating and safe at the same time. I mewled in frustration and anger, yet in lust and comfort.

I swallowed, unable to look at him. I wanted to treasure this moment—this perfect moment—forever. Because in a minute, I would say good-bye and Ryker would go home to his family—to his son and a woman named Meg.

"We still have shit to talk about."

There was nothing left to talk about. There was nothing to say that could fix the pain slicing my chest wide open.

I shook my head and exhaled. It was long and deep and all I could do was focus on his warm skin on mine and his masculine scent. Heavenly. Sexy. So perfect and so incapable of ever being mine again. I swallowed the thickness in my throat.

"I need to go." I kept my eyes closed until I felt the weight of Ryker's firm body pressing against mine. His thighs hit mine until my hips were pinned to the door. His other hand moved until it was pressed against the wall behind my head. "And you need to go home."

I stared at our bodies connected at the waist.

His breath tickled the skin at my jaw up to my ear as he breathed along my skin. Goose bumps exploded on my arms and the hairs on the back of my neck stood tall.

His lips pressed again my jaw, softly, and only one time. My body shivered beneath him. Why was he doing this to me?

Cain's voice bellowed in my head, reminding me of my mother's impending death if I screwed up.

"I'm not leaving here today until we can fix what we broke."

I scoffed at him. Everything was broken. Everything was a huge pile of messy fucking shit that couldn't be fixed. I couldn't be. What he implied was ridiculous. He had his own family.

With a strength I didn't know I possessed, I fixed my eyes on Ryker's. My lips pulled into a tight line while I fought the urge to allow myself to become wrapped in his arms.

I blinked and swallowed. My hands moved to his chest, and I pushed him away.

His step faltered, surprised by my strength.

"Like I said, there's nothing left to say. I get it. I get why you left, and while I'm not sure why you're back, I wish you the best of luck in whatever…" I waved my hand in the air and noticed my fingers trembling. "But whatever you're looking for from me, unless it's a quick fuck, isn't going to happen."

He growled and closed the distance. His eyes narrowed and his hands clasped my cheeks. "Stop talking about yourself like that."

I slapped his hands away. Screw him for trying to think I was better than what I had become.

"I'm a whore, Ryker." My lips curled into an evil smile. "Do you know how many men I've been with? Do you know how many men I've *enjoyed* being with?" I shook my head and choked down the bile that rose in my throat.

His eyes widened, his teeth clenched together, all while the blood drained from his face.

I tried to slap his hands away, but he only gripped me tighter. So I kept talking. Anything to get him out of there.

"Maybe I like it. Did you ever stop to think about that?"

"Shut up."

"The men… their hands on me. Pleasing me…"

"Shut the fuck up, Faith!" He screamed it right into my face. I felt his muscles shaking with rage as he bellowed right in front of me.

Then his lips slammed into mine. I gasped instantly, shocked from the feel of his skin on mine. His lips forcefully pressed against mine, and as soon as my mouth opened, his tongue invaded my mouth.

This wasn't a kiss. This was him claiming me. This was him reminding me that I was better than all the lies I had spewed out of my mouth. It took one second for me to surrender to him. My hands flew to his wrists and I grabbed hold of him. His hips pressed into my waist until we were completely connected from the waist down.

A growl escaped his lips as he pushed me harder into the wall.

I grabbed his hair, pulling him closer.

His hips rolled, proving his excitement. His hands moved from my cheeks back to my scalp and he dug his fingers into my skin.

I whimpered against him. Tears poured from my eyes as my knees shook. I tried to enjoy every single second of this kiss and his touch. It consumed me. He devoured me with his tongue and his lips and the warmth of his skin.

"Faith," he growled, pulling back until his lips were simply brushing against mine. I stared at him wide-eyed. My hands were fisted into shirt at his shoulders. "You're not a fucking whore."

The reminder smacked me straight into my chest. Because I was. And it was time he remembered it, like I had done earlier.

I swallowed, pried my fingers off his shirt, and wiped away the tears.

His fingers were still at the back of my head, massaging my scalp and loosening my ponytail.

My heart beat wildly against my chest. I swallowed, regaining my control and slowing my erratic breathing.

"What I am," I started, staring at Ryker's pulse on his neck that was beating in time with mine. "Is a body that is bought and used for a man's pleasure. That's all I'll ever be."

I almost believed myself. His fingers dug into my scalp before I managed to push him off of me again.

"Why are you doing this?"

"Doing what, Ryker?" I asked, my voice rising in frustration and lust. "Telling you the truth?" I leaned in closer to him, my hands balled into fists at my sides. "I was bought and paid for. You can think that you guys can come in and save the day or whatever knight in shining armor scenario you're imagining, but that doesn't, for one single second, change the reality of who I've become."

"You're not a whore!" His face went red with rage as he screamed at me again.

"I fuck men for money and I like it!" I screamed back. Shock and anger lined the features on his face. His chest rose and fell under his fitted white t-shirt. "Jesus, Ryker. I'm not the twenty-year-old girl you used to know. Can't you just accept it?"

"No." He shook his head fervently back and forth. His eyes squeezed shut and pain replaced the anger. "I can't."

I reached around him and grabbed my suitcase, pulling it toward me before he could say anything else.

"I'm sorry," I shrugged. "But that's not my problem."

He scrubbed a hand down his face and fixed his eyes back on me. "Why are you doing this?"

A quiet scoff escaped my lips. "Doing what, Ryker? Accepting the reality of my life? What do you want from me?" I leaned forward, sneering. "Are you going to save me and whisk me away back to New Orleans and have us live happily ever after?"

His skin blanched. Right. Because he had that whole family thing going on that he couldn't introduce me to.

"Or would you prefer to keep me here? Don't you realize that if you save me from Black Death, if they keep their end of the agreement, you're still going to leave and I'm still going to be here with the same pile of problems I had five years ago?"

"I will do anything I have to in order to get you out from their control."

"And then what?" I prodded. Frustration and anger prickled the small space between us as we argued in the entry way of the hotel room. "I already told you if you came here for my forgiveness, you have it. What else do you want?"

"I want you!" he yelled again, his own eyes widening in surprise as the words escaped his lips.

My heart beat frantically. I blinked away the tears. God that sounded good to hear. If only he meant it in the way I wanted him to mean it.

"You can't have me," I lied. He could. If it was a different time, under different circumstances, he could totally have me. "There's nothing left of me to give anyone."

"Faith," he pleaded, his hand reaching for me. I dodged it and moved to the door, opening it before he could get to me.

In the doorway, I turned to face him.

"Go back to New Orleans, go back to your rig, and go back to taking care of people who want you around." I brushed at my nose and wiped away the wetness that stained my cheeks. "I don't need you fighting for me."

"Three weeks, and I'll be back for you," he stated. "I'll take you out of here, somewhere safe. Somewhere you'll never have to think of this place or your life here ever again."

"You don't get it," I snapped. "If you come back here again and if you believe Black Death will give you what they claim, people will end up dead." I pulled in a deep breath and exhaled. "Do you really want more death—more blood—on your hands?"

He winced visibly and I took my escape.

Away from the only good thing in my life and back to my dark, lifeless reality.

9

Ryker

My knees braced for the impact right as Brayden slammed his little body into mine. My arms wrapped around him, and I rocked back on my heels, almost falling over onto my ass on the wooden floor in Meg's house.

"Uncuh Rykie!"

I smiled. Something about this boy was so freaking cool. "Hey little man," I said, scrubbing the back of his hair with my hand as I held him. "Sorry I worried you this week."

He pulled back and frowned. "Mommy said you busy."

I nodded and watched Meg smile at us from the doorway to the kitchen of their small, two-bedroom house. She wrapped her hands in a dishtowel with an easy smile on her face.

"I was, but I brought you something."

Brayden's dark brown eyes grew as large as saucers as I shook the yellow box of chewy chocolates.

"Milk Duds!" he shouted. He wrenched the box out of my hands and ran toward his mom, body slamming her into the wall like he'd done to me only moments before. "Can I have some?" he shouted again. Most days, Brayden had two volume levels—shouting and sleeping.

"Sure, babe, but not all of them." Meg ruffled his hair and waved toward the kitchen. "Eat at the table."

"But my movie on." He pouted.

Meg kept a finger pointed at the table. I watched their easy banter and her firm eyes on Brayden and felt my skin begin to crawl all over again.

I knew exactly what Faith heard two days ago in the hotel. I knew exactly what she thought. If only she would have let me explain the truth, that morning might not have ended up in such a huge clusterfuck. Her eyes, her anger, and her sickening words were firmly cemented into my mind.

Brayden bounded off to the kitchen while Meg paused the cartoon movie on the television, apparently having reached some sort of compromise.

I pulled myself up from my crouched position on the floor and rubbed my hands on my thighs.

"You look like crap," Meg said softly as she walked toward me. She gave me a quick kiss on the cheek before she pulled back.

"Thanks."

She rolled her eyes and laughed. Two years ago when Byron died on the rig in an accident that I could have prevented, I had watched Meg's easy smiles and laughter all but disappear. Lately, I'd noticed them coming back. Not often, but frequently enough to see that although she still missed her husband like crazy, she was not only surviving, but she was healing.

If only I could do the same.

My night with Faith had brought all my shit back to the front of my mind, and while the thoughts could normally be quenched with massive amounts of whiskey and pussy, neither of those sounded like something I wanted anymore.

I wanted Faith.

I wanted her free. I wanted her to smile. I wanted her happy. I wanted her in my arms.

I just fucking wanted her.

Instead, I screwed up—again. But with her standing so close to me, looking so goddamned beautiful, I couldn't help myself. I broke the promise I made to keep my hands to myself and simply talk to her.

I had essentially raped her mouth like all of her asshole clients had the freedom to do.

"You want to talk about what went on back at home?"

I blinked and shook my head, Meg's soft voice disrupting my wallowing.

"What?"

She laughed again and leaned back, resting her butt against the back of her light brown couch. "Come on, Ryker. You look like shit. What in the heck happened back home?"

Her eyes flashed concern as her voice softened. I had never told Byron, Meg, or Pete the specifics of why I had left home and refused to go back. I also knew that when I had to sit down with Meg and explain why I was leaving now, she'd be worried.

I scrubbed my hands down my face and exhaled loudly. My shoulders slumped. It was all so fucking depressing. "Nothing that can be fixed anytime soon."

I blew out a breath and watched Meg roll a pink kitchen towel in her hands. She studied me for a beat before nodding. She understood. Some things couldn't be easily fixed—or fixed at all in this case.

Although I wasn't going to quit trying.

"Well," she nodded toward the kitchen, "I've got lunch ready if you're hungry."

I was famished. After the disastrous night and morning with Faith, I had gone back to Daemon's house only to be whisked away by Olivia who had some secret desire to get a tattoo. I barely managed to avoid Daemon kicking my ass once he found out. Then I got skunk drunk at the Nordic Lord's clubhouse.

I had been surly. I had been an asshole to everyone who came near me, but I couldn't stop seeing the desperation and the defeat in

Faith's eyes every time I blinked.

I wasn't sure I'd eaten in days.

Still, I followed Meg to the kitchen and tried to smile for Brayden as he rattled on and on about his video games. All while trying to figure out how I was going to get Faith out from under Black Death while still being able to take care of Meg and Brayden.

It seemed impossible.

"I was engaged once."

Meg's eyebrows rose in surprise. I didn't know why I was telling her this.

Brayden was in bed and we'd been sitting in silence for the last hour, me drinking beer after beer, Meg slowly sipping a glass of wine.

I couldn't stand the damn silence anymore.

Slowly, she smiled. "Are you going to tell me about her or just leave me hanging?"

I planned on changing the subject and forgetting I brought it up in the first place, but Meg's sweet smile pulled it out of me before I could.

"Her name's Faith," I exhaled heavily. My hands gripped my beer bottle before I pulled it to my lips and took a long drink. I decided to let go. For once, let everything hang out there. Meg wouldn't understand, but she'd listen.

I fell back into the couch and closed my eyes. I could see Faith as a kid with her long black braids and her skinned knees because she insisted on wearing dresses while playing as rough and tough as us boys. When we wore holes in our clothes, she took the cuts to her knees without complaint.

"I think I fell in love with her when I was ten," I started, and then I kept talking. I told Meg everything. From the time when I knew

I wanted to marry Faith to the night I finally got her to agree. I told her about my plans to leave Jasper Bay and take Faith with me, to Faith's worry about leaving her mom. And last—once Meg had continued to replenish my alcohol, instinctually knowing I needed to be on the cusp of drunkenness to continue talking—I told her about that night. The night everything went to hell.

The night my life changed and the night I lost Faith.

Then I told her about the hotel room.

And by the end of it, my tongue was heavy, my words were slurred, and my cheeks were wet. I didn't realize it until I scrubbed my unshaven cheek with my fingertips and came away with moisture on them.

Jesus. I was crying? I couldn't remember the last time I cried. I didn't know if I had *ever* cried.

Silence filled the room when I was done. My eyes were closed and I reveled in the darkness behind my closed eyelids.

"You're going back for her, right?"

I slowly peeled one eye open and tried to focus on Meg. She was a bit blurry, but I saw her wipe away tears off her own cheeks. Great. Now I'd made Meg cry, too.

I leaned forward, rested my elbows onto my knees, and dropped my head into my hands. I shook it back and forth, trying to erase… something. Pain, heartache, fear… I didn't know, but something had to give inside of me before I exploded.

"I told Daemon I'd head back in two weeks to help clean up some other stuff going on with the club." Throughout the story, I'd given Meg the full version of how I'd been raised. No one in New Orleans knew my full background. When people learned you came from an outlaw-type family, they tended to make judgments. Not that they were always wrong, but it had never been who I was.

It had also never been someone I wanted to be or something I wanted to be a part of, but now, sitting in New Orleans, I felt the pull to go home. To take care of everything Daemon was struggling with.

To help my family and to take care of Faith.

"I'll be okay if you go, you know."

My eyes snapped to Meg. She looked uncertain even as she bravely spoke the words. Her chin wobbled like Brayden's did before he cried.

"Meg." I shook my head.

She raised her hand to silence me.

"I know you, Ryker. You've made these promises and you're loyal and you're determined." Her voice shook with tears as she left the chair and moved next to me onto the couch. Her gentle hand on my leg made my body tense. "But I can do this without you."

Tears swam in her eyes. I couldn't look away.

"I made my choice, Meg." And I had. I had promised Byron, and I would keep it. Maybe someday when Meg was ready to move on, I'd be willing to let go. But as I saw the fear in her eyes when she told me to go, there was no way that time was now.

She nodded and swiped at her cheeks. "I know. I know you did. But I want you to know that when you go back in two weeks and you help your brother I don't expect you to come back."

She stood before I could reach out and grab her hand. To reassure her that I would always come back for her. I would always come back for Brayden. The beer had slowed my reflexes and my responses until I was left alone, sitting in the dark living room.

And still, all I could think of was Faith.

There was something about the oil rig that calmed me. It always had. Maybe it was the confined space—the knowledge that you could only go so far. Your mind had to be in the game one hundred and ten percent or someone could get hurt. It wasn't a fucking game when you were on the rig.

And the men were close. Fourteen of us spent two weeks together, twenty-four hours a day. I had bonded with them like brothers, at least most of them. Pete and I were two of the youngest guys on the rig. Some were older and thought we were peons and treated us as such. Most were cool, though.

So it had taken me a week to figure out why the only place I felt like I belonged since I left Jasper Bay suddenly felt like a cage without walls—a platform barricading me in.

Through every morning safety meeting, my mind swam with thoughts of Faith. Wondering what she was doing—*who* she was doing. If she was safe or hurt. If Cain or Black Death had punished her, filled her back with more lashes and scars. Every night I closed my eyes only to be bombarded with the picture of her back and the poorly healed marks.

I couldn't fucking get them out of my head.

I couldn't get *her* out of my head. The smell of her. The softness of her hair. The beautiful skin. The way, when right before I ended that horrific and manhandled kiss, she had briefly leaned in and accepted what I was doing to her.

Her tongue. Her taste.

Her waist.

Her long legs.

Skin and lips I had once worshipped.

Faith was everywhere.

"Hey."

I lifted my head from the table where I was eating dinner in our mess hall. Pete slid into the spot across from me, his plastic food tray clanking on the plastic table top. "You've been quiet since we got back."

I stuffed a forkful of pot roast into my mouth and chewed. It was damn delicious. The chefs on the rig were cool as shit and took requests from the men for meals. Whoever had requested pot roast was my new best friend. It melted in my mouth and reminded me of my mom's home cooking back when life was good and easy. It also provided me the added bonus of ignoring Pete.

He meant well. I knew that. It didn't mean I could think of a response that he'd understand, though.

I shrugged.

"Meg called me last night."

That got my attention. My fork froze right in front of my mouth. "Yeah?"

"She's worried about you."

I shrugged again. I knew that. She had tried to talk to me a half dozen times before I left for the rig last week. However, I had the benefit of going five years without talking about all the shit that haunted me. I was a master at avoidance.

"I'm good," I said and shoved the fork in my mouth.

Pete eyed me warily before settling into his own meal. "The thing is," he started around a mouthful of food. He pointed his fork at me while he chewed and swallowed. "Is that you're not. I've seen you this week and you're distracted. Which isn't only bad for the men on the crew, but you're acting like..."

"Don't say it," I warned him. I knew what he was thinking—that I was acting like I did after Byron died. We'd been in the crow's nest, fifty feet above the platform of the rig, drilling new pipes down to the drill floor, which was beneath the water. There were hundreds of feet of pipe stationed up there where we had to walk over empty space. It would take one false step to fall. The work was dangerous. It took skill and concentration. I still didn't know what happened. Maybe it was the strong wind gust, maybe Byron had been distracted, or maybe I hadn't been paying as much attention as I should have.

Regardless, his one misstep took him crashing down to the platform floor where he died instantly.

Pete was undistracted by my warning and scowl. He kept talking, and the more he talked, the more I wanted to reach across the table and choke him.

"Byron's death wasn't your fault, as horrible as it had been—none of the men blame you." I'd heard that before. I'd heard that same thing from Daemon over a week ago about my part in my dad's death. What they forgot was that even if the blame wasn't on me from other men, I still shouldered the burden. Byron had been my friend, my crewmate, and my responsibility. "And I hate to say this, man, but Meg isn't your responsibility, either."

"What the hell?" I growled at him.

Pete set his fork down and pushed his plate away from him, resting his elbows on the table. He looked so at peace. How could he be so relaxed when those few words made my entire body coil in rage?

"Look—"

"No, you look." I pushed up to my feet, bracing myself with my palms flat on the table. My chest heaved. My throat constricted. My pulse thrummed in my ears. "Byron made me promise to look after them if anything happened and I'm doing that." I leaned down, towering over the guy sitting all chilled out in front of me, not intimidated by my size or my anger. "But don't you fucking think for one second she isn't my responsibility. It's a promise I made and it's a promise I'll see to the end."

Pete sucked in a breath. "Have you ever thought that it is the end?"

My eyebrows pulled in. "What are you talking about?"

He stood up, holding a stance much like mine, but without the frustration and anger. Out of the corner of my eye, our crew watched us. Fights weren't allowed on the rig. One thrown punch and you were gone—fired. For the first time since I'd worked on the rig, my hands itched to break that rule.

"She's strong, man."

"I know that," I bit out.

"Maybe what you need to consider is that you babying her, you taking care of her, isn't needed anymore. Maybe what Meg needs is to learn to move on, to take care of herself, without worrying about disappointing someone else—disappointing you."

He wasn't making sense. I knew Meg was strong. She was independent and sweet. But she had Brayden, and Byron never wanted his son to grow up without men in his life like Byron had. I was doing what he wanted.

And I would continue to do it for as long as I could. I just had to figure out how to make it all work.

"Fuck you."

I pushed off from the table, tossing my food tray onto the top of the garbage can where it clattered and rattled and thankfully didn't knock the rest of the pile over.

Then I pushed through the doors and made my way to the platform where I could dangle my legs over the edge, seventy-five feet above the water, and forget everything.

Night had fallen and I was still standing on the edge of the rig, a fishing pole firmly fixed in my hands. When requested, the chefs would save the leftover food from meals and mix it with enough water into a five gallon bucket. It became our fish bait that we'd mash into fist-sized balls and rig to our poles. It felt disgusting and smelled worse, but it worked.

I had ignored Pete when he showed up hours ago, pail and poles in hand. I continued ignoring his smug presence when he handed me my pole and we began fishing two hours ago.

We hadn't caught shit. And while the calming act of fishing generally gave me a sense of peace, my muscles tensed while I waited for Pete to start talking again.

"Byron's death wasn't your fault."

I glared at him from the side of my eyes and went back to focusing on my fishing pole. "We're not really going to do the pussy shit girl talk, are we?"

"No need. Meg already told me everything."

Everything? I wanted to ask exactly what everything meant. Instead, I rolled my eyes. "Fucking women."

Pete grunted. "Sounds to me like you've got one back home waiting for you to pull your head out of your ass and save the day." My lips pressed together into a firm line. Like hell I was going to let him talk to me about Faith. He squeezed the nasty leftovers into a ball, reset his hook, dropped it seventy-five feet down into the water, and kept talking, this time with a sarcastic grin. "You could be like an armored knight and all that bull-shit."

I felt a tug at the end of my string and yanked it up quickly. Came up empty. "It's only a name, Pete."

"Doesn't mean you're not needed somewhere else." He turned to me. "I get what you did for Meg. I get the promise you made to take care of her for Byron. But Meg?" He wiped a line of sweat off his forehead. "Meg's strong as shit. I've known her since we were kids. I'm not saying she doesn't appreciate the help or feels like she needs it, but that girl can stand on her own. Byron and you—you have that protector mentality and want to do it all for her—which is admirable. But it's not necessary. She can move on. She simply needs someone to let her."

"So you can move in?" I checked my growl and took a step away, reeling in my own pole. Fucking lousy night for fishing.

"Fuck you, Knight. She's like my sister and always has been. I'll help her if she needs it, but she also needs to learn she can be everything Brayden needs, too. She needs the freedom to move on."

He had a point. I knew it, but I couldn't imagine walking away from promises.

The little shit was also right. Not only about Meg. Her innocence and sweetness might have made her seem weak, but she picked up after Byron's death and did what needed to be done in order to keep caring for Brayden and keeping his life as settled as possible.

He was also right about me. About Faith. I had more important shit that needed to be dealt with. The way Faith walked away from me that morning in the hotel still burned a hole in my chest. My fingers itched constantly to take one shot at Cain. And I needed to be on solid ground to do it.

Even knowing that, I stared out at the black Gulf, unable to agree with Pete. There was nothing to see. No land, no lights—just utter blackness with the only sound being the waves hitting the base of our rig in the moonlight.

"I don't want to leave Brayden. It'd kill him to have another man leave his life."

"Going home to where you belong doesn't mean you're leaving him."

Again, the fucker was smarter than he looked. Maybe I hadn't given his intelligence enough credit by figuring he could be on a billboard being used as man candy. The thought made me grin.

"Yo, Knight!"

Pete and I both turned to see John, the medic on our rig, screaming my name from a doorway.

"You have a phone call on the SAT phone!" he shouted.

I nodded and bent down to pick up my pole, but Pete stopped me. "I'll take care of the stuff. You go get your phone call."

I thanked him and jogged off to the office, breathless by the time I reached the SAT phone receiver in the main living quarters.

"This is Ryker," I said, my mind already swirling with who could be calling me on the phone.

"We got problems," Daemon's voice cracked through the phone, and my blood ran cold as he started talking without letting me say hello. By the time he was done explaining the information Antonio Sporelli shared with Daemon about our dad and Liv's mom, Cherry, having an affair and that being what led to Bull hiring out a hit on them instead of it being Black Death as we assumed in the first place, I was ready for murder.

So when Daemon brought up the plan to take Bull out, I growled, "That fucker's mine," into the phone.

Bull was the ultimate reason for all of our lives falling to shit. It almost made me smile thinking of putting a bullet in him.

10

Faith

Never in my life had I been filled with so much hate.

My house was no longer a home. It was a jail where a thick sense of dread and death would fill my lungs as soon as I inhaled the musty, smoke-filled air when I walked through the doors.

"Mom?" I called out to her by habit, as if she would answer. Some things were too ingrained to stop doing, although she had stopped answering me years ago. Unless she needed more drugs.

Then she'd answer.

This time, she didn't. So I closed the front door behind me and dropped my eyes to avoid seeing the collection of pill bottles and ashtrays that I knew would be littered across every inch of our worn and chipped wooden coffee table.

I dropped my purse on the table in the hallway and headed toward the kitchen to see if she'd eaten any of the food I'd left out for her the night before when I had a client.

My steps were slow, as if someone had filled my shoes with lead. My body ached. Not physically, but emotionally. Nothing felt right anymore. I hadn't felt anything since I had turned my back on Ryker and walked away from him almost a week ago.

My heavy laden footsteps froze when I hit the kitchen doorway at the back of our house. To my surprise, tears suddenly blurred my vision. How could I still be crying over a woman who had been nothing but a constant disappointment to me for my entire life?

That well should have dried up a long time ago. But occasionally on days like today when I saw her slouched over, her forehead resting on the kitchen table while she was passed out with a mirrored tray and fine, white dust smeared over it, emotions surfaced.

The first time I saw my mom passed out on the floor, I thought she was dead.

Now, I wasn't surprised by the cocaine remnants on my kitchen counter and table.

A quick glance in the fridge and in the pantry told me she hadn't eaten any of the meals or protein bars I'd made sure were highly visible to her.

She was like that, now. Ever since the cocaine appeared on the scene, her penchant for remembering to feed herself with any actual substance had diminished. It showed in the way her now, too-large clothes hung on her shrinking frame. It showed in the way her eyes looked like they were sinking back into her skull.

She was dying before my eyes.

And I was still alive, but felt the same as she looked.

I walked to my mom and pushed her dull and graying hair behind her ear. My fingers rested on her pulse on her throat to make sure she was still alive.

Then I left the room. I grabbed my purse on the way upstairs to shower and washed the stench of last night's man off of me.

I spent the rest of the afternoon packing for Sturgis Motorcycle Rally. The club made me go every year. It was my job, along with several other women, to be "available" for the men as needed during the week.

My limbs heated. Bile rose in my throat and my fingers shook as I packed my small suitcase, knowing few clothes would be needed.

Without realizing, I went to wipe my hair out of my eyes only to come back with the back of my hand wet.

Tears.

They were such a fucking waste.

I squeezed my eyes closed and collapsed onto the edge of the bed. I sobbed into my hands and my shoulders shook with grief.

I couldn't stop thinking about Ryker. About his promise to free me. About the way his lips felt against mine as he took control of my body. The body I willingly gave to him when I knew I shouldn't. I knew at the time it would only end with a further severed heart on my part, and I had been correct.

Kissing Ryker, seeing Ryker, and touching him had affected me more in the last week emotionally than I'd anything else I'd felt in the last five years.

He ruined me in the best way possible.

Except only once I was away from him did I realize that without him, I was ruined in the worst way possible.

My ringing cell snapped me out of my self-induced misery. Cringing when I saw the caller, I answered it with a trembling voice. Not that Cain cared or noticed when his vile voice came through the line.

"I see you found a new way to ensure my compliance," I told him, thinking of my mom downstairs. Fuck Cain. He had continued to get her hooked on deeper and darker shit and she simply opened her mouth like a baby bird and took whatever he gave her. And he did it only to prove that he could kill her whenever he wanted. He could lace her drugs with poison, and she'd smile and say thank you.

I suppose I was no different. She was a whore for drugs. I was just a whore.

His greasy voice sounded thrilled, even pleased, with himself. "Only the best for you and your mom."

I suppressed my retort, knowing if I spoke it, I'd pay the punishment for it later.

"What do you want, Cain?" With my patience and my earlier emotions long gone, I began pacing the small open space in my bedroom. Four steps one way, four steps the other.

"Mills is on his way to get you. Don't forget the rules we discussed at the rally this week. You wouldn't want anything to happen, would you?"

My top lip curled, and I was thankful he couldn't see my disgust for him. It'd give him a hard-on. He probably had one now, but at least over the phone I didn't have to take care of it.

"I understand," I gritted out. My hands squeezed the life out of my cell phone.

"Good," he said, happily again. "Then we'll be able to enjoy ourselves this week. Be a good girl, Faith."

I hung up. He would hit me for it later, but I was quickly losing my ability to give a shit about what Cain thought or wanted from me. Punishments be damned. If this was my life, I would go out on my terms. Death would be a reprieve for me.

The rally was loud. Not that I was able to enjoy any of it, but the new scenery and the sounds of the bands in the distance at least allowed me to pretend that I had been free for the last few days.

Currently, I was sitting on a barstool in one of the same, small, non-air-conditioned bars encased between Mill's legs. He was overweight, sweaty, and drunk. A perfect trifecta for a night of hell for me.

I tensed as his large hands pawed at my thighs. The short skirt I was wearing barely covered my ass. I had thrown it on that morning, knowing what I'd be expected to do—again—but I wore it because it reminded me of the day, only a few simple weeks ago, when I'd been allowed to hang out with Olivia, my one-time best friend.

I hadn't been able to see her or talk to her since she'd been shot.

Seeing the skirt had made me smile—slightly, but it had happened—I had felt my lips spread upward a minute amount so I threw the skirt on. Anything to make me feel better helped.

Some days, I couldn't believe so much had changed in a few short weeks. Three weeks ago, I was working at Penny's, taking my clients, and doing my job and it had all felt manageable. Depressing— but survivable.

Then, Ryker showed up in my doorway, and suddenly, barely surviving was no longer enough. The problem I faced was I had no idea how to get away from my sentence, and I wasn't sure life would be any better if I was.

What was there to do in life once your mom sold you to become a whore? Any aspirations I'd had years ago of a simple life with a family were long gone.

"I'm ready to go," Mills said, standing up from the stool and wrapping his arm around me. It was the middle of the afternoon and he'd been drinking since before the sun rose, if he had even bothered stopping when it had set the night before. He was slow on his feet, and his beer breath made me turn my head away.

I, on the other hand, hadn't had nearly enough. But I played my role. Pushing a hand to his chest, for one to give me space and also because he liked it when I touched him, I smiled. "Just one more shot, Mills?"

He dipped his head, and his thick tongue ran along my neck. My shoulders tensed, but he was too drunk to notice my disdain.

"Whatever you want, Diamond."

His words were slurred. I closed my eyes and took a deep breath, cursing myself for ever choosing that name.

After I slammed back two straight shots of vodka, I finally allowed Mills to take my hand and lead me out of the bar.

The bright afternoon sunshine blinded me as soon as we stepped outside. I squeezed my eyes closed to give myself time to adjust to the piercing sky, but then stumbled on my high heels.

"C'mon, hooker," Mills growled, pulling my elbow and walking faster. Spit flew from his mouth. I pulled back, wiping it off my face.

"Slow down, Mills." I instantly knew it was a mistake to talk back to him. Not only did it turn him on when I argued, but it pissed him off, too.

He spun on me, letting go of my elbow, and I stumbled back a step. When I regained my balance, he was in my face and clutching at the waistband of my skirt. "You want me to take your pussy here on the streets for everyone to see?"

I hated him. I fucking hated the asshole in front of me. My cheeks burned with rage and my small hands curled into fists. He noticed and grinned.

"You'd like that, wouldn't you?"

I swallowed and remembered where I was. Black Death territory at the rally. No one would say anything if he actually followed through with what he threatened. Something rose up in me, though, and I was tired of acquiescing to all of their demands.

I may have been a whore and theirs to use however and whenever they wanted, but I was still a damn person and should have been treated with a modicum of respect. Never had I battled for it, and I didn't know why I was choosing to do it now.

"You disgust me," I growled in his face. Mills was large and sweaty. He towered over me with his lip curled in desire and anger. "And the only reason you have sex with me is because you know there's no one else on the planet that would spread their legs for you…"

The back of his hand was on my cheekbone in a flash. Pain radiated from my cheek to my forehead and down to my chest. My feet collapsed from underneath me as I fell to the ground.

"Get up, you fucking whore!" He shouted it, but I could barely hear his voice over the ringing in my ears.

I licked my bottom lip and tasted blood, when suddenly I heard a female voice shouting my name.

"Faith!"

I closed my eyes and embarrassment flooded me, knowing Olivia had witnessed Mills smack the shit out of me. What would she think of me now?

I sunk onto my ass on the concrete and took deep breaths, but nothing stopped the pain from pulsating all over my cheek. I smelled and felt blood dripping down my cheek.

I saw her footsteps quickly approach us and she stopped right in front of me and Mills. I wanted to tell her to run away before he hit her too, but my jaw hurt too much to open. Damn it. Did he break my jaw?

"What in the hell is wrong with you? You don't hit a fucking woman, damn it!" Olivia shouted at Mills as if he couldn't crush her under his boot in a second. I wanted to smile, but damn, the pain. Black dots swam in my vision.

"Watch your mouth, Nordic cock sucker," Mills sneered at Olivia.

My stomach churned. I had to get her away from him before Mills really did hurt her. It would cause a war between two clubs that already hated one another. Daemon would see to it for certain.

Another man approached, one I didn't know, but based on his accent, he was Finn, the Australian, Olivia had told me about.

I looked up briefly to see she hadn't been wrong in her description of him. Sexy and accented. He was incredible.

I just wanted to get out of there. Quickly. Which was why when Olivia crouched down and asked me if I was okay, I ignored her. Cain would be pissed and I would be punished once he found out I was having anything to do with Nordic Lords.

He'd lose his shit once he found out they tried to protect me on his street.

I closed my eyes, my vision still blurred, as Olivia pulled me to my feet.

She wiped my cheek, and I finally found my voice. "You need to leave."

"Listen to the whore, little girl. Nordic Lords don't own her. We do."

Olivia wasn't to be stopped as she slowly wiped my cheek and said, "Let me clean you up."

I raised my eyes to hers and saw hers only filled with pity. No one wanted to be pitied. "Go home, Liv. There's nothing you can do for me."

I took a step away from her and barely recognized Mills and Finn begin to raise their voices as Liv stumbled on her feet. When I blinked again, Daemon was there and slowly the rest of the streets were filled with Black Death and Nordic Lords members standing off on the street corner.

I couldn't pull my eyes back to Olivia as the men argued about who owned me and who would be getting me soon. It sounded so familiar to what Ryker had told me in the hotel room, but the shame that always encompassed my life filled with me such torment that there was no way I wanted to see what sort of disgust laid in Olivia's eyes.

Instead, I looked away and wobbled on my heels, trying to get away from the men who were joining the crowd on the street.

Words were shouted right before the first punches were thrown. Someone shoved my shoulder. My feet slipped on the pavement, and I fell backward. My hands flew out to steady myself, but it didn't help. My head slammed into a glass window behind me, and I crumpled to my feet. The black dots reappeared in my vision along with the sticky feel of more blood becoming tangled in my hair.

I heard Olivia shout my name right before a large, firm hand grabbed my bicep and pulled me to my feet.

Punches flew. Knives were pulled. Sirens rang in the distance.

"Let's go," he ordered, his voice deep and authoritative. Seeing as how I wasn't in a position to argue, I didn't. He pulled me roughly to my feet and kept a hand on me until we were around the corner. The entire time, I hoped that Nordic Lords killed every single Black Death member.

11

Ryker

"I'll be back to see you as soon as I can, okay?"

My heart pounded in my chest as I watched Brayden's chin shake and quiver. Tears pooled in the little boys eyes and my own breathing restricted.

"You're going away," Brayden said as he lost the fight on his tears.

I pulled him into a hug, my arms encapsulating him into a warm and tight embrace. I looked up and watched Meg wipe away her own silent tears. *I'm sorry,* I mouthed to her. She shook her head and smiled. I held onto Brayden until his sniffles disappeared before I pushed him away. My hands curled over his shoulders, and I ducked so he could look directly into my eyes.

"I have to go home to my family for a while, but I will stay in touch. We'll talk and can FaceTime each other, okay?" Brayden sniffed and nodded. For a millisecond, I debated whether leaving was the right choice. Then I remembered the phone call from Daemon and knew I couldn't stay. "You be good for your mom, okay, kiddo?" I asked and stood up at the same time, my hand leaving his shoulder to ruffle the hair on his head.

He nodded once. "I be good."

I wrapped my arm around his shoulder again and pulled him with me when I walked to Meg. We were standing on the front porch of her house in New Orleans. In an hour, I was headed back to Jasper Bay.

Nothing except the idea of Bull getting what was coming to him made me happy about leaving Meg and Brayden again. I definitely didn't want to see tears in their eyes and know that I was the cause of them. Already I felt like I'd backed out on Byron, the first person to give me a chance when I showed up in New Orleans five years ago. He had become a friend, almost a brother. My chest felt tight, knowing that I was leaving the woman he'd made me promise to look after.

Meg's small hand came up and rested on my cheek. Her thumb brushed against my skin, and her smile was smoothing, even if I knew she was faking it. Her glistening wet eyes were a dead giveaway.

"Go do what you need to do," she said, her voice cracking. My hand curled into a fist at my side and my shoulders grew tight with tension. "We'll be fine here. It's time anyway."

I shook my head. "I'll be back."

Her smile fell and her hand fell down to cover mine that was still resting on Brayden's shoulder. She squeezed it tightly as tears ran down her cheeks. "No, you won't. And it's okay. We need to figure this out, anyway."

I let go of Brayden only long enough to pull both of them into a hug. Meg was kind and sweet and she didn't deserve to have her husband die on her. She also didn't deserve for me to turn my back on her. I hugged her hard and long, feeling both of our chests shaking with unspoken emotions.

When I pulled her away, I stared directly at her. "You'll call me if you need anything."

She nodded. I didn't believe her. My hands squeezed her tighter. My glare grew harsher. "I'm not fuckin' around, Meg. I don't give a shit what it is, but if you need anything, call me."

She wiped a tear and bit her bottom lip. "Go." She waved toward my truck on the street. "Go save your woman and don't worry about us."

"Meg—"

"I'll call, okay. We'll be just fine, but I promise that if something happens we can't handle, I'll call you."

I narrowed my eyes and looked for deception, but all I came away with was sadness and strength in her eyes.

I nodded. With one last hug to both of the people who had been such good friends to me, I turned my back on them and headed home.

I could hear everything and nothing at the same time. My sight trained on the gathering fifty yards away below me, and yet I couldn't hear the voices or the slight kick of gravel. I couldn't hear the dust blowing the dirt and I was blocking out the animals in the woods that scampered around late at night, scavenging for food and breaking down branches.

But my senses were trained on the whistling of the wind. The way it flicked through the pine branches, disrupting the trajectory I would need to hold if I wanted a clean shot.

Lying stomach down on a shipping warehouse rooftop, the metal that had burned earlier in the hot sun only felt slightly warm against my abdomen. My arms felt relaxed while tension coiled from my shoulders down to my spine.

I knew when the moment would come for me to take my shot. Daemon and the club brothers had filled me in when I arrived back in town. It didn't lessen the stress as I kept my eye trained on the group of men through my scope. Scanning the crowd, I searched for Cain, the Vice President of Black Death. A muscle in my cheek jumped, knowing he wasn't here. He had been shot last week at the fight that broke out during the Sturgis Motorcycle Rally. It had resulted in

Daemon and a handful of men from the Nordic Lords spending a night in the local jail. Cain hadn't been heard from since. Neither had Faith or her mom.

After I handled the shit with Bull, Cain was my next target.

I would take Faith back by force, if necessary, if it meant getting her out from under Cain's wicked control.

With the resolve of my plan certain, I pushed everything outside my mind and focused on the trigger on my Remington 700. It sat on its stand while I peered through the night vision scope. The men below rarely moved.

I had shown up an hour early to get in place before anyone else did.

The roar of the Sporelli family and his crew crested in my ears as their Ducati motorbikes made their way along the last curve before they began their descent down the narrow drive to where Daemon and his men waited for him.

Daemon had originally thought of partnering with Black Death to get the Sporelli's out of our ports and his interest out of our town. The Sporelli's were a mob family in Chicago. They ran drugs and money and wanted water access. In return, Black Death would release Faith.

But when Angelo Sporelli, head family man, contacted Daemon and told him the truth about Bull's plan, all of Black Death's plans went to shit.

Only they didn't know that. Yet.

Soon, they'd realize that Daemon had greater plans in mind. Plans to eradicate the Black Death presence from Jasper Bay like it should have been done years ago.

Unfortunately, it would put Daemon under control of Sporelli, although he also assured me he had a plan to fix that, too.

I had rolled my eyes. My little brother, ever the problem solver.

After tonight, if I did my job correctly, he'd be President of his own MC Charter. Nordic Lords weren't the largest MC in the country—they sat in the middle—but they were big enough that most others didn't fuck with them.

Sporelli had chosen to do that by making them a deal to agree to run drugs for them down to the Twin Cities. Eventually, they'd see their error.

Upon hearing the bikes engines turned off, I focused my eyes on Daemon. I watched him and Bull speak with Sporelli and then Hammer, the president of Black Death. The men moved to the large truck that had driven in, surrounded by the Italian motorbikes.

I swallowed a deep breath to maintain my focus on Bull while the men emptied the crates.

I knew what was coming, but the blast from the last crate still surprised me.

The building I was on shook beneath my abdomen. My boots rattled and my elbows shifted on the roof. I had my doubts Daemon could pull this off. He had jumped into an ocean of trouble by aligning with Sporelli, and he wouldn't know the full depth of it until Sporelli came to collect the favor he'd just done for them.

Unwilling to admit it out loud, I knew there was no way I'd leave my brother behind again to deal with the fallout of this.

Guns blasted from below as smoke filled the air.

My gut churned. Every instinct in me wanted to be in the brawl—fighting with my fists and the rage that simmered inside me.

But still—I held position and watched Black Death be decimated by both The Nordic Lords and Sporelli.

My lips twisted into a small grin once the smoke cleared. From a hundred yards out, I listened to Sporelli's crew pull out on their bikes. Their engines and the diesel motor of the van that had brought the crates blared passed my position on the roof.

And all the Nordic Lords turned on Bull.

Their President—their betrayer.

I sucked in a deep breath and watched Bull lower his gun. He spoke to Daemon. Bull opened his mouth to respond.

A light breeze ghosted past me. My short hair ruffled and the wind gave off a slight whistle as it went through the trees. I waited for it to settle.

Then… my wait was over.

My finger pulled the trigger.

Kickback from the rifle slammed it against my shoulder.

When I looked through the scope again, Bull was lying on the ground. A quick sweep showed me everyone else had put their guns away.

Daemon had done it.

I had done it.

Vengeance fulfilled swirled deep inside of me, settling into my stomach with a heavy weight.

It wasn't nearly as freeing as I expected it to be.

"Hey, baby girl." I pulled Liv into a hug as soon as I climbed out of Daemon's beat up Ford pickup at the Nordic Lords clubhouse. She had rushed outside and ran straight to my door, jumping back and forth on her feet before I turned the engine off.

Based on her bleeding fingertips, she'd been chewing her nails for the last several hours.

"I'm not a baby," she said as she wrapped her arms around me.

Guilt swam inside me, knowing what I had done and what I had to tell her. Daemon worried about this screwing up their relationship. She'd been through enough over the last few weeks with losing her baby and being shot. If she was going to blame anyone—I'd shoulder it.

"Okay, then." I grinned and pushed her back, squeezing her shoulders. "Little sister."

She smiled. I winked. Worry still lined her eyes, but I knew she liked the idea of her and Daemon. Her brief smile proved it.

"What happened?"

I exhaled a long, slow breath. Liv instantly recognized the shift in my playful mood. "We gotta talk."

Instantly, her shoulders trembled and her chin shook. "Oh God... Daemon—"

"No," I snapped. She blinked and her eyes focused on mine. "He's fine."

She blinked slowly, collecting herself, and I gave her the time before I brought her world to her knees.

"We should go inside—have a drink and sit down. There's a lot to explain."

Her hands tightened on my forearms, squeezing them, but I didn't pry her off. "Tell me."

"I will," I said, turning her and pulling her to my side. With one arm wrapped around her, I walked her into the clubhouse, and once she was settled at the bar with a beer in her hands, I explained everything.

I relayed the phone call Daemon had received from Sporelli at the Sturgis Rally. I told her all about the night I'd walked in on her five years ago when she was unconscious. I explained the shooter had been a hired hit man. She watched and listened—maybe not hearing all of it through her shock—without interrupting until I mentioned Bull's name.

Her father.

Her hands flew to her mouth. "No," she gasped.

"Liv," I began and swallowed my words. I took a pull from my beer while I watched tears rim her bottom lids. Then I lowered my chin. "He hired a hit on the club's Vice President and his own wife. You know what happens to men like that."

She shook her head. Her hands trembled on her beer bottle. Tears escaped her eyes.

I couldn't do a damn thing for her.

"I'm sorry."

Her head snapped to mine. "Ryker."

"I did it. I'm so sorry."

In a flash, she pushed off her bar stool, knocking it over and almost tripping over the metal legs to get away. I reached out and grabbed her arm, preventing her from running. "You killed him!"

She shouted it right before I pulled her to my chest. She heaved and sobbed against my shirt and I wrapped a hand around the back of her head. I had no excuses. I had no words that could make her feel better.

There was nothing else to say. So I held her, swaying slightly back and forth, while she punched my chest with her shaking hands and her shoulders shook under the weight of my arms.

She pulled back as soon as the thunderous roll of motorcycles vibrated against the clubhouse doors. "Daemon," she gasped. And then she ran. I was right behind her.

By the time I caught up to her, Daemon was holding her in the same way I had just been doing.

"I told her," I said.

Daemon flashed me a *no shit?* look from over his shoulder. Pain laced his expression while he held Liv and explained everything to her. I stood back, helpless with the other men, while she ranted and screamed at all of them.

And then I watched her shift. All of us—Daemon, Switch, Jaden, and I watched her transform. "Okay then. I need a drink."

She was calm. It was unnatural. But when she turned on her heels and walked past me into the club, she also looked confident. Sad but resigned because she had been raised in this life and she knew how it worked.

She was fucking brave—braver than I had ever been. In that one second, it was the first time in my life that I had been fucking jealous of Daemon. Jealous that he had been strong enough to go after what he wanted in the first place. To fight for it.

I had never done that. I had always run.

But in that moment, I knew I would run no longer.

"She's…" Daemon stared after Liv, dumbfounded.

"She'll be all right," I assured him, clamping a hand around his shoulder. I wanted to haul ass out of the club and go fight for Faith, to go find her and finish the shit with Cain.

But I knew Daemon needed me. And for some reason, I wanted to curl up on a barstool next to him and Liv and hope like hell that some of their strength and bravery would rub off on me.

"Let's get wasted, Prez."

Daemon laughed once, his eyes flashing to mine before he followed me inside the clubhouse doors. "Fuck yeah, brother."

12

Ryker

My brother owned the gavel like it had been his God-given right to be the President of a Motorcycle Club. Sheer power seeped from him the first time I was allowed into the room where the club men held their chapel.

It wasn't an easy day. It had been almost two weeks since Faith disappeared. Almost two weeks since anyone had seen Cain or Faith. We couldn't find a single lead to save our life. I was ready to blow up at the smallest provocation.

Without Brayden and Meg to calm the beast that prowled inside me with their kindness and gentle words and touches, I was beginning to doubt I'd ever feel sane again.

But she had understood. I couldn't leave. I couldn't go back to New Orleans with everything so uncertain with Faith. And when Meg and I had talked earlier in the week, she had almost sounded smug. I had smiled, hearing her unspoken *I told you so* come through the phone line. Pete had been equally understanding. The conversation I had with him, letting him know what was going on, had been almost as difficult as the one I'd had with Meg. They had become my family.

I would see them again, but it would never be the same.

So while my thoughts were on missing them and finding Faith, taking her far from the hell she'd lived in for the last several years, I wasn't paying attention to Daemon and the other brothers in the clubhouse.

Daemon pounded the gavel, declared the voting done, and men I'd known for practically my entire life began slapping my shoulders, handing me my leather vest.

I gripped it in my hands. Only then did I realize my hands were shaking.

I said nothing as I took it.

There would be no Prospect patch for me. Apparently putting a bullet in their old President allowed me to skirt that step in becoming a member. Not that most of them hadn't known me my entire life. Not that I hadn't heard at least a half dozen of them remind me over the last ten days that no one blamed me for my father's death.

But still, I stared at the cut as if it was the final step in me returning home. Returning to a life I had never wanted to be in, but knew it was where I would always end up. Now I was done fighting it.

It didn't make it easier to slide the soft black leather over my shoulders, though.

"I know what you're feeling," Daemon said. His voice was low and quiet. All the men were gone from the chapel room besides the two of us.

My fist tightened around the cool leather. "Do you?"

"You think I didn't feel the same shit when I did this same thing five years ago?"

"Fuck," I choked out, shaking my head. I stared at the leather, and then at Daemon, a small grin on my lips. "The fucking shit we do for our women."

Daemon walked by and smacked my shoulder, pushing me out of the chapel room into the living room. "First shot's on me."

He nodded toward the shot glasses already lined up on the bar and the men already filling their glasses from the tapped kegs.

He had insisted the club needed a reason to party. We'd been running ourselves ragged for the last two weeks trying to find Faith, coming home from overnight rides where we hadn't slept in over twenty-four hours, completely exhausted. My frustration and fear grew every day.

But he was right. The men needed a night off. Most of them were still reeling from Bull's betrayal and with the uncertainty of Sporelli and Black Death retribution chasing them—*us*—the mood had been somber.

And if they wanted to do it on my behalf, I'd let them fill me with shots and cheap beer until my own head could fucking settle down and maybe, finally, be able to sleep for a night.

"We'll find her," Daemon insisted as we stepped outside.

The men cheered and raised their glasses.

A shot glass filled with tequila was pressed into my palms by Jaden, followed by a slam to my back.

"Drink up, brother!" he shouted, and all the men yelled again. I took in the room. The room that was filled with men I had once considered family. Where the older men had always been like uncles and pseudo-fathers, and the younger ones like brothers.

I slammed back the shot and faced Daemon.

"We'll find her," I agreed. "But it better be fucking quick."

Then I was yanked into the madness, filled with shot after shot. Beer after beer. I played pool, and I got my ass kicked at darts.

Liv tried—and failed—to get me to smile.

Jules showed up and avoided Jaden while he scowled and stared at her in the corner until she left.

And then I passed out in my new room in the clubhouse. The room spun in the darkness.

And through all of it, all I could think about was where the fuck was Faith. And knowing that if when I found her she had any visible injury on her at all, there would be more blood on my hands.

"You going for a ride with me?" I asked Finn, the quiet Australian, as I slid onto a bench to him outside. Xbox and one of the twin prospects—Jimmy or Johnny, I had no clue—sparred inside the boxing ring.

A muscle in the man's jaw jumped. He was quiet. I hadn't spoken to him much, but under his quiet, watchful eye, for some strange reason I trusted the fuck out of Finn even if I didn't know his story.

"Where to today?"

My hands balled into fists. I had no fucking clue. I only knew I had to get out from behind the caged walls and into open air, and then hope like hell someone, somewhere, had seen Faith.

"Headed West, I figure. If Cain has her, he'll head toward where they have other Charters in Colorado."

Finn was quiet for a beat before he ran his hand down his face. "Why the fuck not?"

"What's your story, anyway?" I asked, although I didn't expect an honest answer. Daemon and Jaden had both told me no one knew why Finn had left Australia and headed toward the States. Even more confusing was how he ended up with a bunch of outlaw motorcycle men. Murder was my first guess. Not that I was in a place to judge him for it.

Finn swung a leg over his bike and narrowed his eyes on me. "You ever run from something?"

I arched an eyebrow. He shrugged. "Then you know what it's fucking like to be asked about it."

I gave him that play, but still I said, "Yeah, but I came back."

He started the engine on his bike, and at the same time shouted over the rumbling sound, "I won't."

I gave him that play, too. The man was a silent broody mystery, but hell if I didn't also agree that we were all entitled to our own secrets. I carried enough of them.

He followed me as we pulled out of the club and I waved a see you later to whatever twin wasn't in the sparring ring. Someday, I'd learn their fucking names.

The sun was brutal as it beat down on our arms. It heated me through the black vest that had somehow become a natural part of me over the last few days. It was two hours into our drive when my phone began vibrating in the front pocket of my jeans.

I ignored it at first, lost in the familiar silence of what it was like to be on a bike again. Daemon had fixed me up with his old one as soon as I declared I was staying. I'd get my own someday soon, but for now, it worked.

Eventually, I could no longer ignore the incessant buzzing against my thigh, so I waved my hand and signaled for Finn to pull over at the next rest stop exit.

When we did, my phone buzzed again.

I clicked it open and snarled almost immediately.

"Want your woman?" A slightly accented voice that I could place rumbled through the phone.

I hit the speaker button and watched Finn's eyes widen.

"Who the fuck are you?"

The man laughed. It was recognizable and my blood boiled instantly.

"Sporelli? You fucking shit."

"Calm down, son, my men just got her." He paused and my pulse increased. "She's hurt."

Fuck! "How bad?" I asked through the choking sensation in my throat. Faith was hurt? When I found Cain or whoever was responsible for hurting her more than she'd already been hurt, I'd kill them with my bare hands.

The asshole almost sounded compassionate. His voice softened. "She'll live."

Which didn't fucking help me. At all.

I growled. "Where is she?"

"Not close, yet," he said. My hand clamped onto the seat of my bike. What the hell was he playing at? "But you'll see her soon."

"What's your game?"

The asshole sounded like he was smiling. And suddenly, I knew I was fucking tired of the guilt of killing people. Some people, like Bull and now Angelo Sporelli, simply deserved to die.

"Consider her collateral," he said. "You'll get her when I get my first shipment delivered to the Cities. Should be arriving in your ports later tonight. Don't screw it up."

And then he was gone. I stared at Finn. "You've got to be kidding me."

"Apparently not, man." He shrugged like this was no big deal, like it didn't matter that Faith was being held by someone we were supposed to be working with. And it still begged the question of where in the hell Cain was and Faith's mom.

I didn't have time to answer all the shit in my head.

I picked up the phone and called Daemon.

13

Faith

There wasn't an inch on my skin that didn't hurt. My back felt like it'd been ripped wide open all over again. I tasted dried blood on the corner of my lips. My right eye was so tender it made opening it difficult.

My shoulders, shackled to chains and cuffs above my head, had lost any sensation days ago. My legs down to my toes could barely support my position as I tried to balance on my tiptoes to alleviate the stretching in my shoulders.

I needed a bed. Soon.

I needed a shower even worse. Hair matted my face. Every time I tried to blow my hair out of my eye or off my cheeks, my lips ached and my chest burned.

I had screamed so much over the last several days ever since the man, that I later learned was from a Colorado Charter of the Black Death, had thrown me into their van at the rally. My throat was so sore.

I needed water and food. More substance than the tiny plastic cup of water I was given a day and small bowl of chicken broth and noodles. Based on the numbers of times I'd been given food, I estimated I'd been gone for two weeks.

I wanted to close my eyes and never have to open them again. My life had sucked enough. When would I find my reprieve?

Enough.

I blew out a slow, shaky breath. The fractional movement sent a scorching flame of fire through my back.

I tried to bite my teeth to hold back a sob as my broken body shook and protested against the chains that held me.

I wanted to die.

More than that, I wanted to kill whoever had tortured me.

Cain had left after the first week leaving me alone with a prospect from Black Death, whose name I didn't know, and another man who looked constantly wasted as he made his way down the stairs into the basement where I'd been chained to a metal pipe above the stained and thin mattress since the day I'd arrived.

Fortunately, the bruise on my cheek and over my eye had begun to heal, although it still pulsed with pain. The back lashings were courtesy of Cain being pissed he'd been stabbed in the street fight and the fact that I'd tried to fight against him when he first showed up.

I knew he wouldn't like to be spit on. But by the time he showed up and I'd already been chained to a metal pipe for three days, I no longer cared about pissing Cain off.

The only question I didn't understand was why.

I was so sick and tired of being a pawn. A moveable chess piece in a game where I had never understood the rules or why I was being forced to play.

For years, I figured Cain simply wanted to beat me down to nothing. I never understood why. He was harder on me than the other girls who came to him willingly. Even the ones I knew that weren't given an option, none of them had been beaten as harshly as me.

It had always seemed to give Cain a sick pleasure in the pain he seared into my skin.

I was so tired of it.

Every night after the sun set and I was left alone in a damp basement with water dripping down the foundation when it rained, my resolve grew stronger.

The next time I saw Cain I'd kill him.

And I wouldn't bat an eye while doing it.

Hatred had filled my veins, keeping me warm in the cold and damp room. I wrapped it around me like a thick, fleece blanket until I was secure in the knowledge that regardless of what Cain did to me, he would never succeed in breaking me.

My back thrashed in shock and pain ripped through my wrist connected to the handcuffs as a loud banging sound came from the floor above me. My head snapped to the door as I screamed out in pain from the sudden movement.

A blast filled the air. *Gunshot.* The sounds continued while the heavy weight of bodies dropping and footsteps pounding on the thin wooden floor above me shook the pipes above my head.

Apprehension filled me. Gone was the hatred that had just warmed me. My body chilled at the sound of soft but quick footsteps tapping down the staircase to the basement.

To where I was.

Ryker. He saved me.

I shook the thought from my head. He wouldn't have come to save me. He had his own family. I had tortured my mind with recalling the words he had spoken on the phone in the hotel room. It only served to make me stronger.

I could survive this alone. It was how I would end up when I was done.

And yet, still, as the doorknob twisted and opened, disappointment flickered in my mind when the man in the doorway wasn't him.

I stared at him directly in the eye, not ashamed at all that I was barely clothed in underwear and a bra. Surprisingly, Cain hadn't touched me in that way. None of the men I'd seen over the last two weeks had come close to me. That didn't stop their roaming eyes from leering over every inch of my naked skin while they checked on me. And it didn't stop them from gazing on my body in the middle of the night when they took me to an outdoor restroom—the only time I was allowed to use a real restroom or clean myself up. Based on the few lights that flickered while I was ushered quickly in an out, I figured I was in some type of resort.

"You alive?" the masculine voice asked. It held a hint of big city accent. My fingers tightened against the chains above my head.

The devil you knew was always better than the one you didn't.

"You hear me?" he asked again, this time, his feet slowly trudged into the room.

I nodded and slowly lifted my head. When I did, I saw a slight, thin smile. He had the decency to keep his eyes on mine as he moved closer to me. He was short with black hair slicked to the back of his head and eyes as dark as his hair. His skin was tanned, and his muscles lean.

I opened my mouth to speak, but pain laced my vocal chords. I shut my mouth and nodded instead.

The man cocked his head to the left and looked up above my head. "I'm not going to hurt you."

I nodded again and the man frowned. His eyes flicked to the doorway before he quickly perused my body. His eyes flashed. Not in lust, but simple examination as if he was categorizing every mark on my skin.

He raised a hand. "I'll be back in two minutes, okay?"

"Okay," I croaked, and then winced from the one word that slashed like razor blades through my throat.

He left. As soon as he was gone, my body began trembling.

Free. He was getting me the hell out of the house and the chains and the pain. I didn't give a shit if he was Satan himself; the man had just become my guardian angel.

When he appeared, he returned with a large blanket draped over his arm. The blanket was worn and had seen better days—hell, probably decades—but I wasn't going to complain. I might have sighed over the comforting item even though it was probably dirty and disgusting. Anything would be better than being stripped naked and strung up like a slaughtered calf.

In his hand…. he held God. Or bottled water.

"I'm Erik," he said and walked slowly toward me. He untwisted the cap off the water bottle as a shadow appeared in the doorway.

I jerked from the surprise of more company.

"It's okay," Erik said. "Gio is going to get the cuffs off you."

For some reason, I stared at the stranger who talked to me in soothing tones. I shook my head. I had just put my trust in a stranger. No way was I letting more people see me.

"It'll be fine," he clipped and pressed the water to my throat. I gulped it like it was the fountain of youth and I had just spotted my first wrinkle. "Drink slow."

I tried to listen, but I couldn't. I inhaled the water and panicked as it dribbled down my chin.

He pulled the bottled away, and I stared at the small plastic bottle with lust-filled eyes as he set it on the floor.

"Thanks," I finally said. The razors in my throat had diminished to pinpricks from the small amount of fluid. "Faith. I'm Faith."

He nodded once and moved to the blanket. "I know. You have a lot of men looking for you."

"Who?" I asked, my breath increasing all over again.

He seemed to sense my panic as the man named Gio entered the room. He looked almost exactly like Erik. I blinked at both of them. My toes walked me backward as far as I could to create distance. It was about two inches before the pain shot through my shoulders.

"I believe the man's name is Ryker?" He looked at me and raised an eyebrow.

Ryker.

I gasped.

Gio spoke. And I watched him. It was then I took in their three

119

piece black suits and black dress shirts beneath them. Black dress shoes on their feet. They were rich. They were Italian.

I had no idea what that meant.

"We're here to take you to him," Gio said. His voice was equally as quiet as Erik's had been, as if I was a skittish rabbit.

Which sounded about right.

And what other choice did I have? Stay here and wait for someone to come back and beat me? The decent looking men in the suit who had brought me water seemed like the much better option.

Erik and Gio worked together without speaking. Erik wrapped the blanket around my body as Gio worked on the cuffs.

In what felt like hours, but was probably only seconds as my pulse beat against my chest, I was certain they could hear the ferocious pounding against my bones before I collapsed into Erik's arms.

He swept up my feet and they wasted no time clearing out the room. Gio placed the water bottle on my lap.

I said nothing until we got upstairs. Neither of them did, either.

Then I saw two dead bodies strewn across the floor.

It was then I threw up all of my water. It spewed out all over my lap and onto Erik's chest.

I gasped once for breath before everything went black.

A bed. I recognized soft, silky sheets pressed against my stomach and my breasts before I opened my eyes. My hands, clearly unchained, rested under a pillow.

I sighed. It felt divine.

My legs stretched out under the comfortable sheets before the pain in my back reminded me of where I'd spent the last few weeks.

My eyes flew open. Without moving, I took in the room. It was gorgeous. And enormous.

I blinked and shifted my weight. A lightweight sheet, thrown over my naked back raked against my lashes and I winced.

"Don't move."

I stilled at the deep voice. It sounded familiar, but I couldn't place it until I closed my eyes and remembered the cabin with the gunshots and the men… Erik and Gio.

I turned my head and saw Erik sitting on the side of another bed next to me. Between us sat a night stand with an old-school corded phone.

I was in a hotel room. A nice one. Nicer than any place I'd ever worked, anyway.

"Where am I?" I asked, my throat dry but better than before. Somehow, Erik sitting on the edge of the bed and seeing me almost completely naked didn't bother me. He kept his eyes on my face as I shifted. Trying to turn to face him, the sheet drifted below my breasts.

My legs and back protested against the slow movement.

"Hotel in Minneapolis."

I narrowed my eyes. What in the hell was I doing here? "I thought you said you were taking me to Ryker."

He glanced at his watched. A thick, black leather band with diamonds surrounding the edges of the face. At least it was something that sparkled. Regardless, the man was in another black suit and looked immaculate.

"He'll be here any minute."

My body warmed. My blood began to pulse in my veins. I glanced down to see my naked body barely wrapped in a white, soft sheet and panic filled me. Dirt and sweat covered my skin and my fingers nails were almost black. I didn't want to inhale my own scent knowing how much I had to stink.

Tears stung my eyes at the thought of Ryker seeing me like this.

I couldn't let him see me like this. No one could ever see me like this.

"I don't…" I started to speak and shut my mouth. I couldn't

explain to a man I didn't know that I didn't want to see the man who had apparently been looking for me. "I need a shower."

Erik stood up and walked toward my side of the bed. I watched him, my eyes refusing to blink, unsure of what he had planned. But when he reached me, he simply handed me a white, button up shirt. "This is all I have for you to wear."

I draped the clean fabric over my hunched shoulders and picked at the dirt under my fingernails.

"The bathroom's right down the hall if you want to get cleaned up."

I nodded but said nothing. A thank you bounced on the tip of my tongue, but I still didn't know who the man was. Regardless, no way was I seeing Ryker or anyone else half naked.

I stood up, my legs aching with the movement and the weight of my body. When I reached the hallway, I turned to Erik, unable to help needing to know who had saved me. "Who are you?"

Erik glanced away. "An ally. As long as your man does what he's told."

I tilted my head to the side. "I don't understand."

Erik had moved to the desk chair and sat with his elbows propped on his knees, leaning toward me.

"Nordic Lords made a deal with us. We helped them complete it and you are our way of ensuring they fulfill their end of the promise."

A chess piece. Gratefulness that he had saved me was immediately quenched and replaced with indignation. Would I ever exist in a world when I didn't belong to someone else? Or easily used by someone for their own manipulative purposes?

I looked around the room. Dark woodwork, luscious sheets and bedcoverings over the two enormous beds. There was a sitting area at the far end with a small kitchenette area. A vase of fresh flowers filled the small eating table.

My lips pursed as I tried to fight the anger, but it couldn't be helped. I shrugged. "At least this jail is nicer."

I heard Erik let loose a low but brief chuckle of amusement on my behalf, but I chose to ignore him.

Instead I focused on leaving him alone and taking a shower. The warm water stung my back and I moaned under the spray. Not only from the pain, but also because it felt incredible to be getting clean. Two weeks with barely moving and the stress of not knowing what was going to happen next had done a number on me.

I needed a massage once I healed. Maybe a manicure, I thought, as I used the washcloth and tried in vain to dig and scrub all the dirt from under my nails and off my body.

And I willed my mind to stop racing from the memories of the last two weeks, but it couldn't be helped. Salty tears lined my cheeks as I scrubbed my face and then massaged shampoo into my hair. I had never understood why Cain hated me so much. Why he was harder on me than anyone else that walked through the doors of Penny's.

But kidnapping me for weeks was a new low. Even as I cleaned the disgust from my body, I felt a darkness creep into the edges of my soul. A hatred for a man I knew I would kill willingly if he ever put his hands on me again.

A man who had used my body and done as much as he could to destroy my heart and my spirit.

I refused to give him the victory.

He could have my mom, the waste of space who hadn't been a mom to me since I was a young girl.

I was done with all of it. I wanted to find a home and plant a garden and sit outside in the sun in the summers and drive snowmobiles through the forests in the winter.

I wanted a simple life where no one could ever tell me what to do ever again, where no man would ever think he had the power to control me or touch me in any way I didn't want.

And I would have it.

Somehow, I would find a way to have every damn thing I'd ever wanted.

A loud pounding knock on the door to the room startled me in the shower, and I quickly turned off the water. Armed with new determination, I quickly dried off, squeezed the excess water from my hair, and threw on the shirt Erik had loaned me.

I opened the door to the bathroom and heard a feral growl from a man who I had missed and dreamed and hoped would come for me.

This time, it wasn't a naïve hope that ended in broken hearts.

"Where the fuck is she, Sporelli?"

14

Angelo's younger brother, Erik, stood in the doorway to the hotel room where Daemon and I were told Faith would be after we made our first drop for him.

A part of me still wanted to pound in my little brother's head for making such a deal. From what I knew, Nordic Lords had worked their asses off to clean up Jasper Bay and prevent drugs from coming into the ports and the state. Now, Nordic Lords were in the damn middle of it all over again.

The other part of me—the stronger part—was so fucking glad we had found Faith.

"Let me in," I growled again at the man. My hands were balled into fists and I didn't give a shit that the man in front of me easily held a gun at his side. With the same hand, he waved Daemon and I into the room.

"She's hurt," he reminded us. Daemon was at my back and cursed. The anger I heard in Erik's tone over seeing Faith was the only thing that stopped me from slamming him into the wall.

I growled as I shoved past him into the room. They had used her just like Black Death. I hated them for it even if I understood.

Collateral.

Jesus fucking Christ.

Faith wasn't a damn pawn.

Daemon, sensing my rage and the loose hold on my temper, grabbed my shoulder and hissed quietly, "Get Faith and let's get out. We'll leave the other shit alone for now."

I nodded and didn't stop moving until I turned the short hallway from the hotel room and saw her.

It fucking felt like someone struck me in the chest with a frying pan. It was painful seeing Faith standing in the doorway to the bathroom with only a dress shirt on. Her skin was white as snow, and it highlighted the small red cracks on her lips along with the yellow bruise that covered the right side of her face.

Someone had hit her. Hard. The fact that it was healing didn't settle the heat that pressed against my chest.

"Faith," I said and took a step toward her. But the way her eyes widened and her lips parted on a quick inhale had me freezing in my feet. I had no idea if I could touch her or if she'd talk to me, but I definitely knew that I needed her.

In my arms.

In my life.

"Hey," she said softly. And I swear, that one soft, shaky word escaped her lips and went straight to chest, soothing my anger, and then down to my dick, hardening it.

She wasn't pissed.

"You came."

She ran her hand through her hair until it loosely fell over the font of the white, buttoned up shirt she had on.

I closed the distance between us, and without thinking, I cupped her cheek in my hand and ran my thumb over her bruise. I stared at it as if I had laser powers that could make it disappear. Her skin had been marred enough. She didn't need more damage.

Finally, I pulled my eyes from the bruise to her watchful blue eyes. She looked directly at me, and then pulled her bottom lip in between her teeth. Something sparked between us. I knew what it was. It was the same thing I always felt whenever I had looked at Faith when we were kids, when we got engaged, and when I first saw her at Penny's only weeks ago.

Love.

Need.

This time… she felt it, too.

I smiled and leaned in, brushing my lips against her bruise and back to her ear. "Always, Faith. I will always come for you."

Her head dropped to my chest right as her shoulders began to shake. Her sobs racked my body as hard as if they were coming from my own chest. My hands instinctively went to wrap around her waist, but when I did, her pained cry stopped me.

"What is it?" I asked, my hands freezing on her lower back. I didn't need her to answer. As I caught the reflection of her back in the bathroom's mirror, small red stripes of blood showed through the back of her shirt.

My teeth clenched together as I slowly lifted her shirt.

She tensed beneath me.

"Shush," I told her. "Let me see."

Through a quieted sob, she gave me her permission.

The flash of red I saw in my eyes as my anger rolled through my body was darker than the blood that lined her back. Lifting the shirt only halfway up her back, I couldn't bare to see any more.

Holy shit.

"He'll bleed," I hissed in her ear low enough so Daemon and Erik couldn't hear me. "I will make him fucking pay for this."

"I know," she whispered. My chest was wet with her tears as she lifted her face to mine. "You came for me."

I stared down at her, wanting to reassure her again, but I couldn't. My fury over her back and her skin made me flinch, and I looked away, too afraid I'd snap and scare her. She'd been scared enough.

"Shit," Daemon hissed from behind me. I heard Erik begin cataloging all of her injuries. I stopped listening when he rambled off a list longer than anything I'd heard before.

"Come on," I said, dropping the shirt and lighting wrapping a hand around her waist. "Let's get you home."

Her eyes snapped to mine. There was a hopefulness, and yet fearful look in them. "No," she rasped through a dried throat.

"The clubhouse, Faith. We need to have Doc take care of you."

Slowly, she nodded. I reached for a bottled water Erik held out for me and gently placed it in Faith's free hand.

"Thanks for taking care of her," Daemon said. Ever the professional. Hell—the President, now.

As we hit the doorway to the hotel, Faith looked back and flashed a small, pathetic smile to Sporelli. He raised a hand in a wave and closed the door behind us.

Once we got her settled in the back of Daemon's truck, I cupped her cheeks in my hands. Without thinking, I leaned down and pressed my lips against her temple. She gasped in a quick, quiet breath that told me she was not unaffected by my touch. "You'll never be alone again."

15

Faith

I now knew that Meg was beautiful and Brayden was as handsome as Ryker. I knew this because every time I woke up and opened my eyes for the first two days, I immediately stared at a picture of the three of them. Ryker's arms were around the both of them. The photo was framed and propped up on his dresser directly across from the bed. No matter where I looked in the room, I felt their happy, easy smiles mocking me.

Even after I threw a towel across the room, which knocked the photo over and covered it up, I could still feel his family's happy smiles staring at me all hours of every day.

What hurt worse was that I hadn't seen Ryker since he brought me to his room at the club. Every morning I woke up with decreasing hope that he'd be lying next to me, an arm wrapped around me like he first did as soon as he showed up at the hotel. But that had all changed when he saw the blood on my back. The way he flinched and looked away from me.

He hadn't looked me in the eyes since.

He was avoiding me and the only thing I could figure out was that he might have saved me, but he had his own family. All I was to him was someone to save. A friend of Liv's that he'd been able to help. That was it.

Gone were his promises of always coming for me. Unless he meant that only in the if-you-need-your-life-saved way.

I wanted to get the hell out of Ryker's room except I had nowhere else to go. The only other option was Daemon's house where Olivia now lived with him, but I also knew Ryker was staying there until he found his own place.

I couldn't go anywhere to escape.

So I tortured myself in Ryker's room—smelling his cologne on his sheets and bathroom towels. I tortured myself by mentally taking an exacto knife to the picture I could no longer see and erasing Ryker's woman from his bedroom and his memory.

Mostly, I tortured myself by trying to put myself in his room like I actually belonged. If five years ago he had come inside my house when he saw Cain mauling me with his mouth and beat the shit out of him instead of turning tail and fleeing town, everything would have been different.

I hated him for not being smart enough to know I would never turn my back on him.

Yet knowing what must have been going through his mind that night, I couldn't blame him either.

And none of it changed the fact that as much as I wanted Ryker, as much as I wanted his arms around me, soothing me, and telling me that everything would be okay and that I would eventually move passed the horrific memories that flooded my mind, I knew that some other woman owned that spot now.

My head snapped up as the door slammed open and banged against the wall behind it.

The walls shook and rattled as Ryker stomped inside his room, bloodied and battered, a shredded shirt in his fist. All my earlier anger with him vanished instantly as I threw back the sheet covering me.

I gasped. "Are you okay?" I twisted myself on the bed, placing my feet on the floor, and curled one arm around my ribs as I stood up.

"Fucking fantastic." He stood in the doorway, chest heaving with blood everywhere, and kept his eyes trained on me. We stood across the room from one another, one bed and ten feet of space between us as we stared at each other. It felt like the space of the Grand Canyon.

Tension prickled the air. I expected him to yell at me, to shake me into finally speaking to him. My hands itched to clean the blood off him, to inspect his cuts and gashes and bruises like he had done to me when he helped Doc stitch me up.

But my feet felt paralyzed, too afraid to move and make the first step to him. Too afraid of what it would mean to put myself on the line like that—even as small as that step would be—and be rejected all over again once Meg and his kid came into the picture.

He stalked across the room, grabbing a clean shirt out of his dresser on the way, and then slammed the door to the bathroom shut.

My legs collapsed, and I plopped back down onto the edge of the bed as I heard the water running in the bathroom. My fingers fiddled with the edges of the bed as I tried to wrap my head around what possibly could have happened to him to leave him such a wreck. He was strong—the well-defined chest that I couldn't have possibly missed as he stalked across the room before was a visual testament to his strength.

He was more beautiful than he had been when we were simply teenagers.

"Faith." My head jerked behind me—my cheeks instantly heated as if I'd been caught with my hand in a cookie jar.

Lost in my revere of Ryker's half-naked body, I hadn't heard Daemon enter the room.

He stood in the doorway, his arms crossed and his shoulder propped on the frame. "Talk to him."

I almost smiled, seeing him standing there, looking so powerful and strong. Daemon's goatee needed a trim. When I had said that to Live earlier, she had smiled and laughed, but it didn't reach her eye. Somehow I knew she was simply laughing for my sake, and both of us knew Daemon wouldn't do anything he was told to do.

"There's nothing for us to say to one another."

Daemon laughed once. It was deep and his frustration with me showed. Everyone's frustration with me showed clearly on their faces when I refused to tell them what had happened to me. I figured the scars and bruised ribs said it all.

"You two have a boatload of shit to figure out. Do it before the dumbass gets his brains bashed in the next time he steps into the ring." He left, leaving me staring after him with my jaw dropped to my chest, shutting the door behind him.

I flung my head around back to the bathroom that was now quiet. Ryker came out with a towel wrapped around his waist and a white shirt on. One hand gripped the towel as the steam from his shower followed him into the room.

He glanced at me once before turning to his dresser and pulling out a pair of jeans. He didn't look at me again when he went back to the bathroom to finish dressing or when he came back out to the bedroom, flung his new leather cut over his shoulders, and loaded up his pockets with his wallet and change.

Red scratches, lined with blood, covered the area above his eyebrows and his cheekbones. Daemon's words bounced in my head. The thought that Ryker had that happen to him—because he was pissed something happened to me—filled me with a mixture of emotions I couldn't place.

"Who did that to you?"

His back straightened at the first words I spoke to him in days. Not because I hadn't wanted to, but because I didn't know what to say. What was there to say when he didn't want me… not in that way, at least.

He paused in his steps, looked back over my shoulder—not at me—and said, "Jaden." Then his steps continued.

He was halfway to the door of his room before my mouth started working.

"I don't blame you, you know."

I looked down at the floor, unable to watch to see if anything I said mattered to him at all. And because I was looking at my feet, I didn't hear him quietly pad back over to me until I heard his breath directly above my head. His bare feet appeared in my line of vision.

"Blame me for what?" His deep, gravelly voice rolled over my shoulders. It felt like a soothing balm to the aches on my skin and the bruises that were healing as I shivered beneath him.

I could never help my physical reaction to Ryker when he was so close to me.

It terrified me, wondering if I'd ever be able to get over the man who had meant so much to me but so clearly moved on.

I bit my tongue and shook my head. The fear of the honesty that would pour from my mouth prevented me from speaking.

His thumb was at my chin, pulling my face to his but I turned my head and only saw his dresser. Underneath the towel was a corner of the silver frame I'd knocked over.

"What don't you blame me for?" His thumb tightened on my chin as he spoke and his words were more tightly clipped, as if he had to restrain himself from lashing out.

"None of it." I swallowed, sandpaper lined the edges of my throat and my tongue as I tried to tell him that even when I had wished he'd come back for me, I always understood why he'd left. Not that it hadn't hurt, it still did, but it never changed the fact that I always got why he felt the need to put Jasper Bay in the rearview mirror and never look back.

He tugged my chin so I stared directly into his eyes. His left eye was swollen, almost matching my bruised one, and the cuts above his right eye leaked a tiny trail of blood drops down the edges of his eye. My breath hitched as I stared into his black as night eyes that swirled with unspoken thoughts I couldn't decipher.

"Would you have had to work for Black Death if I'd stayed? If I would have stayed weeks ago, do you think you would have ended up like this?" His eyes quickly scanned my body, and I watched his eyes flash in anger and horror.

I shrugged. "Maybe."

His hand fell from my chin and he took a step toward his dresser. He scoffed in disgust, his hand flying to the back of his neck and rubbing fiercely.

"Damnit, Faith!" I jumped as one of his arms swung out, and in one large swoop, all the knick knacks and towels and change that littered the top of his dresser smashed to a mess on the floor. "Don't you fucking get it?" he yelled, facing me with his face a mask of complete and utter rage. He pointed at himself. "It's all my fucking fault!"

Fear spread through my veins at his outburst. Never had he scared me in such a way like he did in that moment with his breath filling the room and the remains of his outburst scattered all over the floor. In an instant, I was curled into a ball on the floor up against the bed; my knees curled to my chest and my arms wrapped around them. The pain shooting from my ribs was minimal compared to the pounding in my head.

"Fuck!" He roared and stared at me wide-eyed, his hands balling and flexing into fists over and over again.

My entire body shook as tears filled my eyes. I closed them, trying to prevent them from falling, but it was no use once Ryker's arms surrounded me and he held me, still curled into a ball, and sat us both on the bed.

"Fuck. I'm sorry, Faith."

My shoulders shook against his chest and I shook my head furiously back and forth. I swallowed and tried to tell him it wasn't him, because it really wasn't, but all that came out was a garbled sob.

He shushed me, and with one of his hands on the back of my head, he held me tightly and securely to him. "I'm so fucking sorry for scaring you."

"You didn't—"

"I did. Jesus, Faith. This is why I haven't tried to see you since you've been here. All this rage in me, all the anger and disappointment with myself. I'm too much of a loose cannon to be around you. Not with you still reminding me of everything."

I tensed in his arms and tried to pry myself out of his iron grip. Of course. Of course I would remind Ryker of all the shit in his life.

"That's not what I meant," he said, but it was too late. I understood completely.

He tried to pull me back to him, but my hands finally uncurled from my knees and I pushed him away.

Wiping my nose, I nodded. "I got it."

I stood up, searching for new clothes to wear. I'd find a new place to stay. Maybe Jules would take me in. It would just be for a few weeks while I found a new job and a new place to live—maybe somewhere other than Jasper Bay. God knew it was time I tried to put the past behind me, even if it wasn't in the past yet.

I was halfway through finding a new outfit to put on, something nicer than the knit shorts and Nordic Lords T-shirt Liv kept supplying me with, when Ryker's hand wrapped around my wrist.

"Look at me."

I shook my head. No way. He yanked on my arm again until I was standing in front of him while he spread his legs on the bed in front of me.

"That's not what I meant."

I looked at the door behind him. Twelve steps and I could figure out a way to start my life over. Again. "I know."

"Is that why your pulse is pounding against my fingers and you look about two seconds from bolting." My eyes flickered to his. I saw nothing but anger.

It shocked me.

"You're... you're mad at me?"

He dropped my hand as if I'd burned him and his eyebrows rose. "No... shit. I'm not mad at you."

"Then what?" Protective instincts instantly surrounded me. Somehow, I suddenly had no idea what I was feeling when it came to Ryker, but something told me I could get hurt. And quickly.

He pushed off the bed and walked around it, immediately putting space—lots of space—between us. For some reason I was more fearful of the space than I was of his outburst.

With his hands fisted on his hips and his feet braced as if ready for the fight his life, he raked my body slowly with his eyes. Everywhere he looked heated under his narrowed and fierce eyes. "I didn't mean that you remind of me the shitty times. I meant that every time I look at you, I'm reminded of how much I've failed."

I stood there, our stances matching, hands on our hips, chests both raising and lowering, and tears fell again.

Jesus. When had I become such a damn ball of emotions? For years I had been able to bottle them all up and shove them into a corner of a room I never entered. Weeks ago Ryker entered my life and suddenly I was a bumbling mess. I swiped the tears away with my fingertips.

My lips twitched and I nodded. "I think it's better if I go somewhere else. I think… I'm doing better. I just…"

"You're not going anywhere."

I licked my suddenly dry lips. "I think it'd be better if I did."

"Where would you go?"

His question was sarcastic and I knew he was right—where else *could* I go?

"I don't know, but you have a family and it'd be better if I wasn't here, in this room or this place. I need to go somewhere else."

While I talked, I watched his shoulders soften and he took a few hesitant steps toward me until the space between us was minimal.

"You're my family."

God I wish I could be. I shook my head. "I'm not…" My eyes glanced to the broken frame on my floor. When I glanced back to Ryker, his eyes had trailed mine and his mouth was slack.

"You did hear me in the hotel," he nodded toward the photo on the floor, "talking to them."

My chin shook as I willed my body to stay strong. I would not cry again. My tongue pressed against the inside of my teeth.

"It doesn't matter," I said, looking over his shoulder and no longer at him. I couldn't.

Quietly, he laughed once and then his hands were cupping my cheeks. "Is that why you threw that fit in the hotel? Because of Meg and Brayden?"

I stiffened in his hands. They felt too warm, too perfect, and so... not mine.

"It's none of my business. I think that you saved me, and I appreciate it."

"You appreciate it." His eyes danced with a small amount of humor as I tried to look away from him.

"Yeah," I nodded. "But really, I should go somewhere else to heal. I'll be fine."

His lips pulled into a full smile. I didn't know what in the hell was so funny. "You are a stubborn, stupid girl."

"I'm not—"

"Jesus, Faith. What did you think that kiss was for in the hotel? When I couldn't keep my hands off you? You think I'm the kind of man to cheat on someone?"

I had asked myself those same questions. Never had I thought of an answer that made sense. One of my shoulders rose and dropped. "Old time's sake? We have history and it was overwhelming."

This time, Ryker's fingers pressed into my cheeks and he threw his head back and laughed. My body felt inflamed with heat at the glorious sound and at the frustration that he was laughing at me.

"You're fucking shitting me!" he exclaimed when he was done laughing, still wiping water off his cheeks. "Don't you think we've wasted enough time with misunderstandings? Why didn't you just fucking ask me?"

I was so lost I couldn't find myself with a map and a compass. "I heard you—"

His eyes darkened instantly. "They're not mine."

"He called you daddy."

Ryker shook his head, the damn smile still on his lips while I was mortified we were discussing this. "No." He raised a finger and shook it at me. "Brayden probably said he missed his daddy." The same finger moved to his chest. "Which isn't me."

"Oh."

"His dad's dead."

"Well, I'm sorry about that. But..."

"And I had promised Brayden's dad, and Meg's husband, Byron that if anything happened to him I'd watch out for them."

I bit the inside of my cheek. When he put it like that, it sounded so innocent. And somehow, so Ryker. Always the warrior—the knight even though he hated being called one just because of his last name. He was always the person people ended up leaning on for help and to protect them.

Which reminded me that that's what I was to him—the damsel in distress.

Despite that, I still couldn't forget the kiss. I didn't want to, either. I simply wanted it to mean something different than it probably did. But if it meant something to him, it didn't matter—I was way too broken inside to give anything to him.

"Faith."

My eyes flipped to his. They were no longer angry, no longer laughing—they were pitch black and completely serious. I felt the change in the energy between us immediately. It flickered and danced along like a live wire filled with electricity.

I raised a brow, my nerves beginning to dance in anticipation. I remembered that heated look vividly.

"I didn't kiss you in that hotel room because I was overwhelmed with remembering what it was like to be with you five years ago."

"Oh…" I mumbled and wanted to smack myself. Or buy myself a dictionary to think of a new response to him.

His hand reached out and ran down the length of my black hair. When he reached the end, he let it drop before he took my hand and pulled me closer to him. I winced from the small pain in my ribs the sudden movement caused.

His other hand came out and cupped my cheek right before his forehead dropped to mine. I felt a fine sheen of sweat on his forehead slide against mine.

"Don't you know, babe," he said right as he turned his head and pressed his lips against my skin, "that you're the only woman who's ever been mine?"

16

Ryker

Her shoulders tightened under my grip.

I could have held back. I could have given her more time to get used to the fact that I wanted to move past all of this and I wanted to do it together.

But fuck it. We had lost five years.

We had waited long enough.

"Faith," I whispered into her ear.

"Hmm?"

I grinned. "You need to know that whatever has happened to you, whatever has happened to either of us over the last five years, it's always been you. You've always been the only woman I've ever wanted."

Her head tipped back so she was looking directly at me with pale as ice eyes that were still blank as fuck. I hated seeing that in her. In that moment, I decided it would be my mission to do whatever I had to do in order to get those eyes sparkling like diamonds all over again.

I also realized it was the first time Faith had willingly looked at me directly in the eyes since we'd gotten her out of Sporelli's hotel room.

She bit her bottom lip gently. "I'm not the girl you remember,

Ryker. What I said to you in the hotel room is still true. I don't have anything to give anyone anymore."

Pain squeezed my heart like it did the first time I heard her say those words. What was worse was that she looked like she completely believed it.

"You don't have to give me anything except yourself."

"There's nothing—" She shook her head adamantly. I felt her tense under my arms again, but I kept a gentle yet firm hold on her.

"You have everything to give. And we're going to remind you—all of us that love you—what it is that has always made you so special, Faith. You can stay in this room hiding from everyone who cares about you or you can walk out of this room and embrace the fact that despite Cain majorly fucking you over—he didn't fuck you up."

Something flashed in her eyes. She shook her head again. "I can't talk—"

My hand snaked around to her neck, cupping the back of her head, and I pulled her toward my chest. Her forehead hit my shoulder and heat instantly radiated out all over my fucking body. Faith was in my arms. Again.

It was so utterly perfect.

I leaned down and pressed my lips against her hair. "When you're ready."

Her head rubbed against my shirt. "Never."

I sighed, blowing out a breath, and relaxed my body into hers. "Okay."

She had to. If she knew anything, we could finally take care of Cain once and for all. A small voice told me she was still protecting her mom.

But considering she was still recovering from her last beating, we could wait and give her some time.

And in the meantime, I'd do everything I could to prove that Faith may not be the girl she used to be, but she was the only woman for me.

17

Faith

A part of me wanted to cling to the words Ryker so easily spoke to me as he held me cocooned in his arms. I wanted to revel in the heat from his skin on mine, the way his breath tickled my skin, and the way it felt to have his lips on mine.

I wanted to forget everything else except for him.

Which was why, when he finally pulled away from me, I let him take my hand and pull me out into the Nordic Lords clubhouse and plop me down onto a stool at the bar.

I felt everyone's eyes on me. My skin prickled with paranoia but settled on reality when I looked around the room. At least twenty men and about half that amount of women were staring directly at me.

I shivered under their gaze, too afraid to consider what they would see when they looked at me.

I could be the daughter of the man who almost ratted out the club to the FBI.

I could be the daughter of a worthless drug addict.

I could be the whore.

None of it was good, but all of it was me.

Instead of shrinking under their stares, I straightened my back and then rested my head on Olivia's shoulder as her arm went around my back and pulled me to her.

"They're all glad you're okay." She whispered it into the top of head much like Ryker had done a few minutes earlier. The effect wasn't nearly the same.

"They think I'm scum," I told her quietly.

Liv's small fingers dug into the skin on my shoulder and she squeezed tighter. "Say that shit again about yourself and I'll kick your ass in the ring."

It was absurd. I could totally take Liv.

I laughed, a snort-filled laugh, in agreement and it felt good. The sound was foreign coming out of my mouth and my throat, and it only increased the attention I already had on me.

I didn't care. Not in that moment. In that moment, I simply wanted to laugh for once.

"Drink." I looked at Switch behind the bar as he slid a beer toward me. His eyes were narrowed on mine, and he didn't sound happy at all about having to serve me in his own clubhouse, especially now that he was the Vice President.

"Thanks," I told him quietly. It was barely audible because Switch was large and scary, and when he stared at me, it made me nervous all over again. He had been friends with my dad. He was one of the men who had taken him out.

I scooted back as Switch leaned over the bar, rested his elbows on top, and dropped his eyes closer to mine.

His head tilted to the side and he blinked.

I stared at him, my hands frozen on the beer he had opened for me.

Then, he pushed off the bar and nodded once toward me. "You'll be all right."

He walked away as Liv's fingers squeezed my shoulder again.

It wasn't much. He hadn't said anything at all, really, yet a warm sensation filled my stomach and the backs of my eyes began to burn.

Jules sat on my other side, a wiggly two-year-old, Sophie, balanced on her lap. "He's right, you know." She nodded her head toward Switch. "You're one of the strongest women I've ever known and I don't know what's happened to you, but we've always been your friends and we always will be." Her hand left Sophie's blonde mane and settled gently on my thigh. "We're all here for you."

I blinked away the slowly increasing burn in my eyes and pulled a large swallow from the beer.

"Thanks," I choked out. I doubted anyone's ability to help me, but I agreed with Ryker on one point. If anyone could do it, these people—these friends—could. I at least wanted to pretend a little while longer.

So I sat on the stool, allowing my friends to ply me with alcohol in the middle of the day. I let them get me drunk. I let them try to get me to laugh.

And as the alcohol flowed, the laughing became easier.

"It's not that it was all bad." I swayed on my unsteady feet while I waved a pool cue through the air. From behind me, I saw Jules laugh as she ducked out of the way.

Ryker frowned at me from across the table. His hands balled into fists and pushed into the lined felt top of the pool table. He arched a brow. "Faith?"

I waved him off before I bent over, aimed, and completely missed the little white ball.

"I did their books," I explained. "After a few years, they trusted me enough for that. I made appointments for the other girls. And those girls…" I drawled out and then paused to take another sip of my beer. "They *liked* it. They actually loved doing what they did."

From next to me, Daemon grabbed my beer bottle. He set it on a table behind him before he turned back to me. "I think that's enough, Faith."

I eyed the beer longingly. It was numbing all my pain and making it easier to talk. I was simply giving them what they all wanted.

"I wanted that."

Daemon nodded. "I know, but I think that's enough for today. Maybe you should get to bed."

"I'll take her," Ryker said, his voice low and deep, and if I wasn't completely drunk, I think I detected concern. "Come on, Faith," he said and held out a hand for me.

I shook my head and took a step back. Ten sets of eyes were on me although I didn't know the names of everyone watching me.

I swayed again.

"This is what you wanted, isn't it?" I asked and looked at all of them. Men in their cuts and their women stood next to them. My friends had their eyes narrowed on me. "To get me to talk? But now that I am you don't want to hear it?"

I shook my head. I tried to stay quiet, but a faucet had been turned on and I couldn't turn it off. Loose lips sink ships and all that, although I was certain I couldn't have said that phrase without slurring for the life of me.

"You don't want to hear about what I did, do you? Because it disgusts you," I hissed at Ryker. He flinched but said nothing. It proved I was right. "You want me to move on and get over everything... but you don't want to actually know what I'm trying to get over."

"Faith," Liv said, walking up next to me and putting an arm on my shoulder. I shook it off.

I faced her. "Did you know I liked it, Liv?"

Her face blanched. "Faith..."

"That I came even when I was crying. That no matter how much I hated their hands on me, I always gave them what they wanted." Liv's hands squeezed my shoulders as I let the words fly. I leaned in closer. "Because I was good at it. I was the *best*."

"That's enough," Ryker barked, his dark eyes reminding me of a dark summer thunderstorm. A second later, I was swept up in his arms, my pool cue clanking and rattling on the linoleum floor.

My arms went around his neck on instinct as he carried me out of the clubhouse main living room.

"Another jail," I said softly as he carried me down another hallway. "Another place I have to stay. Another place I can't leave."

Ryker sighed. "Faith. We're trying to keep you safe."

I ignored the frustrated yet softened tone. It did funny things to my belly. "And I have nowhere else to go. I wonder when Cain will kill me."

My eyelids drooped in heaviness, partly from the alcohol but partly because talking was making my head hurt. It was exhausting telling them what they didn't want to really hear.

Ryker's arms tightened around my back and then I felt his weight shift as he lowered me to his bed. When he unwrapped his arms from under me, he braced his hands next to my head, his arms fully extended.

"Cain will never kill you."

I couldn't argue with his words. His black hair draped over his even blacker eyes. A vein pulsed in his neck. He had a slight dip in his chin that I used to tease him about and push my index finger into when we were joking around.

He wasn't joking around now.

"He'll try," I said, my eyelids drifting closed. "My mom's probably already dead, isn't she?"

He exhaled a deep breath but sleep was pulling me under. My limbs felt heavier by the second as they sank into the thin mattress.

One of Ryker's hands brushed lightly down my cheek and I felt him drag his fingers through my hair.

"You know," I said, finding the strength to open my eyes a little bit. "He beat me and then he left. Then he told those other men to do whatever they wanted to me."

He cursed through a hitched breath and the muscles in his jaw tightened.

"Except for that… but it doesn't matter… because I gave that away willingly, you know? I don't even know if I remember what it feels like to *want* someone's hands on me."

"Faith… Cain will die for what he did to you."

I blinked slowly. Ryker leaned down closer and I felt his breath dance across my skin. I inhaled the supremely masculine smell of his body wash or cologne. I didn't know which, but it smelled delicious and made my already heavy head begin to spin. "I liked it."

His throat dipped as he swallowed and his eyes stayed fixed on mine. His nose twitched.

"You don't want to hear that, but I did. I liked what they did to me, Ryker."

His black hair swished back and forth right as tears welled in my eyes and spilled over. "Getting off and liking it are two different things, babe. But I know that someday, you'll want it again. And when you do… we'll go slow."

It was such a nice promise from the man I had once loved; the only man who had ever touched me in a way I wanted. I didn't know if I'd ever feel like that again. I didn't know if I could.

But still, it warmed my body from toes to ears as Ryker brushed the tears off my cheeks. I curled my knees to my chest and settled under the blanket he draped over me.

"Go to sleep, Faith."

"He has a brother," I slurred, my eyes closing again, and this time I couldn't force them open again. "Owns a resort on a lake… Miltona, I think. I don't remember… he sends him money every month."

As sleep and darkness pulled me under, I felt Ryker's full, warm lips brush across my forehead.

"We'll take care of it."

Another promise. For once, I wanted to truly surrender to the idea that there were people looking out for me and protecting me, instead of trying to find ways to damage and hurt me.

I felt a small smile tip at the edges of my lips right before I surrendered to sleep.

148

18

Ryker

I stared at Faith and watched her settle into sleep. The bruises on her cheeks and jaw were now a pale yellow, and as her breath became low and steady, I fought the urge to run my lips over every injury she'd received while strung up by Cain's men.

I doubted she'd remember all the talking she had done by the time morning hit. All the leads she had drunkenly handed to us.

But it filled me with a sense of calmness and peace that I hadn't felt since the first time I ran into her, weeks ago, in the doorway to Penny's when I saw what her life had become since I'd left.

I made a promise to her and I meant it. I'd take care of this. I'd take care of Cain and I'd give Faith a reason to hope that she'd never have to live owned by anyone or scared of anyone ever again.

Pushing off the bed, even though all I wanted to do was strip out of my clothes and lay down next to her, I spun on my heels and headed out to the club room where the music was still pounding against the walls.

It was early. Tripp, a club member and only about ten years older than Daemon and me, had taken my turn at the salvage yard as soon as Faith started drinking earlier. I didn't have shit to do for the rest of the night except fill Daemon in and hope like hell he'd get a group of men ready to ride.

I almost hated to interrupt him when I saw him wrapped around Liv as I hit the main room. They were finally able to begin a relationship they had fought for years to have. And with the way Liv's leg was wrapped around Daemon's hip, him pressing her against the wall with his arms caging her in, it was clear that they were tired of waiting for the right time to have something good, too.

I thought about giving them their moment.

Then I remembered the pale, dead look in Faith's light blue eyes.

Fuck it.

"Hey, Daemon," I called, loudly enough to get his, along with everyone else in the club room's, attention.

Snickers filled the air when Daemon pulled away from Liv and growled at me. I smiled when Liv wiped her mouth with the back of her hand.

"You fuckin' me right now?" he shouted, annoyed.

"Nope." I grinned and headed toward them. "Neither is Liv."

"Asshole," he muttered, and then gave Liv a kiss on the cheek before he met me near the bar. "You had better have a good reason for this."

I grabbed a bottle of Jim Bean off the bar, unscrewed the top, and took a shot from the bottle without bothering to get a shot glass. Daemon watched the whole thing before repeating my same move once I set the bottle down.

"Faith talked," I said. "I need men for a ride."

He leaned forward and rested his elbows on the bar, hands clasped together. I waited for him to call Jaden and Xbox over.

"Faith said Cain has a brother who I'm assuming isn't in the club," I said once the men were huddled around the bar.

Xbox frowned and shook his head. "Never heard of him."

Which meant that Cain was either keeping his brother hidden from the club life, or his brother was keeping himself hidden. Xbox was a scrappy, skinny guy but he was able to hack or track anything the club needed. He had proven himself valuable to Daemon time and time again in finding shit that no one wanted found.

If Xbox didn't know about him, then the man was hidden on purpose.

"Said something about him having a brother on Miltona. Runs a resort. That mean anything to you?" I asked the group of men.

"Miltona's near Alexandria, about four hours southwest of here. An hour West of St. Cloud," Jaden filled in.

I checked the clock on the microwave behind the bar. "We can be there by midnight if we leave now."

"We're not riding now," Daemon said. He ran a hand through his light brown goatee and then scrubbed the back of his neck. "Too many men have been drinking for too long today. We'll head out first thing tomorrow morning."

"Daemon—"

He silenced me with a raised hand. "Tonight, Xbox will figure out who he is and where he lives. We'll go in the morning, be there by lunch, and hopefully get the answers you need by dinnertime."

"I have to go."

Daemon's lips thinned before he leaned in and fixed his narrowed eyes on me. The rest of the men hushed as we stared each other down. "I get what you need to do, but you put that cut on and you know you're not your own man anymore. You wait until your brothers can have your back and we'll go in smart. You got it?"

I got that I wanted to punch my little brother in the face.

But I also got what he was saying.

I glared at Xbox. He looked confident and calm as his fingers tapped mindlessly on the bar top. It was a tic he always had when he was getting ready to hunt down information in cyberland.

"You can find what I need?" I asked.

He looked at me with his slick black hair tied in a pony tail that fell halfway down his back. One of his hands rubbed his goatee.

"Two hours, tops. I figure there can't be that many resorts, and he can't be that hard to find. The simple fact we've never heard of him probably tells me he's clean."

I nodded and exhaled.

I wanted to ride.

Jaden's firm hand clamped on my shoulder and kept me tethered to the floor. "Wait until we can all go fuck the asshole up. It'll be more fun that way."

When he put it that way…

I grinned. "You got it."

The late morning air was already stuffy and humid as the four of us pulled our bikes into Grady's Resort on the southeast corner of Lake Miltona. Families with children played outside in the grassy area that ran alongside a dirt road behind a line of vacation trailers and motorhomes. I laughed to myself, not surprised, as moms took in our leather cuts with the Viking skull patches on the backs, and our bikes, and then quickly ushered their kids inside the trailers.

I wiped the sweat from my brow as we pulled up to the main cabin. They were a pathetic gray in desperate need of a good power wash and painting at least a decade ago. The dilapidated office sign hung crookedly from two metal hooks outside a screen door where one edge of the screen curled up.

"Xbox is a master," I said quietly to Daemon as he climbed off his bike and joined me. From the quieting of the engines and crunching booted steps behind me, I knew Jaden and Tripp were right behind us.

In truth, it had taken him thirty minutes to find Nathan O'Reilly, supposed brother to Cain.

Daemon glanced at me before heading up the first crooked and broken cemented step in front of us. "Let's just hope Cain would turn to him if he needed help hiding," he said right as he opened the creaking woodened door.

It slammed shut right after Tripp entered. Combined, the four of us consumed the small waiting space that held a small folding table covered with "Grady's Family Resort" T-shirts, a scratched wooden desk, and decade old computer in front of us.

From behind the desk, there was a narrow stairway that led to what I assumed was the owner's cabin on the second floor.

Footsteps immediately began approaching on the stairway. I reached inside my cut and felt the cold handle of my gun.

"Patience," Daemon scolded next to me right as a man turned the corner of the stairway and faced us. He was small and scrawny— the complete opposite of Cain's large size. His hair was unwashed and greasy, and his frame showed the result of a man who had lived solely on liquor for far too long.

His eyes instantly widened and his face turned white as a ghost.

The four of us stood intimidatingly in front of him.

"You have two choices, Nathan," Daemon spoke, not giving the man a chance to deny his name. "You can tell us what we need to know and live. Or tell us what we need to know and die."

He took a step back toward the stairway as his eyes danced around the four of us. Jaden, closer to the desk than I, copied each footstep of Nathan's.

"I don't know anything." His shaky voice almost made me happy.

"You don't know what we want, yet." Daemon's statement held a touch a humor. Under the humor was the voice of a man who held the power in the room.

The man stumbled into the stair railing and Jaden was on him in an instant. His hand cupped the man's throat, and he raised him by the grip on his neck until his feet dangled against the ground.

"Where's Cain?" Jaden hissed.

Nathan choked and rapidly shook his head back and forth. "I don't know anything."

"The woman?" I asked, taking a step forward as I unsheathed my gun from the holster. "Where is she?"

Nathan's hand clawed at Jaden's forearm, but it did nothing. His cheeks turned pink with a hint of purple as his eyes bulged out from the loss of oxygen.

"I don't…" He coughed and sputtered. I glanced back to Daemon, who stood still with Tripp at his back. Both men had their arms crossed against his chest.

Daemon nodded once at me, his expression cold and unmoving.

I raised my gun. "I can kill you, but we'll still find Cain eventually. And I'm assuming once he's dead, you'll stop receiving the two thousand dollar monthly payments you get from him now."

"How did you find out?"

"We have our ways," I told him, aiming my gun at his knee. "Have you ever been shot? It hurts like a fucker, you know."

Jaden loosened his grip on Nathan's throat. It was enough for him to swallow and gulp in a large breath.

"Where is he?" I asked him.

Nathan shook his head. "I don't know. I haven't heard from him in months."

"Do you know what he did to my woman?" I asked, realizing that was how I thought of Faith. Mine. She had always been. "Her back is covered with so many lashes from his belt that there isn't an inch of skin on her that isn't damaged. Do you know he forced her to become a whore? Forced her to have sex for money until she did it so often that she started thinking she *liked* being used by men like that?"

"My brother is sick. That's not my problem."

"It is when you know where he'd go. Or maybe he's here. Your guests won't mind if we search their cabins."

"You can't," he stuttered out right as Jaden let go of his throat completely. Nathan sunk to the floor, his hands rapidly rubbing the abused skin on the front of his throat.

Without saying anything, Jaden pushed him to his stomach on the floor, pulled out a rope, and began wrapping his hands behind his back.

"Maybe we should hang him up like Cain did to Faith?" Daemon suggested. Jaden was already on the move, pushing Nathan up the stair way. The man cursed as he fell and his knees jammed into the edges of the stair way.

I moved to follow them but hit Daemon's hand on my chest. "Search the empty cabins and shelters with Tripp. They have to have a place to hide from tornados somewhere around here."

"I'm going with Jaden," I said, stepping forward.

"We'll take care of him. If Cain heard us come in, he's gone or hiding. Find him for Faith, and we'll take care of the brother."

"Daemon…" I warned, but the argument fell silent on my lips.

His head tipped down toward my ear and his arms encircled my biceps. "You don't need more blood on your hands yet, Brother. Let Jaden and I handle this." Fighting the instinct I had to kill anyone related to the fucker who hurt Faith, I hesitantly nodded and took a step back with Tripp.

19
Faith

As I awoke, the vicious and unrelenting pounding inside my head quickly reminded me of my error in drinking too much. Cain had never allowed me to truly kick back and enjoy the feel of getting drunk before. He said sloppy drunks made for sloppy whores.

Waking up with one of the few hangovers I'd ever had almost made me thank Cain for the one small thing he'd ever done to protect me.

But then I remembered how much I despised him, and slowly, as I showered and got dressed and headed out to the kitchen to find something to settle my stomach, the memories of the talking I had done last night entered my mind.

Shame at how callously I had spoken of the things I did under Cain's control filled my already queasy stomach. It was no wonder I hadn't heard from Ryker that morning.

A small part of me had hoped that I'd wake up enclosed in his strong, muscled arms, but that was stupid. No way would he want to be with me after I'd spewed all my verbal vomit.

"Good morning."

I snapped my head to Olivia as she practically waltzed into the kitchen behind me.

I took in her bedraggled hair and sleepy eyes and smiled. "Looks like you had a good night."

Her cheeks blushed as she reached for the coffee pot. "It was an early morning before Daemon and the men left."

I cleared my throat. "Left?"

She turned to me, her head cocked to the side slightly. She took her first drink of coffee, sipping it slowly. "You seemed surprised."

"I…" I turned to the eggs, cracking them into a bowl. "Where'd they go?"

"You can't think you could tell Ryker everything you did last night and he wouldn't handle it immediately, do you?"

What? My eyebrows drew together and I paused on whipping the eggs. "Tell him what?"

"You don't remember?" She smiled and then laughed. "You told Ryker about Cain's brother on a lake or something," she paused to wave her hand dismissively, "I don't know, Daemon tells me little, but he said they were riding out early this morning to go see him."

My throat went dry as I stared open-mouthed at Olivia. "I told them… about Nathan?" The kitchen tipped and tilted on its axis as I realized what I had done. "And they went to see him?"

"Yes…" Faith said, slowly. She closed the space between us and took the bowl of raw eggs out of my hands. "Sit down and tell me why knowing that makes you look like you want to puke."

"It doesn't," I insisted. "It's just… Nathan's innocent in all of this, and I can only imagine what Ryker would do to him."

I listened to the frying pan sizzle and spit as Faith poured the eggs into it. She was silent for a moment before she turned to me, her hip propped on the counter next to the stove top. "He'll kill Nathan if he doesn't get the information he wants from him. You know this and yet act like it surprises you."

I examined Olivia and the truth she spoke. I remembered the way she looked, so innocent and sad, when we met for lunch for the first time in five years a couple of months ago.

"You're different," I told her.

She nodded and checked the eggs. "I suppose when you remember who you are and the weight of trying to be someone different is lifted, you tend to change."

I stared at the girl who was two years younger than me, but suddenly seemed so much wiser and older. Two months ago she'd snuck her way into Penny's Boarding house, begging for my help, and I hadn't been able to turn her away then. Now, I knew that I would do anything to repair my friendship with Olivia Masters if only so I could have one good thing to hold on to once again.

"Who did you remember you are?" I asked, filling my own coffee mug and dumping in a spoonful of sugar.

I returned to the kitchen counter as Olivia plated up eggs and toast for us, a bottle of hot sauce included. My favorite.

She grinned at me, showing a full mouth of sparkly white teeth. She seemed so happy her eyes might have actually sparkled. "The Princess of the Nordic Lords..." She raised an eyebrow, half in jest and half in reminding me of my own club heritage. "Don't you know who you are?"

Princess. I hadn't felt like a princess since I was eighteen years old and fell in love with Ryker. I doubted I would ever feel like a princess again.

I shook my head. "I'm happy for you, Liv."

"I'm happy for me, too." She pointed a fork full of eggs at me. "I'll be happier when you're happy again, too."

I rolled my eyes, but somehow, her lightheartedness and kindness infused the space between us.

"Do you know what we need?"

I raised my eyes to Liv's. She looked full of mischievous plotting. It wouldn't be good for me. "What?"

"A girl's night."

"You're kidding."

"Come on," she said, planting her hands to the kitchen counter before pushing off and began cleaning up the plates. "Me, you, and Jules need a night out at The Tavern. We'll get drunk, we'll dance on bars—"

"Please tell me you'll do this while taking off your bras and getting naked."

We snapped our heads to the male intruder. Liv immediately grinned at Finn as he stood in the doorway, encompassing the space with his large chest and angrily inked forearm. He smiled, something I learned he didn't do often. That, along with talking.

Liv pointed a finger at him. "That would drive Daemon crazy and probably get me on lockdown for a month."

Finn pushed off the doorway and helped himself to the leftover eggs. "Probably why you'd do it," he said, his mouth full of eggs that he ate directly from the pan with his fingers.

I watched their flippant conversation in envy. Liv had only been back in the club for less than two months, and yet seeing her in the space we had both occupied so freely as children and teenagers, she was the only one of us who looked like we still belonged.

"I don't drive Daemon crazy," Liv demanded. Then she crossed her arms and made a funny face. "At least not intentionally." She shrugged over Finn's smirk and turned back to me. "Come on. We'll have to take guards—probably that lug." She pointed to Finn who grunted. "And I can't imagine Ryker won't be there, too. But it'll be fun and I really think you need to kick back and have some fun."

"If the fun you're intending is going to leave me with a hangover like I have today then I'm going to pass."

"Gin."

"What?" I dragged my confused face to her smiling one.

"Gin. It doesn't give nearly the wicked hangover as all that yeast-filled beer does."

I knew the look she had. I knew that look like I knew her when we were kids. Her grin and her clasped hands told me I was going whether or not I wanted to.

She squealed and threw herself into my arms when I finally agreed.

20

Ryker

The parking lot was crowded and full of women and men when we pulled in on our bikes, parking them in line with the rest.

I wasn't surprised. Since Daemon had put the club on lockdown when we took out Black Death weeks ago, and with no word from them or what their closest charter was doing with the remaining members, he was too cautious to let everyone roam free.

But for a bunch of men and old ladies who joined a club life for the sole purpose of being able to live free, being caged was difficult.

I scanned the lot until my eyes fell on Faith. She was sitting on a wooden park bench with Liv at her side, who was saying something to her using wild hand gestures, but Faith's eyes were locked on mine.

And they were full of concern. I headed toward the women, Daemon at my side, when Switch appeared in front of us.

"You get it done?" he asked, his eyes on me but his words meant for Daemon.

Daemon flipped a blade so it landed in Switch's greased hand. "Finished it in a way that would have made you proud, old man. No sign of Cain, though."

Switch snorted. His bald head sweated under the hot, humid sun, and his long greying beard needed a trim about six months ago.

Daemon told the truth. By the time he and Jaden had finished with Nathan, there wasn't enough of his abdomen left to hold his guts in.

I had walked back in once Tripp and I searched the entire resort only to come up with very little. Blood on an old tattered mattress in one of their underground tornado shelters gave us the only hint that Cain or Faith's mom had been there.

We knew it was Faith's mom, Roxy, because the only thing left behind the room other than the mattress was a silver locket that contained an old black and white image of Faith's dad.

Switch slid the blade into his back pocket and nodded once, giving his approval of the way the new President handled the situation. I saw Daemon fight a small smile. He may have become President, but he still wanted—and needed—the approval and respect of the other men.

"That should bring Cain out of hiding."

Daemon agreed right as Liv ran up to him. His arm instinctively went around her waist, wrapping her tightly to his side, and pulled her in for a kiss.

"Everything go okay?" she asked as Faith walked up behind her. Even with the scars and the marks I knew she had that would never fade, she was still the most beautiful woman I'd ever seen.

"Good as it could," Daemon replied.

"You okay?" Faith asked me as she reached us. Her eyes slowly scanned my body as if she was searching for my own injuries. But other than the purple bruise on my cheek from the boxing match with Jaden, I was all good.

"Didn't find Cain or your mom." I reached for her hand and dropped the locket into her palm. She gasped when she saw it. "But we found this."

Her eyes immediately filled with tears. "She never went anywhere without this." Her chin trembled as she lifted her worried and sad eyes to mine.

"She could still be okay, Faith." I squeezed my hand around hers.

I doubted my words as much as she doubted hearing them. I didn't give a shit whether her mom lived or died, but the sadness and paleness in her eyes and face eroded an acidic hole in my gut. I was so fucking tired of seeing her sad all the time.

"You can't cry," Liv said, pointing her finger at Faith. "We're having girl's night tonight."

"No way."

She twisted out of Daemon's reach and planted her hands on her hips. "We're going out and having fun."

"Are you fuckin' mad?"

"No. I'm tired of being cooped up in this smelly old club, and Faith needs to dance and let loose."

"It's fine, Liv."

Liv shot her scolding eyes to Faith before she glared back at Daemon. "We're only going to The Tavern, and you can send men with us to keep us safe."

Daemon shook his head. I stood back and bit back a laugh seeing my little brother so worked up. "What did you say to me just a few weeks ago? You'd do what I said because you knew I was keeping you safe."

"I also said I'd take a guard if I had to, and I'm agreeing to that."

Daemon snapped his head to mine, a look of disbelief all over his face.

I bit back a grin. "Don't look at me, brother. She's your woman."

He shook his head again, and then glanced at Faith who was watching all of us and our easy banter with a look of envy and sadness painted all over her. Fuck. What I wouldn't give to see her acting like the woman she used to be.

Daemon noticed it, too, because he turned to Liv and pointed a finger in her face. "We're coming with. You can have your girl's night alone when we're not worried about blowback on us."

"That's fantastic," Liv said, clapping her hands and tugging Faith's hand out of mine. "It'll be like the time you baby-sat us at the mall all over again. *So much fun!*"

She turned her sarcastic grin to Faith.

Faith laughed. It was soft and over quickly, but I heard it. And I fucking loved it.

"I can chain you to my bed, again, Liv. You thought that night was fun."

Liv's heated cheeks were enough of a giveaway to tell me I didn't want to know anything more about the night she was chained to my brother's bed.

"Looks like we're going to a bar tonight," Daemon said once the girls were out of hearing range. His eyes never once left Liv's ass as she walked away though.

Not that I was watching what he was doing... my eyes were firmly glued on Faith's ass.

"Another round of drinks, please." Faith shouted the words as she bent half over the bar at the Tavern. The music was not only loud, but it was obnoxiously country. It hadn't stopped Liv from grabbing Faith's hand as soon as the girls hit the bar and spent the past hour shaking their asses on the dance floor.

Jules and Liv had seemed like they were having a blast. For the first thirty minutes, Faith had looked like her choices were either dancing in public or having her fingernails ripped off. Neither appealing, but the dancing was slightly less painful.

Daemon and I had stood back and watched the crowd and the men who dared get too close to them. Several times I watched Faith's eyes roam the room, watching men.

It had taken her several times of doing this, several times of a few men acknowledging her presence with a quick head bob, for me to get it.

Fucking clients. I had tensed; my hands balled into fists and then I headed for the dance floor, only to be stopped short by Finn yanking on my cut.

"Let her see she can be out there and nothing will happen to her."

"Nothing will happen to her because I'll be there." I growled back, getting in his face. My frustration and anger were growing by the second.

"Maybe she needs to see she can do it on her own."

It was as if Pete was in front of me saying the same damn things to me about Meg. I had looked out at Faith, slowly beginning to get lost in the music, her earlier hesitation disappearing before my eyes, and I had agreed.

But now, with the way her ass was half hanging out of her too short mini skirt as she leaned over the bar, I wanted to rip off every man's head who had ever seen her naked.

Mine! The word repeated at an ear blasting decibel level in my head as she reached for her glasses.

I reached out and wrapped an arm around her waist, hauling her back to my chest.

Leaning forward, my lips brushed against her ear. I didn't miss the way her body shivered or how she moved closer to me. My quickly hardening dick didn't miss it, either.

"If you don't want me starting a bar fight and getting more innocent blood on my hands, you're going to have to stop showing half of your ass to the men in this bar."

I felt a quick intake of breath before Faith tilted her head. Sweat from dancing had some of her hair stuck to her temples. Her back stuck to my leather cut and I could feel the heat from her skin through my thin t-shirt.

"I'm not," she said right before her hand went down to the hem of her skirt. One side of her lips lifted. "This skirt goes halfway my down my thighs. No one can see anything."

I could. And I knew what the men were thinking. It was enough to drive me insane.

"Please tell me you're not taking a play out of Liv's playbook and trying to drive me crazy just because it's fun for you."

She blinked, and her cheeks turned a light shade of pink. A small glimmer of light danced across her eyes before she blinked again. But I saw it—that small fucking shimmer of hope that Faith was coming back, letting her past go.

It disappeared as quickly as it came when she leaned in closer. "I think I've played enough games, Ryker."

Shit.

"That's not what I meant, Faith."

She looked at my crotch. My erection obvious. It was the first time in my life I hated my own dick. "I know what men see and what they want when they look at me. I'm not stupid."

Fuck this. She'd been having too much fun to start wallowing now, and hell if I was going to let her take one small move and turn it into something bigger.

"How much have you had to drink?"

She raised two glasses. "Gin and tonic for Liv," she said, nodding toward one then the other, "And water and lime for me."

I grinned. "That why you've been getting the drinks all night?"

She shrugged. "It seemed important to Liv that I get drunk, but I didn't want to again."

I nodded and took the gin and tonic for Liv out of her hands. When her hand was free, I pulled her closer to me and wrapped her hand around my lower back. "Tonight, when we get back to the club, I'm going to climb into that bed with you. I'm going to put my arm around your waist like this and I'm going to hold you close all night long while you sleep."

I pulled back to see if she was still with me. Her mouth was slightly parted and her skin was flushed. The quickly beating vein in her neck told me that not only was I *not* scaring her, but she was fucking loving listening to what I said.

"Do you know what I'm going to do then, Faith?" I asked, my lips dragging down the tender skin of her jaw.

She shook her head against my mouth but didn't speak.

"I'm going to hold you like that every night until you feel safe. Until you want a man touching you in more than that way. And, maybe, if you get lucky, once you feel that way, I might even kiss you."

She shivered in my arms. I felt like a fucking king.

21

Faith

My breath caught in my throat. Something did. Maybe it was a frog or a lodged ice cube from my glass of water. I could think of nothing I wanted to say except "kiss me now."

I opened my mouth to do just that, but nothing came out—only a squeak of uncertainty and shock.

Ryker gazed down at me like he had made my safety and my security his personal mission in life. The way his black hair fell across his forehead, sweat beads glistened on his skin, and his dark eyes were pinned directly on mine made it difficult to think, much less speak.

I settled for closing my mouth and nodding once.

When Ryker leaned forward and gently swept his lips across my forehead, some of my vocal abilities returned.

"That'd be nice," I told him, my voice shaking like it used to when I had to stand in front of my high school public speaking class. Heat suffused my throat and cheeks. Nice? That's the word I came up with to describe sleeping in Ryker's arms again?

"Nice?" he repeated, amused.

I swallowed. "Nice."

His lips brushed against my ear. The small movement blossomed a fire deep in my lower belly. It was the same as I remembered feeling when I was sixteen and Ryker touched me for the first time. Nothing about my life with Black Death had quenched the way my body responded to him.

Which told me only one thing: Sleeping next to Ryker, wrapped in his strong, muscular arms, wouldn't be nice.

It would be my dream come true.

And I wanted it more than I could remember ever wanting anything.

I was just about to open my mouth to tell him so when Daemon appeared behind Ryker, a scowl on his face.

His hand came down and clasped onto Ryker's shoulder, pulling him from me.

"Gotta get out of here. Tripp said bikes are outside."

Ryker instantly grabbed my hand and I noticed Liv and Jules being pulled off the dance floor by Finn.

"Back door, Ryker," Daemon said. "There's an alley out there and we have my truck. Get the girls to the clubhouse."

I was being pulled before my feet could catch up to my brain to tell me something bad was going on. It all happened so quickly.

The warmth from Ryker's hand went unnoticed as he pushed through the crowd in the old, run down bar. All I felt was the motion of moving, a small push in my back from Liv's hand behind me, and adrenaline spiking in my veins.

"What's going on?" I asked as Ryker pulled me through the back door.

He looked left and right, making sure the alley was clear while he pulled his gun out of his holster and held it confidently in one hand. His other hand was gripping mine so tightly I was almost afraid my bones would crush if he squeezed it tighter.

"Don't know," he said.

But then we all heard it.

Tires squealed.

Gun shots exploded in the quiet night air, sounding like they were coming from the front of the bar.

A dark, old vehicle pulled up and blocked the opening to the alley.

The back door opened.

And I screamed.

Sweaty hands gripped my arms, but I pushed them away as I took off running down the alley. By the time I got there, the car was long gone and Daemon was at the body that had been flung out of the back door of the car.

Her face was almost unrecognizable. Her black hair that mirrored mine was matted to her bloody and bruised and swollen face.

"Mom!" I shouted, right as my knees collapsed to her side.

She was bloody—everywhere. My hands pushed away the drying blood as I tried to find where it had come from, but I couldn't see anything besides her broken, lifeless body lying on the hot gravel in front of me.

"She's dead," I cried out and felt another pair of warm hands at my shoulders, pulling me off her.

"No, she's not," Daemon told me, his fingers on her neck. "She has a pulse. Barely."

He wiped away the blood off her face and focused on the bubble of foam at the edges of her mouth.

His eyes pinned mine. I lost the ability to breathe. "She's overdosed, Faith."

I stared at my mom. Daemon's words ringing truth loudly in my head. Her skeletal frame under her ripped t-shirt showed every bone in her body. Even with her swollen and bloody face, her eyes were sunken so far into her head that I would have barely recognized her even if she hadn't gotten the crap beat out of her.

"We'll get her to the hospital," Daemon said, already pulling a phone out of his pocket.

I quit listening.

My knees collapsed and I felt myself fall back into a hard body. Ryker's hand wrapped around my stomach as he pulled me against his chest. With one hand, he ran it down my hair, trying to soothe me.

I couldn't speak. Salty tears poured from my eyes as my mother's barely breathing body went blurry in front of me.

I heard conversations occurring around me, but it was all unrecognizable to my own ears. I had no idea what the men were saying as Ryker kept me tightly pressed against his chest. Then I was turned and lifted into Ryker's arms as he carried me away.

"No!" I shouted, frantic to see my mom as she disappeared from my line of sight.

"It's okay, Faith, we're taking her to the hospital." Ryker's deep rumble vibrated against my neck. He held me tighter as I cried out for my mom and only loosened me once I was settled into the back of Daemon's truck.

Then my mother's head was placed on my lap.

My mom. The woman who quit paying attention to me when I turned ten years old. The woman who sold me for drugs. The woman who, for all I knew, hated me.

And she was dying in my arms.

"Here. Take this."

I stared at the pale blue piece of fabric that had been shoved into my lap. When I brought my eyes to Ryker's as he stood in front of me, I shot him a confused look.

"You're covered in blood."

His eyes and face held no emotion as he spoke the words. He didn't move. He stood there, watching me, not blinking.

I looked down.

My pale pink top that had Harley Davidson scrawled across my breasts was lined with blood. It stuck to my arms, palms, and thighs. My black leather skirt was splattered.

Tears instantly burned in the back of my eyes.

"Let me help," Ryker said. He turned me away from him in the small empty room we were waiting in and had me stripped of my tank top and covered in a nurse's blue scrub top before I could argue with him.

Then he picked me up and sat down in one of the small plastic chairs and held me on his lap, one arm wrapped behind my shoulders, the other draped over my legs with his hand at my hip.

I said nothing as we waited in the cramped room at the local hospital until someone could come out and tell me how my mom was doing.

Waiting for someone to tell me she had died. An ache in my chest expanded with every breath I forced myself to take. Not because I was sad, but because I was almost relieved.

Her death would break the final hold Cain or Black Death had on me.

I didn't know if my tears were relief, sadness, or happiness.

My eyes snapped to the door when it opened, only to have my heart skip a beat when Daemon entered with a grim look on his face. Liv and Jules followed behind him.

"We should have names etched on our own chairs for as often as we're here," he said before he grabbed a chair across the room from me. He planted his ass in the chair and crossed his feet, legs straight out in front of him.

"Ignore him," Liv said as she took the chair next to me. "He's an insensitive ass."

I watched them glare at each other from across the room in mock disgust. Daemon's twitch of his lips was my only clue that he wasn't really pissed or annoyed.

Still, I was thankful for their presence.

"You okay?" Liv asked and turned to me.

I shrugged, unable to answer, unable to describe how the thought of my mother's death almost made me feel good.

"We've got men on Cain," Daemon said, his eyes on Ryker with only a quick glance to me.

"Cain?" The name leapt out of my throat, scratchy and disjointed.

Ryker's grip on my hip tightened.

Daemon looked at me, his eyes softening marginally. "Got a call right after you took off. Cain said this was payback for what we did to Nathan."

I hadn't yet heard what had happened with Cain's brother. Based on what Cain did to my mom, I figured it was better I didn't know.

"Maybe now isn't the time, Daemon," Ryker warned him. His voice was calm and smooth. It sent a wash of security over my skin into my pores as he held me tightly in that cramped little chair.

My eyes speared Ryker until he caught my expression. Slowly, I climbed off his lap and stood in front of him. Everyone watched me.

I didn't know where it came from.

I only knew that somehow, being encased in Ryker's warmth and confidence had filled me with a strength that I had been missing for what felt like my entire life.

"Kill him."

Ryker blinked. His hand reached out to hold mine, but I snapped it back before he could touch me. I watched his face fill with wariness.

I turned to Daemon. My hands ran through my matted and tangled hair and then smoothed out the too large scrub top. I had to look like an utter mess.

I didn't care.

"I don't give a shit how many men it takes or what kinds of favors you need to pull. I want that fucker dead."

"Faith," Ryker crooned, my whispered name falling softly from his lips. I felt the way he stared at me, felt the way he wanted me to turn to him and forget everything I had just spoken.

"No," I snapped. "This has gone on long enough. If Cain was in that car, if he was responsible for this shit to my mom—which we know he was—go. Go get him." I leaned closer, my pulse beating wildly out of control against my chest. "Gut him."

Ryker's eyes pleaded with me. He uncurled his long frame from the chair until he stood at full height in front of me. One of his hands went to my hair, again running it down the length. He gave a small tug when he hit the end.

I couldn't stop my smile. That same action was one he always pulled when I had humored him before.

There was no amusement in his eyes as I maintained my focus on him.

My hands curled into fists against my thighs. Ryker tilted his head to the left, examining me, before he leaned slowly forward and pressed his lips gently against my temple. "I will gladly gut that fucker for everything he's done to you. When we find him, I'm the one who will take him out, I promise you. But tonight isn't the time to worry about it."

"Tonight's the perfect night to worry about it."

He opened his mouth to say something, but the door opened at the same time.

A bedraggled looking doctor walked slowly through the door. His eyes took in us women and then Ryker and Daemon, now both standing with their arms crossed over their leather cuts.

"Which one of you is Faith?" he asked. His voice sounded slow and tired. His eyes looked like he hadn't slept in days.

"I am."

"Your mother—" he started and stopped. Uncertainty and sadness flashed in his eyes. He swallowed once and recovered.

My knees shook and I reached out to grab onto Ryker's forearm so I didn't collapse.

"Your mother," he repeated, "is incredibly lucky to be alive."

Hot, wet tears spilled down my cheeks as I gasped for breath and listened to him explain the extent of her injuries. Broken bones, internal bleeding, overdose from heroine. He talked about track marks in her arms and between her fingers and toes.

He told me all of it while I stood in the small room feeling like the walls were caving in on me. Ryker's arm was the only thing that kept me on my feet as disappointment from the news washed over me.

I was upset my mother was actually alive.

It wasn't until after he gave us her room number and told me I could see her, after the door shut behind him, that I finally collapsed into Ryker's chest.

"She's okay," he whispered in my ear. He repeated it over and over, trying to soothe me, mistaking my sobs for ones of relief instead of frustration.

"It's not that," I said, choking down the last of my tears with a deep, shaky exhale and large swallow. "I'm not…" I shook my head, trying to put words to my emotions that felt reprehensible, but I had to stand by them.

I *wanted* to stand by them. To be strong and truly live in the knowledge that even though I had at one time loved my mother… the woman who had allowed me to be sold for sex was no longer that same woman.

And I *hated* her.

Slowly, I dragged my eyes from the shiny white member patch on Ryker's cut to his narrowed, dark and tired eyes.

I rolled my shoulders. "I wanted her to die."

I whispered the words and awaited the condemnation. I expected a gasp of surprise or a gentle rebuke from Liv who I knew was still in the room, although silent.

Nothing came. No one bothered to tell me I didn't mean it. And as each beat of my heart blasted ferociously against my chest, it dawned on me that no one—especially no one in that room—would ever judge me for those hideously spoken words.

I watched as Ryker blinked. The lines at the edges of his eyes softened right as his lips parted minutely. The edges turned up slightly and he reached out and softly brought my hand into his warm, firm grasp. "Let's go say good-bye to her, then."

I squeaked out, "okay," and allowed Ryker to lead me out through the waiting room and down the sterile but brightly lit hospital corridor until we reached the doorway to my mother's room.

From the open doorway, the gentle beeping sounds of monitors filled my ears. The medicinal smells stung my nose as I felt a slight nudging from Ryker on my lower back.

I didn't turn to him. I didn't move. "I need to do this myself."

His fingers on my lower back dug lightly into my skin, flexing from the impact of my words. "I'm not letting you be alone with that toxic woman."

"I'll be fine." I glanced at him over my shoulder. His eyes stared through the slats of the window blinds into my mother's room. I had already glimpsed at her. She looked tiny and fragile. Her skin ashen. Her black hair greasy and wet from having blood scrubbed off her. Bruises and scratches covered her skin much like mine had been—much like mine still were—just a week after being freed from the cabin.

I took her entire appearance and committed it to memory as the last memory I would ever see of my mother again.

Shifting on my feet enough so I could rest my arm on Ryker's forearm, I watched his jaw tighten. He kept his eyes focused on my mom.

"I have to do this," I told him, my fingers squeezing his arm to get his attention. "I need to say good-bye to her. And then you need to go get Cain."

A slow smile grew on Ryker's face. He removed his glare from the window and shifted his look to my hand on his arm and then to my eyes.

He shook his head back and forth once.

"No. Tonight, you'll say good-bye to your mom, and then I'll take you back to the club where we'll sleep like I promised you we would earlier."

I opened my mouth to object, but he silenced my words my cupping my cheek with the palm of his hand. His thumb gently rubbed one of my bruised cheeks. "Tomorrow, I'll go looking for Cain until I find him and gut him. Tonight, I want to hold you."

Warmth from his palm spread from my cheeks to my neck to the tips of my fingers and toes. I relished in it while we stood in the hallway of the hospital, gazing at each other with softened eyes as if we were still lovers.

"I'll be right back," I told him, my words quietly spoken.

"I'll be here." He pressed his lips against my forehead before sending me into the room.

My feet trudged slowly, as if in mud or boots filled with drying cement, but I forged through the sadness of my long lost youth and focused on the woman laid before me.

"Mom," I said quietly. I didn't reach out and touch her hand but kept my hands firmly pressed against my thighs.

I stared at my mother and saw the nights of her passed out on the couch or the kitchen table. Her eyes flickered open and the only thing I saw inside them was a life that had died well before her body was ready to let her go.

I shivered under the coldness of the room and her expression as she slowly dragged her eyes to mine.

"I hate you." I expected a sadness at speaking the words. I expected some niggle in the corner of my conscience to whisper words of reprobation for speaking to my mother in such a horrific way.

Instead, I felt peace and freedom grow from my spirit and fill my body with a calmness I had never had, not even in my youth.

"I never wanted you." I fought a flinch at her quietly stated words. There was a slight pain in hearing them, but I had long suspected that to be true, and yet simply unwilling to acknowledge it. "Your father wanted children. I wanted him all to myself. And as soon as you were born, you took over every spare thought, every spare minute he had. And nothing was left for me."

"Nothing was left for you because he probably felt your jealousy of your own child. But that's not my fault and never was." I leaned forward, my hands gipping the edges of her small, narrow hospital bed. "Someday you will die alone. And no one will mourn you. No one will care, and it's all your fault because you pushed everyone who ever loved you so far away until they felt nothing for you."

She blinked and looked away.

I left the room before she could come up with a vicious, selfish retort.

When I met Ryker in the hallway, I wrapped my arm around his and slid my hand down his arm until he entwined his fingers with mine.

"I'm really tired," I said as my eyes focused on the end of the hallway.

22

Ryker

"Do you want to talk about your mom?" I asked Faith as she crawled under the covers in my bed. I tried to ignore the way the Nordic Lords shirt she wore barely skimmed passed her ass cheeks.

My hard dick told me I had failed. But I also knew that I couldn't crawl into bed with Faith, wrap my arms around her, and let her feel that.

Talking about her mom was a sure way to get my erection to shrivel into nothing. She hadn't spoken a word since we left the hospital, anyway. All she'd done was stare out the window of the truck with a glazed look in her pale blue eyes, watching as we passed evergreen after evergreen on the narrow, windy roads through town.

In the slight darkness, the room barely lit by one small lamp, I saw her shoulders move.

"It wasn't anything I didn't know before," she said and draped her arm awkwardly over her eyes. "I just never wanted to admit it."

While she wasn't looking, I dropped my jeans and removed my shirt.

As I crawled into bed next to her, Faith dropped her arm and turned to me. I propped myself up on one elbow, laying on my side, so I was almost hovering over her.

"What changed tonight?" Something had. Faith had always sworn to protect her mom. Hell, she'd had sex for money in order to keep her mom alive.

Her breath hitched and she blinked. She rolled her lips between her teeth before releasing a shuddering breath. I itched to comfort her with my touch but forced myself to hold back.

"I don't know," she finally said, her voice barely audible above the whirring of the small and useless window air-conditioner unit. "But I saw her on that pavement, and I held her in the truck, and all I could think about were all the memories I have of my mom when she was such a complete bitch to me. I know there were some good times when I was kid, but for the last fifteen years I can't think of a single nice thing she's said to me or done for me."

"But you love her…"

"Maybe not," Faith said. "Maybe I just wanted to. Maybe I wanted to feel someone love me."

With a small roll to her side, Faith faced me and slid her arm over my waist. My stomach tightened from the light contact of her glorious skin on mine. It was the first time she willingly touched me as she ran her fingers along the waistband on my boxers from my hip to my back.

The erection I was trying to keep under control took on a mind of its own.

"Faith," I warned.

She shook her head. Her small fingertips pressed into my back. "Do you know what I realized while we were sitting in that waiting room?"

Her fingers continued their soft, insanely sexy assault on my skin. Fuck, I wanted her. I wanted to drag my fingers through her hair and kiss her until she forgot about every single man who had ever touched her beside me.

"I realized that in my entire life, the only people who had ever truly loved me were you and Liv."

A frog jumped into my throat. And what kind of pussy did that make me? I couldn't speak with her hands on my skin, teasing me, pleasing me, and yet the words speared my chest like a hot branding iron.

Straight to my mother fucking heart.

"I wanted you to kiss me tonight," she said. I tried to focus on her words. All I could focus on was the way her lips moved when she spoke.

"I wanted to kiss you, tonight," I said, leaning forward.

I couldn't wait anymore. Faith was in my bed. It felt good.

It felt *right*. Despite the shit going on and the injuries she was still recovering from.

All I wanted—all I'd ever wanted—was this moment. I had lived for it as a kid, missed it for years, and wanted it more than ever as a man.

"Please don't let me fall asleep tonight without giving me a happy memory, Ryker." Her soft, sad voice broke through to my brain. I stared directly into her eyes and saw the fanatic need she had for something. Something good. "I really need something good to happen to me."

And I wanted to give it to her.

Without hesitating, I leaned forward and brushed my lips against hers. I felt her gasp against my lips right as my hand moved to the curve in her neck. I held her in place while I nipped at her lower lip, then her sides, teasing her with my tongue but not entering.

Her chest brushed against mine and a rumble escaped my throat. I could feel her already hardened nipples brush against me through the shirt she was wearing. My shirt.

My bed.

My arms.

Faith was in it all.

With her moving against me, her thigh brushing against my hard dick, I didn't waste time rolling her to her back and removing her shirt.

My hands slowly pushed it up and off of her, taking in every crevice, every dip of her skin that I hadn't seen in far too long. I wanted all of it—all of her—to be so ingrained in my memory that I knew every inch of her even when I wasn't looking at her.

I wanted to remember the dimples at the small of her back. The two small birthmarks she had on the outside of her left breast. And when I saw them, I dipped my head, flicked my tongue against them, and licked them.

"Ryker." Her hands dug into my scalp. She arched into me.

I nuzzled against her skin until I was at her chest, her pink nipples screaming, *"suck me and lick me, now."* Her nipples and I spoke the same language because there was nothing I wanted more, either.

"You sure about this?" I asked. I could slow down. I would stop if she wanted, despite every nerve in my body shouting *Take her! Claim her! She's yours! She always has been!*

Her head tipped back as I pulled her nipple into my mouth.

"God, yes," she moaned.

I wouldn't turn back. She tasted perfect. My hands worshipped her skin. My mouth made love to her body.

I wanted every inch of her body inside of me. In equal measure, I wanted every inch of me to be so deeply ingrained in her so that she would never forget me.

I wanted to erase every man that had been inside her in the last five years.

I leaned off her, one hand brushing her hair away from cheeks while my other hand glided across her skin and down to her pussy. She was wet and hot. I felt her pulsing against my fingers as I played with her slowly.

"You want me?" I asked her, brushing my lips against her swollen ones. I kissed every inch of her face while she hummed beneath me; my fingers gentle playing with her clit, rolling it, teasing her.

With a dazed expression, her eyelids fluttered as she writhed against my hands.

"Need more," she moaned and pressed into me.

I smiled and shook my head. "Do you want me, Faith?"

I knew she did. I wanted to make sure she knew it was me doing this to her.

"Ryker," she warned me. Her breath panted out my name as if she was starved. I hoped she was fucking starved for me like I was for her. Her next words sliced my chest open. "I've always wanted you."

My mouth covered hers as I kissed her. It was hot and wet and I continued kissing her as my fingers pressed inside her hot sex. She groaned into my mouth and the sound went straight into my mouth and down to my dick.

Her hands fumbled at the edges of my boxers until she pushed them passed my hips, freeing my hard dick. It throbbed in her palm when she wrapped her chilled fingers around me.

"Jesus," I hissed as she began working me from base to tip. I almost came in her hand when she began gripping my balls, pulling and massaging them with perfect finesse.

"Now, Ryker," Faith whispered against the sweat lining my neck. "I need you, now. Please."

Shudders rocked my body. My shoulders shook and the muscles in my back tensed. I wanted her. God, I fucking wanted her.

I had always loved her.

A part of me was too afraid we would fuck this up. That this was too soon.

But the part of me that was still rocking into Faith's hands as she jacked me off like she used to do when we were kids… that part wanted to sink in to her, to have her screaming my name until every damn person in the clubhouse knew what we were fucking doing.

First, I wanted to see her come apart beneath me.

My fingers pressed into her pussy, my thumb pressed against her clit, and my lips clamped down on her nipples. Her whole body shook with pleasure.

"Let go, Faith." I whispered it while keeping my eyes on her. My lips alternated between playing with both of her nipples, licking her breasts, and trying to soak in every taste of her I could.

She tensed for one brief second, but I saw it.

I saw the fear light up in her eyes that she had done this with men and had enjoyed it.

"It's me, babe. You love me. Come for me."

Her eyes flashed with something. But fuck me, it was there. That sparkle I had wanted to see so badly. Her eyes brightened right as her pussy began convulsing around my fingers. She screamed my name as I rode out her orgasm.

And when she was done, when I removed my fingers from her before I spread her thighs and sunk in between them, I fucking felt it.

Love. Forgiveness. Redemption.

I had it all. I had everything I wanted in the bed with me and surrounding the walls of my room.

I had Faith.

"That was amazing," she panted. Tears fell from her eyes and a smile graced her lips.

I kissed away her tears right as I pressed my dick against her.

"It will always be amazing," I whispered against her ear.

She tightened around my dick as I pushed inside. And fucking shit. Phenomenal.

I had wasted years having sex to chase away the memories in my head of my fuck-ups, of my regret.

Nothing had ever felt this good.

"Fuck," I breathed out against Faith's collarbone.

Her hands went to my ass and pressed me harder into her. I couldn't move. I was two seconds away from blowing my load like I did the first time we had sex. I needed to feel her warmth for a minute.

"Fucking… Jesus, Faith. What are you fucking doing to me?" I brushed away her sweaty hair and stared directly into her eyes.

They lit up.

"The same thing you do to me." I saw the truth in her whispered response.

My hips rocked harder and she gasped. I rolled my hips and pulled out, memorizing the perfect feel of her.

"It's always been you," I told her right as I rocked back into her. My control was wound tight. I wanted to pound into her and release the tension that had built up in me for weeks every time I looked at her.

She moaned and arched into me. I lowered my chest to hers, craving the feel of her skin brushing against mine. I rocked into her again, swiveling my hips. Her legs came up and wrapped around my waist as we made love.

I was making love to Faith.

Holy shit.

Her sweaty hands slipped from my ass as I continued plunging into her, taking everything from her that she would give me and giving her everything I could without shouting the words out loud.

But I saw it. As we moved together, I saw the same dazed and shocked expression in her eyes as I knew she had seen in mine.

Our eyes stayed connected. Every part of us, every inch of us, stayed connected until she pulsed around my dick.

She shouted my name as she came again and I buried myself so far inside of her I wasn't sure I'd ever be able to dig my way out.

Her name fell from my lips as my head fell into the crook of her neck. I collapsed on top of her, our sweat and breaths mixing together and swirling around us.

I never wanted to leave.

23

Faith

The haze of darkness from sleep cleared when I felt a warm heat pressed against my inner thighs.

My eyes half-opened, I grinned sleepily.

Ryker lifted his mouth from my thigh and returned the grin. "Good morning," he murmured and returned to a teasingly slow assault on my skin. I squirmed beneath him, my body already beginning to pulse with need for him.

I never wanted to forget last night.

The way he held me, the way he made love to me, and the way he knew that I loved him.

I moved my hand to run it through his short black hair while he continued pressing his lips against my legs, coming close to my core, but avoiding it just enough to begin slowly driving me insane.

I gave his hair a small tug.

When he pulled his eyes to mine, his brow wrinkled with worry. "What is it?"

"We need to talk."

One eyebrow rose. "Now?" He glanced down at my legs spread wide for him before he shot me a wry grin. "I was sort of busy."

A silent laugh escaped my lips, but I yanked on his hair again, pulling him toward me. My jaw dropped while his muscular frame slowly climbed over my body. He braced himself above me, both elbows planted by my shoulders.

"All right, then."

I bit the inside of my cheek, suddenly self-conscious and worried. "You didn't use anything last night."

He shifted his weight and played with my hair that was splayed out beneath me and all over my pillow. I loved it when he used to do this, gently dragging his fingers through my hair like he couldn't help but touch me somewhere—anywhere.

"I know," he finally said. His eyes stayed on his hands in my hair. "I didn't want to."

"But." I opened my mouth to argue, but when Ryker dragged his eyes from my hair to my eyes, I closed my mouth.

"You're on birth control?"

I nodded as I felt heat climb my neck at his sudden question.

"You're clean?"

I nodded again. "But…"

He shook his head and brought his lips to my ear. I shivered beneath his breath and penetrating gaze, relishing the feeling of the weight of his body on mine. "Then we're good, Faith. I wanted to feel you."

My nose began to sting, and I blinked several times before my eyes dried.

I cupped his cheek with my hand and slowly dragged my thumb across his morning stubble. "It's always been you, too, you know…" I stared at my thumbnail on his skin, too ashamed, too worried, what he would think. "When I was with them… I wished it was you."

I swallowed the lump in my throat, emotions that I had fought down to the pit of my stomach began swelling inside of me, wanting to finally burst forth.

"Hey," Ryker said, his voice soft and still scratchy from the morning. "Look at me."

I did. I had to. I loved staring into his black eyes and finding my reflection in them.

His lips spread into a tender smile. He looked at me patiently, as if he was waiting for me to come to some conclusion. But I couldn't.

"It will always be me."

His words caressed my fears and concerns. With one simple sentence, with one reverent look cast in my direction, Ryker was able to erase all of my worries.

Overwhelmed with emotion, with a feeling of love that grew so quickly inside of me I thought I might burst if I spoke, I simply nodded.

It was enough for Ryker.

"Now," he said, glancing down at my still naked chest. He shifted his weight, leaned off of me slightly, and I watched his hand drag slowly across my abdomen, smiling when pleasure bumps prickled my skin trailing the path of his hand. "Can I finish what I was starting when you woke up?"

I licked my suddenly dry lips and raised a hand, giving him a small wave. "If you must."

"We're heading out today."

I pretended like this didn't concern me as Daemon spoke to Liv and me while we huddled over an enormous plate of nachos that Sloppy, a club member, had served up for us.

It was well past breakfast time, but neither Liv nor I had eaten.

But we had both looked like we'd had an energetic night—and morning—before we stumbled out of the men's rooms in the clubhouse with our hair disheveled messes, our cheeks rosy pink, and our lips swollen. As soon as I saw Liv, she had thrown her arms around me and giggled like we were kids.

I had returned it easily, still slightly surprised when a laugh fell from my lips.

But now we were at one of the large dining tables in the main area of the clubhouse, stuffing our faces with a massive mound of seasoned beef, jalapenos, and enough cheese to clog our twenty-something-year-old arteries.

It was awesome.

Ryker's warm, large palm squeezed my bare thigh at Daemon's previous statement. I turned to him, my head cocked to the side, and raised a brow.

"I'm going with them."

I shoved a soggy nacho chip into my mouth and chewed, moaning with delight. "I figured."

He leaned toward me, one elbow on the table, blocking my view from Daemon on the other side of him. "I wasn't kidding around when I told you what I'd do to him."

"I wasn't kidding when I told you to gut him," I replied. Although the thought of that actually happening to someone, that I *wanted* something like that to happen to someone, sent a cold shiver down my spine.

He brought his face closer, nuzzled my cheek with his nose, and whispered, "I don't know how long we'll be gone."

When he pulled back, a worried look danced across his eyes.

"I'll be here," I told him, hoping it would soothe whatever concern he had. It must have because he nodded once and looked to Liv.

"She'll stay with you," he said.

Liv, snarkier than I remembered her being, smiled. "Of course she will. And when you get back, I've got a surprise for you."

Ryker raised his eyebrows in question as Liv slid a key ring across the table. It held two identical keys.

"You can have my house." She waved a hand dismissively as Ryker. I stared at her. Her eyes glanced from Ryker to me. "Well, my old one—my dad's—whatever. Anyway, I don't want it, so it's yours."

"You're giving him a house?"

"No." She rolled her eyes and smiled. Then she wiggled her finger between the two of us. "I'm giving you a house. Both of you."

She fell back into her chair and crossed her arms, a pleased smile stretched from ear to ear on her smug, happy face.

"What?" I asked.

Ryker squeezed my thigh and then reached across the table for the keys. "Thanks," he said, and pocketed the keys as he stood up. He said it as nonchalantly as if she'd slid him a candy bar.

I gaped up at him.

He smirked at me and leaned down, pulling my face to his. "It will always be you," he said, repeating what he told me this morning. He planted a kiss on my lips so roughly that my eyes flew open, and even though I was seated, I had to grip onto his biceps so I didn't fall over from the sudden rush of lust hitting my body.

"Get a fucking room," Daemon growled. The screech of wooden chair legs scraping across the linoleum floor broke our kiss. When Ryker pulled away from me, Daemon pointed at him. "We leave in thirty minutes. Be ready."

Ryker shot him a mock salute. "Aye-aye Captain."

The rumble of the bikes pulling out of the parking lot thirty minutes later left an eerie silence in their wake.

I stood outside with my arms crossed protectively around my stomach for no reason except I didn't know what else to do with myself.

The scorching kiss Ryker planted on my lips, the heat from his hands searing my cheeks as he cupped my face while he claimed me in front of the entire club, old ladies, and club bunnies, left my knees wobbling and mind reeling.

Women glanced at me. Their eyes raked my body from head to toe with a smirk on their lips that left me knowing exactly what they thought of me.

Not that I wasn't used to it. I had been an escort in Jasper Bay for five years. A part of me had become immune to snap judgments and vicious looks from women on the streets. But seeing it in the Nordic Lords clubhouse, feeling it in every pore of my body from the club bunnies who I knew were thinking I was no better than them, left a cold and slimy feeling covering my skin as soon as I no longer had the protection or warmth of Ryker surrounding me.

Uncertainty began to sift into my mind and fill my veins, flooding my body from the tips of my toes and upward, rippling its way through my body, until my arms shook slightly from fear and the leftover shame of my life that I knew would never go away completely.

"Hey."

I jostled to the side, wobbled on my feet, and replanted them to regain my balance from Liv's friendly bump on my hips.

Her arm went around my waist and she tugged me to her. It wasn't the same comfort as Ryker, but it was something.

I eyed her, not moving my face from the closed gates at the end of the parking lot.

"Yeah?"

"You okay?" she asked as her fingers dug slightly into my hip.

I ran a finger through my long and tangled dark locks, fidgeting with myself. Eventually, I shrugged. "I'm..." Hell, I didn't know. So much had changed in such a short amount of time.

"Come on," Liv said, removing her hand from my waist and grabbing onto one of my wrists. "I know just what you need."

I followed her as she dragged me to the club's firing range, not saying a single word as she prattled endlessly on about Daemon and how much she hated it when he left on a run or to do a job, but that she was slowly learning that the way to keep her mind off the worry was to keep herself busy.

"So you shoot something?" I asked, palming a small and comforting Beretta in my hands. It had been years since I'd held a gun. My dad and Liv's dad, Bull, had taught us girls how to shoot when we were young, insisting that someday we might need to know how to use it. The cool metal chilled my sweaty palms—part from the humid summer air and part from nerves.

"It helps," she said. Then she slid a clip into her own pink gun and aimed it at the target twenty-five yards out.

When I was younger, I had naively assumed my dad would keep me safe. Then I'd assumed Ryker would keep me safe.

But as I held the cool metal of the gun in my hand and loaded it, a strength came tumbling through me, replacing the uncertainty and fear from earlier.

It was time I learned how to take care of myself. It was time I no longer allowed myself to play victim to anyone.

I would never again let anyone take advantage of me the way Cain and the other members of Black Death had done to me.

24

Ryker

"Fucking slick bastard." I growled the words out, frustration lining every feature of my face as I scrubbed it and ran my hands through my hair.

Cain had slipped past us.

Again.

Three fucking days of trying to track the asshole down, and every time we got close, he beat us.

I was tired. I was hungry. I was horny.

And I missed Faith.

"Come on," Daemon said, slapping a hand on my shoulder harder than necessary.

I turned and glared at him. My eyes piercing his with a serious "don't fuck with me" look.

The dickhead grinned.

"We need to eat and head home. We'll figure this shit out later."

My head dropped back and my feet were firmly planted on the pavement as I straddled my bike. The sun was setting and the sky was filled with shades of oranges to purples. Had I been a chick, I'd probably call it beautiful.

But since I had a dick, the setting sun only reminded me that we'd spent one more day hunting Cain—and lost. Eating and sleeping had become a waste of time, a distraction that put us further behind the smart fucker who kept evading us.

We'd been to bumblefuck and back and all over the northern half of Minnesota, trailing Cain who was running but not going anywhere. None of it made sense. Least of all, the insane niggling in the back of my mind that continued to question—why in the hell was Faith or her mom so damn important to Cain in the first place?

My ass burned from the constant vibrations of the road.

And I needed a serious shower.

But Daemon was right. We needed food and it wasn't like we could do anything about Cain now.

I opened my mouth to tell Daemon that he was right when his phone buzzed in his hand.

He looked down at the screen with one eyebrow arched.

"Who is it?"

He ignored me and answered the call. "What is it?"

As he listened to the caller's voice come through the line, Daemon's eyes darted to mine. Then he froze. His jaw tightened, and his knuckles turned white as he gripped the phone tighter. My chest tightened in response to his instantaneous reaction.

"Tell me you can track her phone, Xbox."

Her. My hand went to my chest and pressed in hard, trying to relieve the ever increasing tension. It felt like someone had put my ribcage in a vice grip and began squeezing mercilessly. My other fist tightened on the handlebar of my bike as I continued to watch… silently helpless at whatever phone call Daemon was getting.

Liv's been shot. The memory of the words Daemon had spoken to me only a few months ago rang through my mind as Daemon's growl into the phone became indecipherable.

And all I could do was stand next to my bike, rubbing the hole in my chest filled with pain and impatience while he barked orders into the phone at Xbox to get his technological genius ass on whatever he was supposed to be doing.

He hung up the phone, lowered it to his side, and looked at me.

My eyes stayed trained on the phone in his hand. His knuckles still gripped it as if he wanted to shatter it into a million jagged fragments.

Pain sliced through my chest up to my throat and the hair on my arms stood on ends.

Time might have stopped when Daemon opened his mouth.

"Faith's gone."

25

Faith

Four Hours Earlier

With my legs propped up on a worn, leather couch in Daemon's living room, I munched on handfuls of popcorn while mindless reality television about an ink shop blabbered on in the foreground.

Lockdown from the club was horrific.

Gut-wrenching concern every time the phone rang for the last three days while I couldn't do anything to help—couldn't do anything except sit around and hang out with Liv and sometimes Jules—was worse.

My fingers and my hands and my mind all itched to do something. *Anything.*

Yet there I sat, a beer on the floor next to the side of the couch, a bowl full of heavily buttered and even more heavily salted popcorn in my lap, while I lay out on the couch like a sixty-year-old man.

"We need to get drunk."

I grabbed the beer and dangled it from my thumb and middle finger, letting it rock back and forth. "We're on it."

Liv rolled her eyes, but her eyes danced with unspoken and not-yet-acted on drunken regret.

"One beer isn't drunken fun."

"And I bet you're going to tell me what is." Placing the bowl of popcorn on the coffee table, I swung my lazy feet off the couch and onto the floor. My shirt and short yoga shorts made a sticky-tacky sound as I shifted.

It was August. It was summer. It was hotter than Hades, and my clothes had gotten stuck to the couch from my lazy afternoon.

"Call Jules," I said. "I'll watch Sophie and you two can go out."

"Or her parents could watch Sophie and we can all go out. Do some shopping, get some martinis, maybe get our hair done, and pretend we're classy and shit."

I laughed. Leave it to Liv. Being from biker families didn't make us classless. Liv had more class in one hand than most women carried in their whole bodies. She just covered it in chilled out, ripped denim and Harley tanks because she was that awesome.

I took in my own lazy day appearance. Stained gray yoga shorts, a yellow sweaty tank top, and chipped nail polish on my toes because I no longer had to look perfect all the time. My hair looked decent, but only due to the copious amounts of dry shampoo I used to make it look less greasy. I was unwashed and unshaven—basically a completely sloppy mess.

But I was dying to get out of the house.

I opened my mouth to agree that I'd go out, at least for the shopping—a girl could always use a new purse or shoes, and maybe a new haircut—when a quiet tap hit the front door.

"Who's that?" I ask, whipping my head to Liv.

She shrugged and picked up her phone. "No clue, but Finn's supposed to be outside."

The slight creaking of the old wooden screen door alerted us to the fact that whoever had been outside was now inside.

My eyebrows pulled together when a quiet, feminine voice called out, "Olivia?"

Olivia set her feet on the floor and used her hands on the armrest of her chair to push her up to standing. As she walked by me, she mouthed, "I think it's Melissa."

Which was odd. Melissa was not only *not* our friend, but she had been Daemon's club bunny for a long time until Olivia came back into the picture. I had seen her around town for years, her cheeks almost always slightly bruised, which I knew came from her asshole of a father.

I reached out to clean up my popcorn and empty beer bottle and was halfway standing when Liv returned to the living room with Melissa on her heels.

Melissa's blonde hair hung down the sides of her face, parted directly in the middle and hid half of her cheeks. I knew what that meant.

My blood immediately began thrumming in my ears. Any man who would hurt any woman—especially his daughter—should have a reserved seat in hell, as close to the eternal fire as possible.

"Hey," Melissa said, looking at me for a split second before she looked down at the floor, effectively cutting off any more eye contact.

"Hi, Melissa."

She opened her mouth and then shut it. I shot Liv a "what the hell" look as I made my way to the kitchen. Whatever Melissa was there for had nothing to do with me.

Washing and rinsing out the popcorn bowl, recycling the beer bottle, and pretending to scrub the already clean kitchen counter, I delayed my return to the living room filled with hushed voices for as long as possible.

When there was nothing left I could do to stretch out the time, I headed back to the room, my feet trudging quietly along the slick kitchen floor.

My jaw dropped as I hit the doorway to the living room and saw Liv, crouched on her knees in front of the coffee table, and Melissa sitting on the other side, the edge of her butt resting on the couch I had vacated.

Paperwork covered the table in front of them.

"What's all this?" I asked as I entered the room. Both women turned to me, but Melissa's bruised cheeks turned a different shade of pink before she glanced a way. When she did, she slide the edge of her thumbnail into her mouth and began chewing.

"Melissa wants to go to college." Liv's grin tilted up slightly higher on one side. Her eyes flashed wide before she nudged her head in Melissa's direction.

"Wow." It was all I could say, but my feet closed the distance and I took a seat on the couch next to Melissa. "Getting out of town, huh?"

I smiled so she knew I was being friendly and happy for her. And I was. She was a sweet girl and always had been. It certainly wasn't her fault she was born to a loser mom and an asshole dad.

We could relate that way, I figured. Shutting off the line of thought that hit whenever my mom was brought up, I reached out and grabbed a stack of papers.

"FAFSA?" I dragged my scrunched eyes to Liv.

"Financial aid."

I arched a brow, my fingers absentmindedly fidgeting with the corners of the thin, cool paper.

Liv glanced at Melissa before returning her eyes to me. "I told Melissa that if she wanted to get out of town and go to college, I'd help her figure it all out."

My eyes snapped to Melissa, who refused to look at me. Her fingers alternated between tapping the paper in front of her and playing with her the ends of her hair.

I knew. I knew the hesitancy she was dealing with. The fear that was wrapping its tendrils around her already fragile and shattered heart while some quiet voice spoke inside of her, telling her to flee, telling her she could do this.

My nose stung and I sniffed away the tears that threatened to grow in my eyes.

Instead, I sat back on the couch and threw an arm around her waist, pulling her to me.

She stiffened in my arm, but I pulled her closer and held her tighter.

"I get it," I told her, my voice quiet, almost as if I was terrified of scaring away the frightened little rabbit.

But I was. And so was she—the frightened rabbit.

And I knew that with certainty while I looked at her because I saw me in her. The fidgeting of the hair and the fingernails. The inability to look someone in the eye. The way her shoulders slouched and her toes tapped mindlessly against the carpeted rug in Daemon's living room. She lived her life in fear every day.

This step—this attempt at freedom—was the single most amazing and bravest step Melissa would ever take.

I knew that because it was how I felt the morning I allowed Ryker to drag me out of his room at the clubhouse, plop my ass in a stool, and feed me.

Melissa slowly relaxed into my arm as my hand that was wrapped around her waist squeezed her tight. "It's so brave of you to do this," I whispered against her cheek. Liv pretended to ignore us as she flipped through paper after paper, but I knew her ears were perked in our direction even if her eyes were glued to the stack in front of her. "You'll do great wherever you go."

Melissa's chin trembled slightly. I dropped my arm from her waist and pulled back, allowing her the time to regain her emotions.

Smacking my hands on my knees, I pushed off the couch and headed for the stairs. "I'm going to take a shower," I said, hitching my thumb in the direction of upstairs. Both Liv and Melissa glanced at me with smiles on their faces. One was proud, and yet one was still uncertain and shaky. "Call me when you're ready for shopping, okay?"

"Got it." Liv threw a thumbs up in my direction, smiled at Melissa, and started talking again.

The voices disappeared as I headed up the narrow and darkened staircase.

Quickly, I peeled off my sweat lined clothes and turned the water on in the bathroom. The warmth of the water and the pounding of the spray against my shoulders and my back erased the tension in my shoulders from worrying about Ryker. They'd only been gone for three days, but we hadn't talked much. Every time we did speak, his deep voice was tinged with a tightness that equaled my own stress and worry.

Except below his, I sensed an anger and a need for revenge that rivaled my own hatred for Cain. Black Death had essentially left town weeks ago after The Nordic Lords, Daemon leading the charge, had annihilated their charter and their President, Hammer.

But that wasn't where my mind went to as beads of slightly stinging hot water tumbled down my back, into the crevices of my behind, and down the front of my chest.

My hands in my hair as I massaged the shampoo into my scalp, I watched bubbles and water beads drip and roll down my chest, over the swells of my breasts and my nipples. My eyes closed, lost in the seductive tingle of the water on my skin, I saw two black eyes peering at me in my head.

Ryker's eyes. The way they crinkled slightly at the outside edges when he smiled. The way they narrowed on my body when he raked them over my chest and body just days ago.

I felt his eyes on me as I stood underneath the water, my hands drifting to where Ryker's had been days before, his firm, calloused hands roamed my body, tugged at my nipples, and pleasured my body in a way that only he could do.

My heart rate increased as my hands gripped my own breasts, pulling on my nipples, mirroring the way Ryker touched me.

I envisioned running my hands through his short black hair, tugging him to me, holding him against my skin as his lips and his unshaven morning shadow scraped against my tender skin. The way he woke me up by pressing his lips against my thighs, teasing me until he had placed his mouth directly onto my sex before licking.

I moaned, my fingers teasing myself the way Ryker had done for me. It wasn't enough.

I needed *more*. I needed *him*. The only man who had touched me in such a reverent and awe-inspired way. My orgasm rocked through me quickly and fiercely. One hand of mine propped on the wall of the shower, one foot on the edge of the shower tub combo, as my fingers pressed against my clit, so close, but not nearly close enough to the perfect orgasm Ryker could pull from me.

When it was finished, and I only felt slightly satisfied, I knew I would never feel immense pleasure again unless it was Ryker's hands or body doing the pleasing.

With that knowledge, I turned off the water in the shower, dried myself off with a towel, wrapping it around my chest, and grabbed another towel and did the same with my hair, piling it on top of my head so I looked like I was wearing a fluffy gray turban.

My slightly damp feet padded across the worn carpet into Ryker's childhood room where I'd been staying for the last few days. The same room Ryker had been staying in since he'd been back in town.

His masculine scent cloaked the room and enveloped me in warmth and memories of good times in my youth every time I entered.

This time was no different as I traipsed across the room and headed straight toward a small bag of clothes I had brought with me. Clothes Liv and Jules had bought for me, yet they were perfectly me in fit and style.

I dug through the bag, searching for another pair of clean shorts to throw on, when my phone began buzzing against the wooden nightstand where I'd been charging it.

I unplugged the phone and frowned when I didn't recognize the number. Yet the phone continued buzzing in my hand.

Vibrations from the phone tingled in my hand and sent similar sensations up my arms directly to my heart.

"Hello?" I asked, uncertainty and nerves made my voice sound shaky and ragged.

"I will always own you."

The voice.

That voice.

It chilled me from my teeth to my bones. Coldness and chilled bumps broke out along my arms and the back of my neck. Hairs stood on end as I squeezed my eyes shut.

Cain. At the same time I thought his name, the image of the gun I'd used the other day flashed through my mind. Strength pumped through my blood as I gripped my cell phone, my eyes looking wild and untamed in the mirror across the room from me.

My skin was paler than normal. My blue eyes flashed wide. The words in my throat felt as if they tripped over a maze of razor blades on their way out of my mouth as I asked, "What do you want?"

Silence filled the line for a beat in time before he barked out one command.

"You." I forced myself to swallow through a large golf-ball sized lump in my throat, unable to respond when he continued. "I want to see you. Now."

My eyes darted around the room, subconsciously seeking a weapon that would end him. Screw the fact it was impossible to kill him through the phone line. "Never."

His sick laugh reverberated through the phone until my body felt as if it'd been dipped in an oil spill—greasy and sick all over.

"Sure you will, Diamond." My body trembled at the word. Never again did I want to be called that. I had taken something pure and beautiful and turned it into something defiled and ugly. I never wanted to be that woman again. "You can't resist..." His voice changed then, an unknown timbre I'd never heard him speak in rolled through the line. "Don't you want to know... don't you have questions?"

I did. I had so many. And he taunted me with answers as I was a bunny and he was the carrot, dangling them barely out of my reach. I knew what he was asking. The answer to the question I had repeatedly asked him—begged him for. *Why did you do this to me?*

"Yes." The word flew through the phone before I could take it back and feign indifference.

"You'll come to me," he said, his voice full of threatening undertones that I knew too well. "And by the time the night is done, you'll be coming for me."

I swayed on my feet as I stared at my ashen appearance in the mirror. With every word he spoke, more of the confident and strong woman I'd try to be in the last few weeks disappeared in front of my eyes.

I knew his threats. I knew his abilities to make me do the things he threatened even when I despised him.

But despite the fears that threatened to overtake me, I wanted it done.

I wanted to be free. And for the first time in five years, freedom was within my grasp.

"Tell me where." My eyes widened in the mirror—my reflection surprised at herself and the steadiness in which I spoke.

Cain chuckled through the line. Unaffected or unaware of the fire that burned within me to extinguish him, he spoke the place, telling me to get there as soon as I could, that he'd be waiting for me. The only thing I had to figure out how was how to get out of the house without Finn following.

26

Faith

Turned out using the excuse that you needed tampons and running out the front door like a crazy woman was the perfect deterrent to assuage Finn's concerns about me running into town alone.

The shaking rumble of Daemon's old truck as I attempted and failed to dodge potholes in the back country roads I knew like the back of my hand jumbled my already frazzled nerves.

But nothing... nothing prepared me for the moment I pulled into the driveway of my house. It came at me in slow motion as I hesitantly pulled the truck into the driveway and headed toward the house. I stared at my childhood home. It was the same home I'd lived in every day of my life, but for the first time, I really looked at it. The roof over the cement front porch hung haphazardly in one corner, as if one more giant snow storm we were likely to receive in the winter would force it to the ground. The cement stairs crumbled and the paint was chipped all over the place. I couldn't remember the last time someone had done work in the yard or trimmed the bushes that lined the front of the porch and the side of the house.

A sad oak tree stood tall but wilted in the front yard. Even the tree looked like it'd given up on life. I stared at my house, my yard, the place I had lived my entire life, and wondered if apathy and self-loathing sucked the life out of everything that tried to grow and live once you stepped foot on the property.

Nothing looked alive. Nothing looked like anything I wanted any part of. The gray house loomed in front of me; the large bay window at the front of the house had the curtains pulled closed and prevented me from an inkling of what I should expect when I stepped inside.

But still, I moved. Quietly I closed the door to Daemon's truck, although Cain knew I had already arrived. No one could miss the deep rumbling of the run down truck. My hesitant steps trudged across the front sidewalk and up the cracking cement stairs until I stood before the front door.

A gentle breeze blew through the air, cooling my sweaty skin while at the same time sending shivers down my spine. Darkness and everything nasty and evil awaited me on the other side of the door. No matter how many slow breaths I took, no matter how many times my trembling fingers reach for the front door, nothing could make me take the final steps.

Expecting me, Cain opened the door before I could knock. A metal frame and a screen full of holes separated us.

My stomach churned as I took in his probing eyes and squinting, hard smile. Nothing about Cain and the way he looked with his beady eyes and nasty graying beard had ever radiated anything except pure evil.

My insides twisted as I nodded once. My hands itched to feel the cool metal from Liv's gun that I lifted from her dresser before I had taken off. She had only given me one simple glance when I told her I was headed toward town while she continued to help Melissa fill out college paperwork.

Now I wished I'd taken one quick moment and scribbled a note to her. Something that told her if I didn't come back that I'd always loved and admired her.

"You going to come in?"

My eyes snapped to Cain's before I quickly looked around him and inside my living room.

As I entered my own house, Cain caged me in the doorway so I had to shift to move passed him. I twisted so I could move by, my breath catching in my throat as my breasts rubbed lightly against his leather vest. A slow burn erupted in my throat. I pushed down the vile taste to hide my disgusted reaction from him.

"What do you want?" I asked him, remembering to keep my back out of his view. I knew the gun was hidden in the loosely fitted Nordic Lords t-shirt I'd thrown on, but Cain wasn't stupid.

His pale hazel eyes slid down my body as smoothly as a snake glided across the grass. His lips curved as he took in the skulled Viking holding an axe, the Nordic Lords logo, on the left shoulder of my shirt.

"I've missed you."

I swallowed the thick taste of disgust in my throat, breathed deep in order to slow my pulse, and did everything I could to keep my hands at my sides. I would end him, and I would never allow Cain to ever see again any emotion from me.

"Why are we here?" I asked, my eyes trained over his right shoulder at the door to outside. My voice, surprisingly, carried a tinge of impatience, whereas the inside of my stomach was rolling with my earlier eaten popcorn. A quick glance backward ensured no one was behind me as I widened the space between us.

He huffed at my question as his eyes flickered to the empty living room. "You haven't been to see your mom or checked in to see how she's doing." The knowledge that he'd either been following me or had me followed sent a chill down my spine that I fought to hide. Instead, I arched a brow in silent response as he shrugged. "I suppose it doesn't matter. She never was much of a mother to you."

As he talked, he walked into the living room, glancing at the fireplace mantel that held one family photo. The only family photo we'd ever had taken. I was eight. My long, black hair was braided into two perfect French braids that hung down to my waist. Even in that photo, my mother's eyes were depressed and dark. Cain crossed his arms against his massive chest and took in the photo before he faced me.

His head nodded toward the photo while his eyes stayed fixed on me. A slight smirk graced his lips. "Do you know why that is?"

Every word he spoke sent a chilled response to my chest until my entire body felt as if I'd been dipped in an ice bath. My knees trembled from the simple weight of holding my body in a standing position. It took every ounce of strength I didn't know I possessed to cross my arms and mirror his response, instead of sinking to the floor and begging him to answer my questions.

Why me?

Why her?

Why does she hate me?

"Come sit," he said, his smile wide as he waved a hand out toward the couch. "I have a story for you."

I didn't want to hear his story. I also didn't want to sit on the couch where he could too easily reach me from the across the room.

I needed space and the buffer of furniture for not only my physical safety, but also my emotional stability.

"I'll stay here," I said, and then took two small steps toward the back of the couch as a show that I was willing to listen.

I didn't want to hear it, but I still had to know it.

Cain licked his lips before rolling them between his teeth. As he faced me, his arms fell to his sides before he took a relaxed seat in one of my mother's wingback armed chairs. His languish movements expressed a calmness to him, while every nerve in my body was firing on high-alert. The air around me seemed to buzz in anticipation.

Of his answers. And his death. Because I wasn't leaving until I had both.

"Did you know your father and I were friends once?"

I blinked once and then leaned forward, my hands gripping the back of the couch and in shock of this news. It was the only reaction I would give the monster in front of me.

Cain's smile grew wider, showing a full mouth of yellowing teeth from too many years of nicotine and probably infrequent toothbrush purchases. "I suppose you didn't know that we grew up together then, did you?"

My nose twitched. A hundred questions screamed inside my brain. Still, I stayed quiet, wondering the purpose of this.

Cain stood again, pacing a few steps back and forth before he scrubbed the back of his neck with the palm of his hand. "Your mom…" he started and stopped, frozen, while he stared at the curtains that covered the front window of our house. There was nothing to look at, yet he was seeing something. My eyes darted in the direction of his gaze and I frowned.

"She was beautiful. So full of life. Gorgeous as fuck and had a laugh that made all the boys in our high school want to get their hands on her."

My pulse thrummed in my ears the more he talked and more questions filtered into my brain. I pressed my lips together forcefully to prevent them from slipping out while I tried as hard as possible to remain unaffected by this confession that meant so little, but knew would explain so much.

Time. I needed more time.

"And?" I asked, an irritated tone to my voice.

Cain turned on his heels, his arms crossed over his slightly protruding gut, and narrowed his eyes on me. "You look so much like her, you know."

Oh, God. Sick slimy filth crawled in my veins and all over my body. My lips twisted in disgust.

"Except for your eyes," he continued, as if he didn't notice I was ready to vomit all over my own furniture. "Your eyes are your dad's."

As he spoke of my dad, his words turned dark—the familiar evil expression in his eyes appeared as he stared directly into my light blue eyes that one hundred percent mirrored my father's.

"What's your point, Cain?"

His nose twitched before he reclaimed his seat in the chair like a king on his throne. "I dated your mom. I took her out, did everything I could to get her to want me as much as she wanted him."

A perverse sense of satisfaction began to erase the filth. I arched a brow. "And she chose him over you? That's what this is about?"

"He stole her from me!" He shouted the words with vehemence as he launched himself out of the chair, directly at me. Had I not been behind the couch, he would have been on me in seconds.

As it was, I stumbled backward until my back pressed against the knobby pine wall behind me. My hands flew to my chest as I attempted to calm my racing heart.

Cain stared at me, panting heavily, his hands fisted at his sides and a cruel scowl on his face. He stabbed himself in the chest with his index finger. "She was mine. She was always going to be mine, and then one night your father got her drunk and took advantage of her. And then…" His eyes narrowed as they raked my body again. Despite the eighty degree humid weather, I wished I would have worn a snowmobile suit as Cain's eyes dragged down my exposed legs. "You came along. And your father took her from her home, took her from her family, and brought her to this hell-hole where she never wanted to be." He leaned forward and leered. "And with people she never wanted to be with."

"So all of this," I said, my voice shaking and trembling. My heart raced and pounded against my rib cage; I wouldn't have been surprised if it had made a sudden appearance in the palm of my hand. "Is to get even… with a dead man?"

"It was to give your mom what she wanted. A life without you and him." His tongue darted out and licked his lips.

"You're sick," I gasped. I struggled. I struggled to breathe and to speak and to have a rational thought in my head. "You fucked me?

You raped me and whipped me because you blamed *me* for my mom leaving you?"

"I wanted to destroy you." His eyes flashed and he moved to walk around the couch. "I wanted to kill every part of you."

I shook my head, my long hair getting tangled against the uneven sanded finish of the wooden wall at my back. "That makes no sense."

He shrugged. "I got your mom."

"You drugged her and beat her. You did everything you could to keep her high out of her mind until her body started dying long before her mind would."

"You had the Nordic Lords gut my brother!" he bellowed, his face contorted in rage as he leaned forward, panting for breath.

All of my breath left me in one huge whoosh of expulsion. "I didn't know." I blinked, once, twice, and then three times, while I fought my quivering limbs to settle.

Cain smiled. It was twisted and sick and didn't look right. "I gave her what she wanted. A life without you, and it kept her close to me. And now she knows the consequences for trying to leave me."

I gasped. The realization of where we were hitting me. The significance of it. "Where is she?" I asked, too afraid to tear my eyes off of his slowly approaching, menacing frame.

His eyes darted to the stairway behind me. I refused to follow it. "Upstairs. And soon, we'll be together again. Just the two of us."

He was sick. Vile and disgusting and fucking warped in his head.

"And me?" I asked as I slowly moved my hands to my hips defensively. I turned my back from the wall and toward the kitchen.

"You'll be dead."

I expected it. I still flinched from the coldness of his words and ambivalent shrug. "Why keep me alive at all then?" I asked, putting more space between us as I took a timid step back toward the kitchen. I had no idea if anyone was there—I only hoped we were alone.

He perused my body again. "Because you were worth money." As his eyes reached mine, he tilted his head. "Did you think I'd ever let you live?"

"I figured you would have killed me a long time ago."

"I thought it'd be more fun to kill your spirit first."

My tongue rolled in my teeth before my hand reached to my back. My fingers easily slid over the handle as I gripped the gun in the back of my waistband. I had one shot at killing him. With every ounce of courage I could muster up, I stared him down and aimed the gun directly at him. "Looks like that idea failed."

The gun trembled in my sweaty grip. My lips pulled into a grin that had to be unnatural and matched Cain's in evilness. I didn't care.

I cared about blowing his head off so the sick fuck was dead and could never again touch me, violate me, or any other woman—my loser of a mother included.

Suddenly, Cain's eyes darted behind my shoulder right as a thick, warm arm slid around my chest. Before I knew what happened, I was braced tightly against a chest of hot, steeled warmth and a thick, rumbling voice was at my ear.

"Put the gun down."

I melted into him as my grip on the gun tightened.

27

Ryker

Adrenaline coursed in my veins as soon as I was able to sneak quietly through the back door to Faith's old house. As soon as I heard their voices coming from just beyond the kitchen, I felt like I was able to breathe again for the first time in hours.

She was alive.

As my hand wrapped around her chest and I pulled her against me, I couldn't decide if I wanted to throttle her for scaring the shit out of me or fuck her because I was so fucking thankful I wasn't finding her covered in blood again.

My breath blew into her ear as I repeated the earlier command. "Put the gun down, Faith."

She shook her head, her black hair brushing against me as she adamantly refused. "He... he ruined me."

I kept my eyes on Cain. For the first time since I'd known him, he looked unsure of himself. His feet were slowly moving backward, his hands raised, and his wide eyes stayed focused on the gun.

Faith looked at Cain, the barrel of the gun trembling in her grip. "You beat me," she said. "You loaded my mom with drugs so you could keep her and you let men use my body so you could have your way with me *and* her?"

My jaw tightened against her shoulder as I took in her words. I knew the strength it took for her to finally confront Cain, but blood on Faith's hands was the last thing she needed.

"Give me the gun, Faith," I whispered into her ear. My grip on her chest loosened as my hands gently brushed against her skin.

Her shoulders tightened and she flinched away from me.

Six more large steps and Cain would be out that door. At least that's what he thought. He didn't know six men were outside, guns cocked, loaded, and waiting for him.

Any of the brothers taking him out would be better than Faith doing it.

"Let him go," I told her quietly. "Men are outside and they'll take care of him."

She shook her head.

"No," she clipped. I wanted to pull her chin to face me and stare directly into her eyes. The coolness of the words told me that the fucking light that had been in her eyes had disappeared again. "He fucked me. He beat me."

She repeated the words, increasing in volume and speed, until her hand was shaking so hard she could barely get the words out, much less hold the gun.

"Faith," I warned her. I pulled back, intent on reaching for her gun, when she yanked it from me.

Cain took that small moment, that small mistake, to turn and run.

"No!" Faith's shout was barely heard over the discharge of the gun.

Cain ducked and his hands flew over his head as he dropped to his knees.

Footsteps pounded outside right before two doors flung open and Faith's house was overrun with men.

"You fucking shot me!" Cain shouted, his hand wrapped around the back of his knee. His fingers were coated in blood as it poured out of him.

I turned to Faith, who still stared directly at Cain. Smoke bellowed gently out of the barrel of the gun, a complete contradiction to Faith's tight expression and trembling fingers. But still, she held the gun on Cain.

She didn't appear to see anyone, no recognition on her face that she knew where she was or knew anyone else in the room.

Slowly, so I didn't startle her, I reached out with one finger and brushed a lock of her hair off her cheek and pressed it behind her ear. She flinched slightly.

"Faith," I whispered. She flinched again, but I knew she heard me, so I took a small step toward her, coming close enough where I could reach out and smoothly slide the gun from her hands. "Let the men handle the rest."

She didn't move for several breaths. My eyes flashed to Daemon and Jaden as they stood inside the front door, their guns on Cain, and Daemon's eyes narrowed on mine in concern.

"I'm going to take the gun," I told Faith. She nodded once, but didn't move. I slid my hand down her arm, comforting her, and alerting her to my presence and movements. As soon as I covered her hand with both of mine, her fingers loosened on the trigger. Slowly, each of her fingers uncurled from the handle of the gun until it fell into my hands.

I flicked the safety on and stashed it in the back of my jeans.

"You okay?" I asked her as I shifted so I was standing in front of her. Cain writhed on the ground, moaning about his knee, and I wanted to block her view. When I was in front of her, both of my hands went to her shoulders. She looked at me and through me simultaneously. The sparkle in her eyes was there, but diminished.

"Hey," I said, jostling her softly. She blinked at me, and finally, her eyes cleared and reality returned. "Let the men handle this, okay?"

She licked her cracked lips. Her shoulders raised and fell under my hands as she took several deep breaths. I stood in front of her, squeezing her shoulders and offering her the most comforting look I could.

By the way peace and color returned to Faith's cheeks and eyes, it was enough.

"My mom is upstairs. He took her out of the hospital somehow."

"We'll take care of her."

Faith shook her head, looked around the room, and took in the six men who were there to protect her. "No... I don't—" she swallowed, her eyebrows pulled in. I let her have the time to process everything that had happened while Cain groaned on the floor. "I don't care what happens to her... kill her, too. Send her to rehab." She shrugged under my grip, and I squeezed her tighter. She couldn't mean that. The dead serious look she flashed me as I opened my mouth to tell her that silenced me before I spoke. "Kill her or send her away. I don't care."

I nodded. Like hell Faith wanted her mom dead, but I wasn't going to argue. "Okay. Let's get you home, okay?"

I wanted to kick my own ass as soon as Faith's eyes darted around the living room, of the very home she'd grown up in. But it was no longer her home, and I watched her eyes soften as she realized the same thing. "Let's go, then."

She spun around and headed out of the hallway, out the kitchen, and through the back door before I was quick enough to follow her. I took in the room, the men, and the asshole on the floor who still moaned like a pussy.

"You heard her," I said and raised one eyebrow at Daemon.

"We got this." He tilted his head toward the outside of the house. "Go see to Faith."

"You hear about her mom?"

Daemon nodded. "We'll figure it out. Go." He waved his gun toward the back door, and I left with a thanks and a few shoulder claps on Jaden and Tripp's shoulders as I headed out.

I caught Faith standing in her front yard near Daemon's truck with her head tilted up as she stared at the night sky. Dusk had settled as Daemon and I had hauled tail to get to her house as soon as Xbox tracked her cell phone. Now, the night was pitch black except for the stars that filled the sky.

"How'd you know I was here?" Faith asked, her voice hollowed and gravelly.

I stopped feet from her, not knowing if my presence would be unwelcome and hating the idea she wouldn't want me around her. "Xbox tracked you when Liv called Daemon to tell him you and her were gun were gone."

"You got here quick," she said. She dropped her head from the sky to her feet. Her hands wiped against the tight shorts she wore that barely covered her ass.

"We were already heading back and weren't that far away."

I rocked on my heels, uncertain as to what to do or what to say. Faith twisted her neck and looked at me over her shoulder. One side of her lips quirked. "Any reason you're that far away?"

It was the only thing I needed to hear. I was in front of her, my arms around her, and my hand holding onto the back of her neck. I pulled her to my chest before I could force out a breath.

"I shot him," she whispered against my shirt.

"I know." My eyes closed and my chest heaved slowly, afraid of how this would affect her. "Want to talk about what happened?"

Her forehead brushed back and forth against my chest. She sniffed and blew out a breath against my shirt that shot a hot, searing heat straight to my chest and down to my dick. It wasn't the time, but my body couldn't contain its innate reactions to Faith being in my arms again.

Safe.

Her hands came up to my hips and she pushed away from me. It was slow and firm and I hesitated to let her go. I wanted to fucking haul her in my arms and to a bed where I could take my time and make sure she really was okay.

She had shot someone. That shit messed with your head.

But at her firm insistence, I let her go. My hands fell to my sides as she took a step back, but kept her hands on my hips.

Slowly, she brought her eyes to mine. Her eyes darted back and forth between mine while I waited. For what, I didn't quite know. "It felt good."

My eyebrows pulled in. I doubted her words, yet her calm expression and lack of freaking out said she spoke the truth. I gave her the benefit of the doubt until I could see otherwise.

I knew it would feel good had I been the one to shoot Cain.

She looked back over her shoulder toward the house behind her. "What are they going to do to him?"

"Kill him."

She nodded once before looking back at me. "Can we get out of here before that happens?"

I reached out and tugged on the back of her neck with my palm. She tripped and face planted into my chest once again and there was no way in fuck I was letting her go this time.

She handed me the keys to Daemon's truck before I helped her inside.

As I backed out of the driveway, Faith's eyes stayed trained on the front door of her house. Her eyebrows pulled in and a crease ran down between them.

"Hey," I said, my hand covering her warm and toned thigh. "You okay?"

"Yeah." She paused and slowly tucked a small piece of hair behind her ear. "You told me to go home, but I don't have one."

I squeezed her thigh tighter and stopped the truck. "Look at me."

She turned to me with such a lost expression, I wanted to go back inside and kick Cain's ass and her mom's because I knew it would make me feel better. Instead, I licked my lips, dying to put them on her, but for some reason, I needed the reassurance that whatever the fuck had happened to her with Cain hadn't completely fucked her up.

"We'll make one together."

Her lips twitched. When her hand covered mine and squeezed tightly, I assumed it was the right thing to say.

28

Faith

I shot a man.

I shot a man who defiled me for years all for some depraved, perverted reason to use me as a way to seek his revenge on a dead man.

As much as I tried, no matter how hard I squeezed my eyes to erase the images and words Cain had spoken earlier, they wouldn't stop flipping through my mind in slow motion. As if constantly reconsidering what he said would have it make sense.

It didn't.

And yet, even though I knew a sliver of remorse should have whispered into my conscience that what I had done was wrong—reprehensible—nothing could stop me from finding solace in the moment. I found peace in the cab of the rusted out SuperCab truck with Ryker's hand on my thigh, humming to the rock tune filtering through the speakers.

The truck's headlights were the only thing that illuminated the driveway as we pulled in.

I sucked in a breath, the peacefulness of the moment before was gone and replaced with a tingling in my fingers and arms.

"Why are we here?"

He eyed me warily as he pushed the shift into park. "You wanted to go home."

I stared at the house in front of me. It had practically been my second home growing up. Liv's home. The home I knew she never wanted to return to, and the same home she had given Ryker the keys to only days before.

For us.

He jumped out of the truck. I frowned at the house, but at the same time, my hand opened the door and I slid to the cracked pavement.

When I reached him at the front of the truck, my limbs and arms still tingling with uncertainty and nerves, I dragged my eyes to Ryker's.

"We can't just go inside."

With his face angled down, I could barely see him in the darkness, but I didn't miss the way his eyes crinkled. "It's ours. Why not?"

"Because," I said, my eyes flickering between him and the front door. "It's weird."

Ryker shrugged and pulled me up the sidewalk and to the door. The keys jingled in his hand while he found the right one. My breath hitched as he opened the door and smiled down at me.

"Should I carry you over the threshold?" A mischievous grin tilted his lips as he wiggled his eyebrows.

I shoved his shoulder with the palm of my hand and pushed him out of the way. "Don't be stupid."

My breath caught in my throat as I entered the dark room. I only had to run my hand down the wall to my right and the entire room was completely illuminated in brightness. And yet, it seemed so empty at the same time.

Everything from Liv's childhood had been replaced. She had told me this when I asked her for certain if she wanted to give me the keys to her house, but she had simply said everything from her life there was gone anyway.

She wasn't wrong.

"This is like, the ultimate man home."

I nodded at Ryker's slow voice that rumbled behind me.

My eyes took in everything as my body began to feel drained from the day's events. "I know," I said, my mouth opened wide and a large yawn escaped. I didn't bother trying to hide it. "It's so weird."

"We'll make it ours," he said and began directing me up the flight of stairs. The warmth of his hand on my lower back singed through my T-shirt and directly into my skin. I let him push me along, my feet feeling heaving and slower with every step as I trudged up the staircase and down the hall.

I stopped when he led me directly into the master bedroom. All over the house, masculinity echoed in every corner and every wall and every furnishing. Dark browns and blacks and reds coupled with beer signs and motorcycle logos and artwork had lined the walls.

But this room… it wasn't what I expected.

"I had Jules do this." His breath in my ear elicited pleasured bumps along my hairline and the nape of my neck. The warm hand on my back grew hotter as he pushed me begrudgingly through the door. "I didn't think you'd want to sleep in Bull's old bed."

He had that right. But still, this didn't explain the sheer silver colored drapes over a four-poster King Size bed. It didn't explain the pale, greyish blue pillows and decadent bedcovers. And it certainly didn't explain the majestic mahogany furniture that sat on both sides of the bed and one large dresser on the wall.

"Do you like it?"

My jaw dropped. I was unable to speak. He had rendered me speechless with his thoughtfulness, but also with his assumption that I would live there with him.

I took a step away from him and instantly felt the loss of heat on my body. I shivered and crossed my arms as I turned to him, my head tilted to the side. "Isn't this too soon? I mean, it's too soon. It's only been a week since we really started speaking again and so much has happened."

The more I rambled, the wider Ryker's smile grew.

"It's too soon?" he asked as he took a step toward me. I stepped back and nodded. My fingers dug into the skin on my elbows because all I truly wanted to do was reach out, tug on his short black hair, and draw his lips to mine.

But this was crazy.

"You got Jules to do this?" I asked, ignoring his question as I took in the room. It was beautiful. Masculine and elegant at the same time. Completely romantic in all of it.

I wandered to the bed, reached out, and ran my hand down the shimmery gray stripe in one of the half dozen pillows propped on the bed. Silk. It had to have cost a fortune.

"Why would you do this?" I looked at Ryker over my shoulder. He padded toward me and sat on the edge of the bed.

His hand snaked around my waist and pulled me to him until I was standing nestled between his thighs. The rough denim abraded the soft skin on my exposed thighs as he shifted me where he wanted me.

A line appeared between his eyes. "You're afraid of this. Why?"

I looked back at the pillows. Elegant and soft. So… not me. "I don't know. It's fast."

My lip twitched, and I bit down on it. A thousand jumbled thoughts tumbled through my mind but none made enough sense to voice out loud. I couldn't tell what they all were, just that nothing this good had ever happened to me before.

It had always been Ryker. But as he sat before me, his hands loosely holding my hips, worry and fear appeared in his furrowed brow and tightened jaw.

"It's not that it's not beautiful," I told him. Because it was. I reached out with a finger and dragged it down his cheek and jaw before I stopped at his chin. Shrugging one shoulder, I let my hand fall to my side.

"Then what?"

"Everything's happening so fast," I admitted. His reappearance in my life less than two months ago, being taken, being beaten, held by a mob family, my mom, Cain… my life was certainly not dull.

Ryker gripped my hand in his and brought it to his lips. He pressed his lips gently against my knuckles, my palm, and then my inner wrists. He tightened his grip as I squirmed beneath his piercing, lustful gaze and the tickling warmth of his breath on my sensitive skin.

"If I could go back five years and never leave, I would."

I nodded, a slow burn beginning in my throat. "I know."

"I thought we'd agreed we've wasted enough time apart."

"We did."

He tugged me forward, one hand wrapped around my waist, and we fell back onto the bed, Ryker beneath me, and we shifted so we were lying side by side.

"So what's the problem, then?" His hand ran through my hair and down the side of my body. His eyes followed his hand as he trailed my body over my clothes slowly as if he wanted to memorize every dip and curve.

My hand ran through his own silky hair as I bit my bottom lip. "I'm afraid it won't last," I finally admitted.

He rolled forward, capturing me beneath him and pulling me to him with an arm around my waist. I was pinned to the bed and I had been correct. The coverings were decadent and soft and incredibly comfortable. I wanted to sink into the bed with Ryker on top of me and never come out.

"I'll have to do everything I can then, I suppose," he began with his nose almost touching mine. His breath ghosted across my skin as his eyes stayed trained on mine. He leaned forward until our lips were touching, brushing against mine as he spoke. "To prove that you have nothing to be afraid of anymore."

With my clothes from the day before thrown on, I padded my feet down the hallway and the stairs to the kitchen. I knew this house like it was the back of my hand, yet I still expected at some point for Cherry to pop around the corner with a warm smile on her or Liv's dad, Bull, to be sitting in the recliner with a beer in his hand and the remote in his lap regardless of the time of day.

None of that happened though as I wandered through the house and took in the completely empty feel of the place. The house Bull had turned from a family home into a rotted out bachelor pad.

My heart ached for Liv and what she must have felt as she walked through these doors for the first time in five years only to find everything important to her, completely gone.

"Coffee?"

Ryker's deep and husky morning voice brought my mind out of my wandering and back to the present.

"Sure, thanks." I watched as he poured a cup of coffee. His back was to me and he was only wearing the jeans he'd worn the day before. The muscles in his back rippled with every small movement he made as he reached for a mug in the cabinet. When he turned, I looked away, somehow embarrassed I'd been checking him out in Bull and Cherry's kitchen.

"Thanks." I took a quick sip and looked around the kitchen. When Cherry was alive and Liv lived here, it was a bright lime green. A bright color completely at odds with the dark life she lived, but Cherry had always insisted on finding the happiness everywhere she looked. Now it was a dreary and drab gray color. "This is weird. Being here."

With one fluid movement, he had an arm around my waist and pulled me into his lap at the kitchen table. Amazingly, not a single drop of coffee spilled from either of our mugs. He reached for my mug and set it on the table before he cupped my cheek in his hand.

"I thought we'd go do some shopping today. Get some things for the house and new furniture—whatever you want."

I pulled my coffee to my lips and sipped. The fragrant aroma of caramel flavored coffee stung my nose. My favorite kind. I wondered for a brief moment if he knew that or if Jules or Liv played a role in procuring coffee for our new place.

His hand ran down my hair to my lower back and he hugged me tighter to him. "Are we going to talk about what happened yesterday?"

"There's nothing to talk about." I shook my head and ignored the questioning gaze I saw in his eyes. Why wasn't I freaking out? Why wasn't I upset? I assumed part of it was because I was still in shock over everything I'd learned and done. The other part simply didn't care enough about either Cain or my mom to expend any further effort in thinking about them. They were gone, and I didn't care where they went.

I opened my mouth to explain just that right as a blaring ring blasted from the pocket of his jeans.

His hands left mine immediately as he cursed. "I have to take this."

In another second, I was unceremoniously plopped into an empty chair. Ryker turned his back to me and answered the phone.

"Meg?" he asked, his voice tight. I watched as he ran a hand through his hair before his shoulders tensed. "Are you okay?"

I tensed along with Ryker. Not from the concern he apparently had, but because of the way he stood, so tall and strong, and how his voice softened instantly as he exhaled. The way that, as he continued to talk to her, his voice lightened with quiet laughter, and he never once turned to me.

My focus went to my coffee mug as if it was the most important thing in the world. I wrapped my hands around the warmed ceramic, my thumbs rubbing up and down mindlessly as I tried to contain the jealous, dark tendrils that increased inside of me with each easy laugh that rolled from Ryker's lips.

He kept his back to me, his shoulder braced on the doorframe of the kitchen that faced the four-season screened porch at the back of the house.

From his profile, I could see small laugh lines crinkle at the edges of his eyes. His lips were wide in an easy smile as he threw his head back and laughed at whatever Meg said to him.

His voice dropped further. He calmed and I watched as his entire body melted into the wood.

"Hey buddy," his soft, deep voice rumbled into the phone. "I miss you, too."

Something filled the air in the room as Ryker spoke. An intimacy or a pure love that was so vastly different than anything I had ever felt from him—or anyone in my entire life—I suddenly felt as if I was a voyeur, peeking in on someone's most private moments.

It was the way Ryker tilted his head when he spoke, the way his brow pulled in as he listened to the boy I knew was Brayden as if he was the most important person in his entire life.

And I couldn't help but feel envious of a boy I had never met and probably never would. I tilted back the ceramic mug, draining the hot liquid in a large swallow. The jealous tendrils in my veins spread until my body had been warmed from the coffee and the heat that spread through my veins.

I was jealous of a little boy.

I hated it, but it was the truth. Ryker had something with that woman and her son that I had never had. I had never had the chance to have it with him. He had a family.

Not by blood and not by marriage, but a family nonetheless.

My nose stung as I listened to Ryker soothe the clearly upset boy on the line. His calming tones were unequally matched with the wrinkles lining his forehead as he dipped his head, exhaled a breath, and shoved his hand through his hair.

"He's not handling this well," he snapped in a harsh tone. I watched as he swore and began pacing the four-season porch.

The room chilled to just below freezing while Ryker continued to argue with Meg. And then my world tilted on its axis as he confidently and assuredly said, "I'll come back."

My head dropped into my lap, and I released my harsh grip on the cold coffee mug. With one last look back at Ryker as he continued pacing the room—never once looking in my direction—I stared at the only man I'd ever loved and realized with finality that I wasn't the only priority in his life.

It shouldn't have stung as forcefully as it did, but my hand flew to my chest, pressing against the sharp-shooting pain lancing through me as if I had been shot.

I must have gasped, or done something, because from across the room, Ryker's eyes flew to mine. His jaw clenched and he spoke through his teeth as he saw the twisted expression on my face.

It hurt. It made no sense.

Yet, I wanted him to be mine. *All mine.* And he wasn't. Not by a long shot.

Slowly, he walked toward me, his voice soft and quiet on the phone. A deep line engraved between his eyebrows as his lips turned into a small smile. "Of course she's coming with me. I can't wait for you to meet her."

He reached me, and before I could pull away, Ryker's hand went to my cheek. He tilted my head back and bent down, placing a gentle kiss on the tip of my nose.

It changed me. The way his eyes furrowed with concern, danced between both of my eyes, and then down to my hand still on my chest. He dropped his hand from my cheek and held his hand over mine. The pain dulled to a slow throb when Ryker, still listening to Meg on the phone, mouthed, "All yours."

My jaw dropped as if suddenly unhinged as my mind whirled. How he knew me so well to read my mind at everything I was thinking or feeling without saying a word… stunned didn't cover the sudden change in emotion covering me.

While he quietly said his good-byes to Meg, his hand wrapped around my fingers and he pulled me to my feet until my chest was pressed against his.

"Tell Brayden we'll see him as soon as we can get there. But have him FaceTime me later." His eyes stayed on mine, his lips moved gently across my temple, as he spoke before he clicked the phone shut and slid it into the back of his jean's pocket.

"You're worried." He stated the words so simply as his hand snaked to the back of my neck and his fingers dug into my scalp.

I pulled my bottom lip in between my teeth.

"You know, when you know you're responsible for someone's death, it changes you." His eyes bore deeply into my own it felt as if he was connecting to my soul. His fingers dug into my hair. "Meg's husband died because of my mistake on the rig one night."

"And?"

He shook his head as if trying to dislodge the painful memory before he blinked and smiled down on me. "I promised I'd take care of them and I am."

"They're your family."

"They might be," he said, his lips lowering to my ear. His breath caressed my skin making it difficult to concentrate as he continued talking. "But you're more important. Always will be. But it wouldn't be right for me to leave them and never check on them again—never visit them again."

"So you're leaving."

"No," he said, as he pressed a kissed in that soft space below my ear. He laughed softly as I trembled in his comforting grip. "Is that what you thought?"

"You're so… you seem so happy with them. More relaxed than you are with anyone else." I swallowed the lump in my throat, forcing myself to talk around it. "Even with me."

"And you thought I was leaving you?"

Everyone leaves. I couldn't put a voice to the words though, too afraid he would pull away and that Ryker would see how big of a mess I still was.

"Jesus, Faith. I couldn't leave you. For five years I tried to forget you—every day I had to fight to get you out of my mind. And now that I have you in my arms again, you think I'd do that to you?"

A shrug was the only movement I could muster before the tears spilled over. Stupid tears. Ryker made me cry more in the last few months than I'd cried in years.

"You're a stubborn woman. You know that, right?"

Through my tears, I looked up to a smile on his lips. An easy smile as he laughed at my fears, but not at me. "I've been told," I choked out right before his lips planted firmly to mine.

I breathed him in, the scent of his body wash and coffee, as his tongue pressed into my mouth and tangled with mine in a languid, fluid movement. Moaning into his mouth, I gasped for breath as my hands flew to his hips, pulling him and his hardness to me.

I wanted to ask for more—beg and plead for more—until he was so deep inside me he could erase my fears and my doubts. But when I tried, he pulled away, leaving me panting and gasping for breath.

He took my hand with a smile and tugged me down the hall. "Come on."

My head spun back around and looked at where we had just kissed, confused and wondering where we were going. "Where?"

"I need Club ink. Maybe that'll help prove I'm not going anywhere."

29

Ryker

Four hours of lying in a tattoo chair in Gunner's GetInked2 tattoo shop and my back was killing me. Every buzz of the sharp needle pressed into my skin and vibrated down my spine. It stung like a bitch.

The doorbell above his front door chimed, but I barely heard it over the needle and the sudden laughter that entered the waiting area. From the mirror next to me, I saw Faith, Jules, and Olivia walking in, but all I cared about was Faith.

Her black hair whipped around her face as she threw her head back and laughed at whatever Jules said. Her hands were bogged down with large paper bags, which showed me their shopping trip had been successful.

A sharp sensation stung my chest as I watched her, my eyes couldn't have moved if I'd tried. Faith was gorgeous. She was beautiful. More distant than when were younger, but more vulnerable at the same time. I didn't blame her.

But watching her walk into Gunner's tattoo shop, a smile on her face with armfuls of shopping bags of things she'd bought for our home… my chest swelled with an indescribable feeling of pride.

Or love.

I laughed to myself.

Who the hell was I kidding? It was definitely love.

"You need to take a break?" Gunner asked, pulling the needle away from my shoulder. I wouldn't be able to sleep on my back for a week after this, which was fine because I had plans to spend a lot of time with Faith under me.

"How much more do you have to do?" At the sound of my voice, Faith stopped talking to Jules and her eyes met mine through the reflection in the mirror. They crinkled and she lifted one hand in a wave hello.

"Another hour. The outline's done, but we still need to do more shading. I can finish the rest later." He wiped away the stain of the ink and the blood from my shoulder blade.

"Finish what you can today." I turned my head so I could greet Faith. "Get over here and hold my hand."

Olivia laughed in the entryway. "I can do it for you, Ryker. I think I owe you the favor."

No shit she did. My fingers stung at the thought of how tightly Liv had gripped my fingers weeks ago when she got her own tattoo.

"I barely survived the last time you held my hand, but thanks."

She threw her head back and laughed. Faith smiled and pulled up a stool next to me. "You okay?"

"I'm good."

Gunner laughed as he turned the ink gun back on. "Pussy's had to take a break every twenty minutes."

Asshole. I took one break. "I had to piss."

"That's what they all say," he muttered, but I was already ignoring the man in favor of the beauty sitting in front of me.

She reached out and brushed a piece of my hair off my forehead before her eyes fell to my back. Gunner had outlined the entire Vikings skull and helmet all over my back. Across my shoulder blades in a Gothic script, he was writing Nordic Lords in all capitalized letters. It would take more than one, maybe more than two sessions, to complete the entire tattoo. I didn't care how long it took.

Patching into the club, inking their name across my body, was only one of the ways I planned to let Faith know I wasn't going anywhere.

She was stuck with me.

She chewed on her bottom lip, her nose crinkled as she watched Gunner run the gun slowly across my back. "You okay?"

"I'm good, babe," I told her and squeezed her hand. Gunner hit the edge of bone on my shoulder blade and I hissed in a breath. "Except for when he hits bone."

"Toughen up," he muttered.

Faith's quiet laugh at our banter took away any pain the tattoo gun could have caused.

"What'd you get at the store?" An hour after we got to Gunner's, I had sent her away with Jules and Olivia so she didn't have to sit and watch me get inked for half the day. Fuck if I knew it would take as long as it did.

But I was anxious... she had bought stuff for our house. *Our home.* Finally, it felt like shit was going right for us. It had certainly been fucked up for far too long. I figured we'd earned it.

Faith glanced around at the piles of bags in the entryway. Jules and Liv were sitting on a leather couch, kicked back and smiling like they had nothing else planned for the day.

"A blender, plates, more glasses... wine... beer..." She shrugged. "I don't know. All sorts of things."

My grin grew with every word she spoke. Her knee bounced quickly as she spoke and she played with a strand of her hair.

"Why are you nervous?"

She pulled her light blue eyes to me. "Liv wants to have a party tonight."

"And?"

She shrugged, uncertain. "I think it's weird... after last night and today. I don't know."

I squeezed her hand and nodded my head so she had to lean close.

"Keep still," Gunner scolded.

"Bite me." When Faith was close enough, I whispered, "Stop waiting for the other shoe to drop. We're good. Life is good. Take a damn day and enjoy it, won't you?"

Hesitantly, she nodded and then pressed her lips against mine. "I love you."

"You too," I answered seriously. My eyes glued to hers so she would absolutely have no fucking doubt how I felt about her. I knew she still questioned it, questioned everything that had happened, but someday she'd wake up and know I wasn't screwing around on her. And I'd stick around until that happened—and every day after.

"All right, then. I should probably get going. I have a party to plan."

I shook my head. "Stay with me. Let the girls do it."

She looked back at Jules and Liv and then to me. I shook my head again. I watched her war with indecision but answered it for her.

"Hey, Liv," I shouted over the music, the needle, and the incessant girl chatter. "Faith's staying with me 'til we're done here. Can you and Jules take care of everything for the party?"

Liv grinned. Jules stood up and clapped her hands together. "You bet!" they said in unison. They gathered up the bags and took off, mischievous giggles filtering through the air, as they hauled ass out of the tattoo shop with barely a wave and shout good-bye.

Faith sank back into the stool next to me. "Well, I guess that answers that."

"Does it hurt?" Faith asked me. I had grimaced and groaned my way through sliding my T-shirt and leather vest back on after Gunner covered the tattoo with Vaseline and bandages.

"Like a thousand bee stings." I grabbed her hand and pulled her toward the door.

"Yikes." She made a face. One of sympathy, but it was over exaggerated and I couldn't help but laugh at her. I couldn't help but want to pull her to me and ravage her in the middle of the damn street because she was so damn beautiful and cute. Innocent and not at the same time. Light on her feet with a heavy burden on her shoulders. Such a beautiful contradiction, but it was all perfectly Faith.

I wanted it all. I yanked her to me, wrapping a hand around her waist when she stumbled into me. My other hand slide to the back of her neck.

"Kiss me."

She didn't hesitate. Our lips met and I instantly groaned as I tasted her bubble gum mixed with the sweetness that was simply Faith. My tongue licked her bottom lip before I entered her mouth. A growl of pleasure escaped the back of my throat as I swallowed her whimpers of pleasure. My dick instantly hardened. I rolled my hips and pulled her closer to me, letting her feel what she did to me.

"Jesus," I said, pulling back and looking down at her. "I want you. All the fucking time, I want you." My thumb brushed the pink tint to her cheeks. "How is that possible?"

"I don't know, but I'm not going to argue with you." Between her breathy voice that was soft and sexy as hell, and the wicked glint in her eyes, my dick hardened."

I stepped back toward my truck, our bodies still connected as I nuzzled and tickled her neck with my chin. Her laughter vibrated against my chest.

"I think you should take me home and do whatever you want to me."

Fuck, yes. That's what I wanted to hear. I nipped at her neck before I pressed my lips against hers again. "Did you forget Jules and Liv are there decorating?"

"I can be quiet."

I threw my head back and laughed. "For what I have planned for you, there's no fucking way you'll be able to be quiet."

I had no clue what happened to my nervous and hesitant girl, but in an instant, she looked like sex on a stick and confident as hell. The weight pressing down on her shoulders seemed to have disappeared.

"Cocky?" she asked, arching a brow as her hands flipped to her hips.

I leaned in and ran my tongue along her jaw. "Confident."

She shook her head and took a step away, waggling her finger at me. "None of that."

"We can wait 'til we get home, then."

She nodded once, her eyes blinked. "Home."

It whispered across her lips as if she was finally just realizing the truth. What I had given her and what I would always want to give her.

I opened my mouth to repeat the word, right as a masculine and dipshit sounding voice interrupted me.

"Faith Winston?"

30

Faith

I flicked my head back over my shoulder to the man who had called my name.

A gigantic boulder settled in my stomach as I watched the Chief of Police of Jasper Bay saunter toward me and Ryker on the sidewalk.

I squeezed Ryker's hand that was suddenly against my palm and exhaled a deep breath. My limbs trembled as Chief Garrison reached us and held us out his hand.

"Good afternoon, Faith," he said, and then nodded toward Ryker. "Knight. Heard you patched in."

Ryker released the Chief's hand and pulled me closer with his other one, wrapping his arm around my waist and holding me tightly next to him. He nodded once. "I did."

Garrison studied both of us for a moment before he lifted his sunglasses, hooking them to the front of his beige, button down shirt.

"Good luck with that," he finally said to Ryker before setting his full attention on me. "I've been looking for you."

My heart pounded against my ribcage as I waited for him to tell me about Cain. Maybe arrest me for shooting him. My arrest flashed across my eyes as blood drained from my face. Handcuffed and stuffed into the back of a squad car as Ryker was forced to watch and bail me out of jail. Awesome.

"It's about your mom."

My head jerked to his eyes. Ryker's hand tightened against my hip and I felt every single one of his fingertips searing heat directly into my body. I leaned into him for support.

"What about her?" I choked out.

Garrison's hands fell from his slight belly down to his sides. His piercing hazel eyes softened around the edges as he pulled in a deep breath. "She was found just outside of town today."

I inhaled a deep breath only to find I couldn't exhale it. I choked on it, unsure of what to say or do.

"What do you mean?" I finally asked, looking to Ryker for help with something—anything—I didn't know what I needed. Only that I needed him to say something. Do something. But all I saw was a small tick in his jaw as he kept his focus tied to the Chief.

"I'm sorry to be the one to tell you this, Faith." The Chief's voice was softer when he spoke again. He took a small step forward, reaching out to touch me, but Ryker yanked me closer to him. His eyes flickered to Ryker's for a brief second before landing back on mine. I'm sure they were as big as dinner plates. "Your mom's body was found in an old abandoned farmhouse this morning. And I'm sorry to be the one to tell you, but she's gone. The coroner's initial reports claim an overdose."

Gone. As in dead. My knees gave out. Ryker lifted me up and held on to me with both arms so I was standing on my feet, but he was doing all the work.

"We need you to come identify her body."

"No," I breathed out, shaking my head.

"Faith." I turned my head only to find Ryker's lips right at my temple as he whispered my name against my skin. "You can do this."

I shook my head again, staring at the Chief. "You know who she is. You can identify her and take care of her."

Ryker called my name again. The Chief opened his mouth to say something, but I stopped both of them. She was dead, but I had already said my good-byes a week ago. No one would mourn her death—least of all, me.

I straightened my shoulders and regained my own footing. Shifting away from Ryker's clutch, I stood directly in front of the Chief. "We all know what my mother was and wasn't," I told him. He blinked once before nodding. "But there will be no service for her. There's no one who would want to say good-bye to her."

I stood there, on the sidewalk in the middle of the day, with Ryker's warmth surrounding me, but finding my own strength inside of me. I knew... I knew last night when I left her with the men and with Cain bleeding out that this was a possibility. A better daughter might have mourned her or been saddened by what she had lost.

I wasn't that daughter.

My mom wasn't the kind of mother whose death brought on those emotions. As far as I was concerned, the world had lost one less drug-addict and was now a better place without her.

I sure as hell was.

"Take me home," I said, looking at Ryker. My chin jutted out in a way that dared him to argue with me.

He didn't. He simply opened the door to his truck and ushered me inside. Once I was seated in the bench seat, the Chief stepped forward.

"One more thing," he said, this time focused only on Ryker. His stance was more defensive, less kind than it had been moments before. "Heard you guys are helping the Sporelli's out now."

Ryker said nothing. He stood like a sentry at his post and arched a brow, waiting for Garrison to continue.

"You should know that Travis Larson was doing the same thing and we all know how that ended up."

I swallowed my gasp this time, waiting to see if anything else would be said. Larson had been Olivia's boyfriend and father to her lost baby. The last time she'd seen him he'd been gunned down by a group of the Sporelli family, and in the process, Liv had been shot as well. Her wounds were healed now, from where two bullets had grazed her waist and shoulder, but I also knew she still carried the guilt of Travis's death in some way.

"What's your point?" Ryker asked.

The Chief shrugged, unfolded his sunglasses, and placed them back over his eyes, shielding his eyes from Ryker's harsh glare that rivaled that of the sun's rays. "You boys might want to be careful."

"Is that all?"

He nodded and took a step away from the truck. "Have a good day."

Ryker closed the door to my side of the truck and ignored Garrison as he walked around the front. I looked straight ahead until Ryker climbed in and started the engine.

He turned to me as he moved the shifter into reverse.

"Don't ask if I'm okay," I said. I held up a hand, hushing him before he could argue. "Every time we get in this truck, you ask if I'm okay. I'm fine. We knew it was going to happen and right now, I don't feel a thing. Maybe I will, maybe I won't. But right now, I want to go home."

A thick, palpable silence swirled in the space between us. After several long, agonizing seconds, Ryker opened his mouth to say something.

"I think-"

"I'm fine," I said, cutting him off. "I just want to go home."

"Okay, then." He nodded, and his lips curved up slightly as he leaned over and brushed a hand through my hair, tugging the ends. His eyes softened and I could tell he wanted to say more, but I enjoyed the moment, soaking up the quiet between us. "Home it is."

My friends knew how to not only throw one hell of a Welcome-To-Your-New-Home party, but they knew how to throw a kickass party together quickly.

We had only been gone for a couple short hours, but by the time Ryker and I got back to the house, Jules and Olivia had snack foods lined up all over the place. They had two different barbeques ready to grill in the backyard and the fire pit ready for a campfire later. Drinks were in buckets and kegs were both inside and outside the house. And the house was full of old ladies, mostly Switch's old lady, Marie, cooking up more side dishes than I'd ever seen in my entire life.

The house smelled incredible, even if it still didn't feel like mine. But I knew they were all working hard at making it feel that way. I pushed down the awkward feeling and let myself enjoy the fact that not only had Olivia and Jules planned a party in no time at all, but they'd called men from the club and their women in to help.

And they had all come.

Not only that, but someone had already unpacked all the things we'd bought from the store earlier that day.

The shopping trip had drained my bank account, what little of it there was, but I didn't care. For the first time in a long time, I'd been able to enjoy an afternoon out with friends without the weight of Cain or my mother pressing down on my shoulders.

It had been freeing.

Which was partly why I didn't want Ryker worrying about me or my thoughts about my mom. I didn't know if the overdose was intentional or not. I didn't want to know.

I wanted to walk through the house that had new towels hung up in the bathrooms, pretty—but not too girly—soap containers on the counters, and smiled when I saw my new blender and toaster on the kitchen counters and some new, cheap, but cool looking paintings I'd bought at a local store of views of the north shore in Minnesota, already hanging on the walls in the living room and entryway.

My stuff.

In my home.

I kicked off my shoes when I walked in the door, grabbed Ryker's hand, and for the next few hours until the sun set, I laughed and mingled with the biker club that was quickly reminding me that my family was larger than the one I'd been born into.

I smiled.

I drank.

I kissed Ryker freely, whenever I felt like it, for no other reason than because I could.

And that was exactly what I was doing when Olivia plopped her butt down on the picnic table next to me. Without any thought to the fact that Ryker's hand were cupping my cheeks and our lips and tongues were mingled together, I felt a hard, pointy elbow jam into my waist.

"Ouch," I cried, yanking back from Ryker. "What the heck was that for?"

Ryker simply laughed, ran his hand down my hair, and pressed his lips to my forehead.

Olivia smirked. "Check that out."

I looked away from her to where she pointed at the tree line where Jaden had his hand grasped around Jules' biceps. From the distance, I took in Jaden's tense expression as he barked harshly at Jules. Meanwhile, Jules kept her eyes on Jaden. Her lips pressed together before she ripped her arm out of his grasp, snapped something equally angrily back, and then stomped across the grassy area.

"Crap," I muttered. And then my eyes widened as I watched Jaden watch her walk away. Except his angry face vanished as his eyes drifted to Jules' butt and his angry expression flickered to confusion before he spun around and clasped his hands behind his neck.

"That boy is going to have to figure out what to do soon," Liv said softly next to me.

"About Sophie?"

"That… and the way that as much as he hates Jules, he also can't take his eyes off of her." She took a pull from her beer as we watched Jaden face the crowd again. His eyes almost immediately went to Jules who had bent to scoop up Sophie and carry her back to us. Jaden watched the whole thing before he bypassed the partying crowd in the backyard and went inside, ignoring everyone who tried to talk to him. The scowl never left his face.

"He'll figure it out," Ryker said next to me. His arms were braced on the sides of my hips, but his head was turned to where Jaden disappeared. "Men are stupid sometimes. It'll take him awhile, but he loved Scratch way too much to not be there for Sophie. It's just bringing back a bunch of painful shit for him."

I nodded but said nothing. Coming back to this club had brought painful shit back to Liv's life and I wasn't an exception, either. But tonight wasn't the night where I was going to waste time dwelling on it.

"Hey, sweetie," Liv said as Jules reached us. Ryker pressed another kiss to my temple before he excused himself to go talk to Daemon closer to the fire. Liv's arm went around Jules. "How are you?"

Jules lifted and dropped one shoulder. Her hand smoothed down the back of Sophie's sleepy head. "We'll figure it out."

"You get a job?" I asked. Jules had moved back to Jasper Bay for the summer when I had called her, telling her Olivia had been shot and Black Death wouldn't let me go see her. I figured Liv could have used a friend. Jules had come back immediately, but I hadn't expected her to stay. I also hadn't expected her to show up with a two-year-old in tow, either.

She shook her head. "No, I've got a few interviews coming up but most of the districts have already hired for the year. I might be able to do some substitute teaching to get my foot in the door at some of the high schools around the area, though."

I took a sip of my drink while Liv and Jules talked about high school and the memories. Their soft laughter danced through the air, and with every giggle and every memory shared, I felt the stress—the darkness that had pressed down on me for far too long—lift into the dark night air and drift away.

"I need a new job," I said, abruptly cutting Jules off from the story of the time we'd all toilet-papered our principal's house one night. He was pissed and Jules figured he still wasn't over it considering when she'd gone in to apply for an open English Teaching position, he'd reminded her of that very night.

"You should go work at Gunner's."

I frowned at Liv. "The tattoo shop?"

Liv shrugged. "Yeah, I'm sure he'd hire you to do my old job. It was simple bookkeeping work and you could do it. Daemon wants me working at the garage, instead."

With that, her eyes went all hazy looking and seemingly on their own accord, drifted over to where Daemon and Ryker stood by the fire with a bunch of their brothers surrounding them. As if Liv's eyes were magnets to his, Daemon caught her glassy-eyed look, lifted his beer, and flashed a wink in her direction.

"You two are gross," I said. "But yeah, I'd be willing to work for Gunner. It couldn't be too hard."

"Until a bomb is thrown through the window," Liv snorted.

I nodded. "That would be a problem." I nudged her shoulder. "Stop staring at your man."

She grinned. "Can't help it, he's freaking hot."

The three of us girls laughed. It was easy and light laughter, and I never wanted the night to end.

I opened my mouth to ask Jules about Jaden when Daemon took a few steps from the fire and the group of men. He halted when he stood in the middle of the yard.

"Listen up," he called. Everyone instantly stilled. Daemon stood in the middle of the group, his shoulders back, looking like the man

Liv always wanted him to be. From next to me, she let out a breathy sigh.

Once Daemon knew he had everyone's attention, from adults and kids alike, he raised his beer bottle in the air. "We haven't had an easy few months." The crowd rumbled with agreement while Daemon kept talking. "But we joined this life and the club to be able to live free and live hard and nothing is gonna stop us from doin' that under my watch."

As the group of biker men and their old ladies cheered, he turned to face Liv directly. His beer tipped in her direction and his grin went wide and happy. I nudged Liv in the shoulder when I saw her smile matched his.

"We're gonna have some tough months comin' up. But what all this shit has taught me is that in the dark times, even among the death and the fighting, we have got to take the time to treasure what's ours." Liv gasped as Daemon's hand went to the front of his jeans pocket. My own body tingled with anticipation. "Get your ass over here, woman."

Daemon kept his eyes focused on Liv as I pushed her off the table. She stumbled slightly and muttered, "You have to be shitting me," but she went into the middle of the yard where Daemon waited for her.

"We've fucked around long enough, right?" he asked as soon as she reached him.

"I'm not sure our sex life is everyone's business."

Daemon laughed and pulled his hand out of his pocket. "Not what I meant, woman. But this—," he paused and held up what I knew was a ring. A diamond ring. Liv's jaw dropped as Daemon's smile stretched from ear to ear. "This is what I want from you. We've fucked up and it took too damn long to get you back in my bed and my house. And now that you're here, I want to make sure you never want to leave again. So what do you say, princess… you ready to be my queen?"

The crowd of men hooted and hollered while the women clapped and cheered. Above the noise that rang in my ears, I couldn't hear Liv's response, but her nod gave her answer.

Daemon slid the ring onto Liv's ring finger and pulled her into the kiss that only increased the hollers from the men. Except this time they were coupled with shouts of telling them to get a room.

My fingers dug into the wooden edge of the picnic table as the sight in front of me grew cloudy and blurry through the stinging of my tears.

I was happy for her. Happy for my friend who had loved Daemon more than anyone else in her entire life. Much like I'd felt about Ryker. The words Daemon spoke rang true in my own ears.

We had fucked up long enough… hadn't we wasted enough time?

As if Ryker knew I was thinking the question, I caught him staring at me in the distance. My lips lifted into a small smile as he caught me watching him and his feet began bringing him toward me.

31

Ryker

I saw Faith's desire and peace flash in her eyes as soon I caught the way she looked at me. Over the noise of the men cheering Daemon and Liv on and congratulating them, all I heard was the sound of my heart beating against my chest as my feet began walking toward her.

I knew exactly what she was thinking.

Hadn't we wasted enough time? I had already asked her that, and she'd agreed before, but something about this moment... this night... it sunk in.

And I wanted nothing more than finish the night by sinking into Faith.

I reached her; the dozens of steps felt like thousands as I closed the space and set my empty bottle of beer on the table next to her. I didn't say anything, I just nodded my agreement.

We'd wasted enough time. Now was the time to celebrate and enjoy the moment because we never knew when it was going to end. Not in this life. Not in this world.

Without talking, I reached out, hooked my hands under Faith's arms, lifted her, and gave her no other option but to wrap her legs around my waist.

She did and one of my hands dropped to her ass to hold her against me.

I leaned in and whispered, "Say goodnight to Jules."

She turned her head and looked down. Jules was quietly laughing and watching us. She simply raised a hand.

"Good night, Jules," Faith said, but she choked and tripped over her words as my tongue darted out and licked and sucked on her jaw.

Jules hopped off the table, Sophie in her arms. "I think that's my cue to head home. See y'all later."

I didn't give Faith a chance to say anything. I didn't give her a chance to go and congratulate Liv and Daemon. We'd do it later.

Tonight had become about enjoying us.

I didn't care there were dozens of people in our new backyard. Someone would clean up. Someone would lock up. Hell, by morning there'd probably be dozens of people camped out all over the house and the yard.

I didn't give a shit.

"Our room," I growled into Faith's ear as we hit the inside of the house. She simply nodded against me.

When we hit the room, I wasted no time in lowering her to bed and climbing on top of her.

With my elbows braced by her shoulders, I held her face in my hands. "What were you thinking of out there?" I asked as my lips brushed against hers. I felt the quick intake of her breathe against my skin and rocked against her, letting her know how much I wanted her.

"You," she breathed out on an exhale. She lifted her head to kiss me back, but I smirked and moved out of her reach.

"What about me?"

She dropped her head and a moan of frustration escaped her lips. My smirk grew.

"Tell me, Faith," I said and moved my hands to her hair. I didn't know what it was about her hair, but I had to touch it. Constantly.

"What Daemon said," she whispered. I nodded. "It's true. We

never know what's going to happen…"

Her voice trailed off as I leaned down and began pressing my lips against the column of her neck. "Go on," I murmured against her skin, moving down to where her neck met her collarbone. When she mewled, I teasingly bit her skin. "Tell me."

She cleared her throat and shifted under me. Her hands went to my lower back and then her fingertips were lifting my shirt. Her hands drifted to below my waistband as her fingers pulled me against her.

"That we'd wasted enough time."

"Haven't I already told you that?" I asked and rocked into her again. Her pleasured response had my dick hard and pressing against my zipper.

She nodded. "Yes… but tonight I got it."

"You got it?"

She nodded again. I leaned back on one elbow and trailed my other hand down the length of her body. She was so beautiful. Her soft, olive skin was perfectly tanned and toned. I wanted to see all of it. I pressed my hand under her shirt, lifting it slightly, as I moved my hand over her stomach.

"Ryker," she moaned. "I need you."

I leaned down and licked her lips, smiling. "You have me." My hand reached her breast. Through her bra, I could feel her already hardened nipples. "Always," I said, staring directly into her eyes.

All she could do was nod as I pulled down the cup of her bra, rolling her nipple between my thumb and finger. I pinched it lightly and smoothed it.

God she was beautiful. And despite the life I knew she'd led but never wanted to think about again, when she went soft in my arms, an innocent and light look appeared in her eyes.

I was her first. In so many ways, I was her *only*. And truthfully, she was my only, too.

It was that thought that had me moving. I dropped my lips to hers, tasting her, but not waiting another second to begin removing her clothes as our lips tangled against one another.

Her hands pulled on my hair and held me close to her before moving back to my jeans. I shifted off Faith long enough to kick off my boots, my jeans, and the rest of my clothes.

Naked, standing over her at the edge of the bed—our bed—I looked down at her still fully clothed.

"You're awfully overdressed," I stated.

Faith grinned and looked at me through half-closed eyes. Her voice was soft and silky—seductive—as she said, "Then you better fix that."

I would. Slowly. As much as my body screamed *take her now!* I wanted to treasure it. Treasure this moment that I knew was Faith fully giving herself to me all over again. It wasn't the first time we had sex. It wasn't even the first time we'd made love. I'd done that last night when I dragged her up here. But tonight… tonight was a night for pleasure.

My hands went to her thighs. I slowly brushed my palms and my fingers across her skin as I undid the button on her denim shorts and pulled them slowly down her legs along with her underwear.

My dick twitched with every gasp of breath she made. I would kill to be inside her, to ravage her like I wanted to do with my baser instincts. But first, I needed to taste her.

With my hands on her thighs, I pulled her to me so her sweet ass was at the edge of the bed. Dropping to my knees in front of her, I spread her legs and smiled.

"So wet for me," I purred against her skin and held her tighter as she shifted.

I looked up to see Faith propped on her elbows. Her hair fell over her breasts, hiding them from me, but I didn't care. As much as I wanted to see every inch of her skin, I loved the way she could hide herself from me so demurely, but it only took one look at her eyes to see her lust and desire.

I didn't take my eyes off hers as I pressed my lips against her inner thighs, teasing and sucking and licking and biting, while she tried in vain to shift against my touch. I rubbed the scruff of my jaw against her sensitive flesh and grinned as her head fell back. Another groan of pleasure, or frustration at my teasing, escaped her swollen lips.

I couldn't wait anymore. Lowering my mouth to her clit, I sucked and licked around it, still teasing her while I watched her. I couldn't help it. I wanted—needed—to see her fall apart for me. To know that *I* was the one giving her this pleasure completely selflessly.

Or maybe selfishly because she tasted so damn good. I couldn't get enough as I licked and sucked and tasted her. I drove my tongue inside of her and hummed my approval as she began grinding herself against my mouth.

I fucked her with my tongue, moved my hand off her thigh to play with her clit at the same time, and loved it as she rocked and shifted harder against me. I felt her body pulse and spasm on my tongue. She tasted amazing. By the shocked gasps and moans leaving her mouth, the way her eyes widened in shock, and the way she licked her dry lips, it was clear that no one had done this for her before.

The knowledge rose up an insane amount of caveman instincts as my testosterone pulsed through my body. I wanted to beat my chest and scream from the rooftops that she was now mine.

Instead, I focused on her pleasure as her thighs began to quiver and her pussy tightened around my tongue.

So close. She was so close. I watched her as I pulled my tongue from her, pressed two fingers inside, and bit and sucked on her clit.

She shattered beneath me. Her thighs clamped around my ears as her entire body shook while I continued pleasing her through her orgasm. Her screams shook the windows and rocked my whole fucking world.

When she calmed, I climbed over her and adjusted our bodies so I was holding her back to my chest. My dick throbbed against her ass, but I didn't care as I moved the covers and shifted us under them.

She pushed back against me, feeling my thick erection. "Ryker," she moaned.

I shook my head and pressed my lips to her shoulder. "Tonight was for you, honey. All for you."

She rocked back against me and I bit off my groan. Fuck that felt good. I wanted more of her, but I wanted to give Faith this moment. The first time any man took the time to only care for her instead of himself, at least since we were together before. She needed it. She might not have said it, but I knew she needed this night to simply feel my love for her without expecting anything in return.

"You're sure?" she asked through a hitched breath.

"Tomorrow, you can do whatever you want to me," I assured her. "And only what you want."

She was silent for a moment, and I felt her pulse increase against my chest.

Finally, as my eyes drifted close and I pulled her close, she whispered, "Thanks."

I clasped Daemon at the shoulder and shook him. "Wipe the damn grin off your face, man."

He shook his head. "No fuckin' way. It took me five years to get Liv where I wanted her. I'm a happy man today."

I didn't blame him. After having Faith last night and again this morning, I knew it was only a matter of time—a short time frame—until I was standing right where Daemon was.

"Who would have thought, huh, brother?" he asked, one eyebrow raised. "That after all this time we'd have the women."

He wasn't kidding. All I wanted now was a smooth sailing ride, which I knew wouldn't come, but a man could hope. "You're turning into a pussy."

"No," he winked. "But I had a taste—"

I threw my hands up. "Don't, Brother. Don't fucking go there."

Daemon threw his head back and laughed. I joined him. Damn it felt good to do nothing but laugh and be with my little brother again.

He shoved me out of the chapel room at the clubhouse where we'd just gotten done talking about Sporelli and how in the hell to get us out of the mess with them. It would take time because they were apparently not only psychic, but psychotic as well.

After filling Daemon in about what the Chief of Police had told me the day before, he let us know that he'd already been told that Liv's ex-boyfriend, Travis, had been working with Sporelli to clean out both Black Death and Nordic Lords from Jasper Bay. Unfortunately, when Black Death found out he was working for them, they had threatened Liv's life. Hence the bomb through the window at Gunner's old shop a few months back, which had been the catalyst for Liv and Daemon getting back together.

It had been a warning to Travis. I didn't know how Daemon had learned that, and I didn't ask if he'd told Liv the truth behind it. If he was like me, I figured it'd be best to let it go at this point. Liv was healing from not only her miscarriage, but Travis's death. No sense rocking the boat there.

But we had to be careful with the Sporelli family. They were the largest underworld family in Chicago, and somehow, they seemed to know what we were doing before we ever did it. It explained how they had been able to find Faith before we did a few weeks ago.

At the time, I hadn't bothered to ask, and today wasn't the day either. She was in my bed, for now, where she belonged.

We'd figure the rest out and figure out how to take care of having to run drugs for the Sporelli family in time.

Until then, half the men were leaving soon for another run. Another drop was being done at the ports. But this time, I was sticking close to the club and getting back into the groove of working in the garage and the salvage yard that the club ran for their legitimate profits.

"Hey," I said to Daemon, pulling him back from the rest of the men as we streamed into the clubhouse living room. "Whatever happened to Cain?"

Darkness flashed in Daemon's eyes right before he nodded to Switch. Switch was a big man. One you didn't want to mess with. He'd been best friends with our dad and Liv's dad, Bull, back in the day. As if he sensed what we were talking about, he nodded once in our direction before turning back to Tripp and throwing back a shot of whiskey.

"He took care of Cain?" I asked, glancing at Daemon.

He shrugged, which gave me my answer. "We burned him afterward at the salvage yard. But he screamed like a pussy before that."

"Jesus." I scrubbed my hands down my face. "Don't tell Faith."

"Wouldn't dream of it. She doin' okay?" Daemon started walking toward the bar.

"Better," I said and left it at that. I helped myself to a beer, popping the top and flicking it into a nearby garbage can. Soon, the men were talking about the upcoming drop and run for Sporelli, tossing back drinks and smiling as if life was easy.

It wasn't.

I didn't think this life would ever be easy, but in the few weeks I'd been back, I finally understood why my dad loved the club and why he wanted nothing else except the club life for his sons. They weren't men and friends and club members standing around, shooting the shit.

We were brothers. All of us.

32
Faith

Every day that passed as the next couple of weeks went by made me want to pinch myself to see if I was really, truly alive.

Things almost seemed too good to be true.

Not only had Ryker and I settled into our life together easier than I thought it'd be, but things had also been quiet on the club front. With Cain's death—something I knew had happened but still didn't want to know *how*—Penny's closed down. Black Death had essentially been eradicated from town. The boards on the windows and the shutting off of the lights outside and inside effectively closed down a link to my past that I never wanted to revisit.

Occasionally, I would pass a client on the street. Surprisingly, given the small size of our town, it was infrequent, and when it did occur, the glances were minimal. No man wanted to admit to walking through Penny's doors, and so it was with silence that my old life as a whore was beginning to fade into the background.

My body still bore the scars, and always would, but when we lay in bed together at night, Ryker would kiss and rub each scarred lash on my back, making me feel as if his hands and his lips contained healing powers I hadn't known before.

Gone was the shame and remorse. Somehow, between Cain's

death, my mother's death, and falling in love all over again with Ryker Knight, my regret and anger had dissipated into what could only be described as a dull, flashing memory; like a fading, blinking Christmas tree light. Occasionally, I would sense a glimmer of my past—a memory that flashed before my eyes when I daydreamed or got lost in my own thoughts—but it took a quick blink, a quick look around at my present surroundings, to remember who I was now and who I had the potential to become.

It was freeing.

More than that, with Ryker at my side and us living together and continuing to grow closer together—it was fantastic.

And more than just my relationship with Ryker, I was quickly re-forming friendships with Liv and Jules, two of the girls I had grown up with and then been separated from. I was quickly realizing they were more like sisters to me than I ever could have asked for.

Which is how we found ourselves at Bella Salon, the three of us getting pedicures and manicures for no other reason except we were girls and sometimes we liked that stuff.

The salon had opened over the summer and I had never been inside, but I instantly fell in love with the dark woodwork, the black leather chairs, and the lighting that was both elegant and relaxing. In the background, gentle, soothing music flowed through the speakers. I had felt stress seep from my pores as soon as I walked inside, heard the music, and inhaled a mild eucalyptus scent that seemed so prevalent in high-end salons.

Three, petite blonde women who could have probably passed for triplets immediately whisked Olivia, Jules, and me into out pedicure chairs. They left us alone while they fetched Liv and I coffee and hot tea for Jules.

"Are you and Ryker still going to New Orleans this weekend?" Liv asked, her lips pressed against the edge of her deep red, large coffee mug.

My lip twitched nervously. "We are." Ryker was taking me to

meet Meg and Brayden, who was still having a difficult time with Ryker being gone. A part of me was looking forward to meeting them. I had nothing to fear.

I knew it. Yet the other part of me was nervous as hell at meeting the other woman Ryker had spent the last two years taking care of. He was practically the only father Brayden knew, and my stomach flipped every day wondering what would happen if Brayden didn't like me.

I had never been around kids that young before with the exception of Sophie. Kids simply made me nervous.

"That's a pretty big step," Liv said as her own eyes glanced down at her sparkling diamond.

My eyes followed hers and I huffed. "We're not there yet."

"Why not?"

I shot a teasing glare at Jules. "Because we're just now figuring everything out again. I don't mind waiting."

I didn't, either. We had already screwed up one engagement. The last thing I wanted was for Ryker to feel pressured to propose again.

Not that I'd say no…

I shook the thought out of my head. Ryker and I had officially only been back together for like three weeks. It was way too soon to be imagining matching white dresses with Liv and a simultaneous wedding as we married the brothers we'd always loved.

Because I certainly wasn't thinking it.

"What happened to your car?" I asked Jules, effectively changing the conversation. Two nights ago, her car had been towed into the Nordic Lords clubhouse, but she had never shown up to check on the work. Apparently Jaden had to go get her and her car when it died on the side of the road. I was *dying* inside to know how that confrontation happened. All I'd seen of them so far had been fireworks and bombs exploding when Jaden got too close to her.

Her pink cheeks and intense focus on the steam from her hot tea gave me my answers.

"I don't know what was wrong with it, but my car broke down

the other day on my way home from an interview. Jaden came and got me."

Her voice tightened near the end, and I couldn't bite back my smile. Someday those two were going to explode, and I couldn't wait for it to happen. I knew deep down, Jaden didn't blame her for Scratch's death, and I'd seen the looks he gave not only Jules, but Sophie too when she wasn't looking.

"You get the job?" Liv asked.

Jules shook her head. "No… all the jobs around here are filled up since school starts next week. I've applied for substitute jobs, but I need to find something more permanent. When I moved back my parents only agreed I could stay with them for a few months until I had to be on my own with Sophie."

"Harsh," Liv whispered.

Jules shrugged. "Not really. I'm an adult and I'm able to care for the two of us alone. I just didn't think I'd have a hard time finding a decent paying job. But we move into our new place next weekend, so I have to find something soon."

"We have an opening for a receptionist," one of the perky blondes chirped, smiling wide at Jules. "I mean, it's not teaching, and I don't mean to interrupt, but I'm sure if you can teach, you can answer phones and make appointments."

Jules jaw dropped right as I blinked. The girl was so… happy.

"You'd hire her on the spot?" I asked.

The three girls looked at one another before sharing some secret smile and they all shrugged. At the same time. So strange.

"Yeah, we just opened, but we're already really busy. Apparently some other salon didn't have the best reputation and have recently lost a lot of their clientele, so all the other women in town who were going there are coming here instead."

I felt a warm hand slide over mine. Liv squeezed my hand tightly while I pretended the bubbling water at my feet was fascinating. I knew what salon she meant. The one where Cain sent me and the rest of his girls. A lot of them had left town and I was sure, now that the finer citizens of Jasper Bay had a better option to go to for their salon needs, not many people were willingly gracing the doors of Kelly's Hair Cuts and Stuff anymore.

Not that it was a great place to go in general. Plus, Bella Salon was ten times classier. Looking around the large and gorgeous spa, I wasn't the least bit surprised.

"I'll... I'll think about it," Jules said, her voice quiet and her expression uncertain.

The middle girl shrugged as she scrubbed the heel of my foot. It felt divine. "No rush. We can be flexible with your teaching stuff if you need us, too. But we could really use the help around here."

"Are you related?" I asked, my mouth spurting out the words before I could stop them.

The girl in the middle smiled at me. "Twins," she said, nodding to the girl at Liv's feet. "Cassie over there," her head flipped to the other side, "is our big sister, but we've always wanted to be in business together... so we did."

They said it so matter-of-factly... but still happier than I'd ever heard people sound. But they made it sound so simple as they began telling us of growing up in Duluth but wanting a smaller town to live in. As if it was just so easy to want something and go after it and make it successful.

I listened with rapt attention while they giggled and laughed, while in the meantime, Jules, Liv, and I kept our smirks to ourselves at their exuberance. They seemed so sweet... so innocent... and clearly smart and beautiful, too.

When we were done, Liv paid for all of us because she insisted it was her turn to treat us on a girl's day. Then, I waved them off and headed to Gunner's to work at GetInked2.

Liv hadn't been joking when she had said doing their books was easy. Gunner had hired me based on Liv's recommendation alone.

I couldn't help but smile as I walked the few short blocks,

throwing on my zip-up hoodie. September quickly ushered in fall in northern Minnesota and the early crunching of falling leaves at my feet told me that we were nearing the end of summer and warm weather. Soon I'd be dressed in wool gloves and parka coats.

Snow would be knee-deep in a couple short months.

A slow breeze blew my hair over my shoulders, making me shiver and thankful I was headed south for the weekend. One last weekend in warmth and humidity was just what I needed.

"Hey, Gunner," I called out over the pinging door chime as I entered the tattoo parlor.

I was met with complete silence other than the vibrating door chime.

Odd. A tingle moved slowly down my spine until the hair on my arms stood on end. I peeked over the half wall that separated the reception area from the Gunner's tattoo beds only to find them completely empty.

Hesitantly, I reached for my cell phone, unlocking the code and holding it in case something had happened to him. When I heard nothing coming from the back hall area where my office was, something simply felt off.

Gunner never left the tattoo parlor unattended. He certainly never left the front door unlocked. And every other time I'd been inside in the last week as he and Liv took turns training me on his computer software, ear-piercing music was always blaring from the speakers.

Sensing something wasn't right, I retreated back to the entry area and dialed Ryker.

It had just rang once when the door chimed and a masculine voice behind me called my name.

I screamed. My phone tumbled to the floor as I spun around, one hand flying to my chest.

"You okay?" Gunner asked, his eyes wide opened. Two paper bags hung from his closed hands at his sides.

I gasped for a breath. "Damn it, Gunner," I breathed out, reaching down to pick up my phone. From the speaker, I heard Ryker shouting my name. "You scared the crap out of me."

"What the hell is going on?" Ryker shouted as soon as he heard my voice.

Heat suffused my cheeks as my shaking hand clamped onto the phone for dear life.

"Sorry," I told Ryker. "I just freaked out, but it was nothing."

"What happened?" His deep growl calmed my rapidly beating heart. Ryker cared. In my head, I knew he did. But as his voice rumbled, I could practically see his worry lines etched deep between his eyes through the phone line; his concern went straight to my overwhelmed and terrified heart.

"Nothing," I said, taking another deep breath. My eyes stayed on Gunner as he lifted the bags and mouthed, "I went for lunch."

I laughed softly. "Sorry to scare you, Ryker. I got to GetInked and Gunner was gone. It just freaked me out, I guess. But he's back, so I'm sorry."

"You sure you're okay?"

I nodded. Then I realized he couldn't see me. "I'm fine, I swear."

A few seconds of silence passed where I knew Ryker was debating whether or not he believed me, and whether or not he should drive over and check it out for himself. His protectiveness made me grin.

"I'm fine, Ryker. But I do have to get to work. I'll see you later."

He sighed. I closed my eyes and pictured him running his hand through his hair as he continued debating showing up at the shop. "All right… but I'm coming to get you after work."

I smirked. "I figured you would."

"And don't scare the shit out of me like that again." This time, I knew he was grinning.

"I'll do my best. Love you."

His breath hitched and his voice went deeper and softer still. "Love you, too, Faith."

I clicked the phone off, wanting those words to be the last ones I heard from him. Once I slid my phone back into my pocket, I met Gunner back in the break room.

"Sorry," I said sheepishly as I leaned against the doorframe and watched him take out two enormous taco salads from their cardboard boxes. Salsa and hot sauce permeated the air, making my stomach rumble. "I got scared when the place was unlocked and no one was here."

One side of Gunner's lips hitched into a smirk. He pointed at the boxes. "I went next door for lunch and knew you didn't have a key."

"I figured," I said, pushing off the doorway and joining him at the tiny table in a room that he used as a break room slash storage room. Boxes lined one wall and the table always rocked back and forth on two slightly crooked legs, but it worked. He also had a small fridge installed to keep our drinks cold. It was all we needed.

"Thanks for lunch, though," I told him and dug into my taco salad.

He eyed me for a few minutes, watching me eat. Just as I was beginning to feel self-conscious under his watchful gaze, he began eating his own salad. "You always that jumpy?"

I chewed the bite in my mouth and wiped my mouth.

"Only in businesses that have had bombs thrown through the front windows." I watched Gunner's smirk turn into a full grin.

"Touché."

Then the room filled with silence as we both dug into our massive, and incredibly delicious, taco salads.

The truth was, I would most likely always be jumpy and scared of some big, bad man coming for me behind a dark corner. I wasn't naïve enough to be convinced there would be no retaliation from Black Death charters for this local charter's decimation.

On the other hand, I tried every day to not live my life under that umbrella of fear. I had lived in it for years, and Ryker was helping me feel truly free from it.

But Gunner was boss, not my friend. He did me a favor in giving me a job, and I'm sure he knew what I'd been through via rumor mills and Olivia's big mouth.

That being said, he didn't need to know my dark secrets, and I didn't feel inclined to share them with him.

By the time we finished our lunches, two of his next appointments were waiting in the entry area and the rest of the afternoon flew by in the same manner. For a small town, Gunner was highly recommended, and people drove for over an hour simply to have him do their tattoos. We were constantly busy, so while I worked on his accounting, I also stayed busy cleaning the chairs and equipment and taking appointments for people who phoned in as well as walk-in clients.

When the sun set and we were getting ready to lock up, I wasn't surprised at all to hear the front door open and see Ryker's presence immediately fill the space.

I grinned, one hand going to my hip as I stopped what I was doing and stared at him.

His jeans fit his thighs perfectly and draped over his black, scuffed boots. His shirt was pulled tightly over his toned chest; even his leather cut couldn't hide his ripped muscles. And his eyes, although still covered by his sunglasses, hit my body. His head dipped down as he raked his gaze over me, making me flush, and leaving me feeling naked in the middle of the shop.

He closed the distance between us. Or maybe I did. I didn't remember moving, but at some point Ryker's hands were on my hips and we were pressed chest to chest to one another.

"I'm taking my girl home," he yelled out to Gunner, who had disappeared back to the storage room. Then his lips met mine in a gently, sweeping kiss. My entire body burst into a warm, comforting blaze as Gunner's muffled, "Okay!" came from the background.

"Miss me?"

"Yes." I breathed it out on a shaky exhale, still trying to recover from the fleeting but powerful kiss.

"Ready for home?" he asked me when he pulled away.

Home.

With Ryker.

The mere thought made my heart skip a bit.

The fact that it was reality made my heart swell to such a huge size that I felt the pressure in my chest increase.

I couldn't take my eyes off him or his sexy small grin. "You bet."

33
Faith

"I still can't believe how gorgeous this city is," I told Ryker as we walked hand in hand through the French Quarter in New Orleans.

The sun beat down on my exposed shoulders and arms as I walked next to him wearing a navy blue and white, strapless maxi dress. It was Labor Day weekend and tourists abounded in the city, although Ryker told me the main part of New Orleans was always packed with tourists and visitors.

Ryker looked over my shoulder at the cemetery we'd left blocks ago and shivered as if he could still see it. "I still think part of this place is creepy."

I bumped his shoulder and laughed. "I can't believe you're afraid of the tombs."

Ryker feigned another fearful shudder, making me laugh harder. "It's just not right… all those dead people behind the walls. It's as if they could open the doors and walk out at any moment."

"Like Zombies," I supplied with a grin.

"I'll never understand your fascination with them, either."

He removed his hand from mine, wrapped his arm around my shoulder, and pulled me to him playfully. We walked in silence until we turned a corner and stopped to watch a street performer play his saxophone on the corner. The man was old with leathered, thick skin that said he spent most of his life working outside in the sun. But his playing was incredible. Ryker and I stood on the corner, our arms wrapped around each other, swaying back and forth to the music.

A gust of breeze blew by, cooling the thick, hot air and pushed my hair in front of my face, momentarily blocking my view from the jazz musician.

Ryker's warm hand moved to my cheek and brushed the hair out of my face, while at the same time cupping my cheek and lifting it to him.

His eyes stayed on my hair in a hazy-eyed look as his fingers ran through the length of it.

"What is it with you and my hair?" I asked, my breath husky and soft at the same time. He shook his head and watched the end of the lock slip from his fingertips.

"Reminds me of back when everything was good."

I swallowed through a sudden egg-sized lump in my throat. "I thought things were good now."

And they were. We had been in New Orleans for two days and the break away from the stress of the club had been exactly what I needed to relax. And Meg and Brayden were incredible. Even at his small height, the kid knew how to tackle hug with the best of them, which is what he did to Ryker and me as soon as we'd walked through their door. His head had rammed right into my crotch, almost making me lose my breath.

And that was how I met Meg. Hunched over and trying to keep Brayden's head from knocking into my crotch with a grimace on my face. She simply laughed, waved him off, and then wrapped me in small arms that were deceptively fierce. She kissed my cheek and whispered in my ear, "I'm so glad he found you."

When she pulled back, tears clouded her vision, but her grin was contagious.

I fell in love with their easy banter and laid back disposition in about five seconds.

I had thought everything was perfect.

I had thought we were perfect.

Based on the tightened jaw in Ryker's expression and the way he stared at my hair as if I was threatening to chop it all off and burn it, I realized I might have been mistaken.

"Hey," I whispered when he didn't answer. I shook him gently with my hand on my hip only to realize that it trembled slightly against his cargo shorts. "What is it?"

He pulled his dark eyes to mine and blinked slowly. His nose wrinkled before he pressed his lips together. He cupped my cheeks with both of his large hands, effectively encompassing my whole face in his strong, protective hands. I'd placed everything I was into those hands at the promise he'd never leave. As he lifted me onto my tiptoes, I felt as if the floor was dropping under my feet.

My heart thudded against my chest as his lips finally brushed against mine. It was a whisper of a kiss that left me breathless and more confused.

When he pulled back, he kept me lifted onto my toes and my eyes stayed frozen on his.

He tripped over his words. "I'm sorry."

My brow furrowed. "Sorry for what?"

He shook his head and then leaned down, pressing his forehead to mine. "I'm so sorry I ran that night."

I gasped. "That's what this is about? I thought… I thought we were past all that. You said—"

"I know," Ryker nodded, and then set me on my feet. His eyes glanced over my shoulder behind me and he directed me to a nearby metal bench. The heat from the sun burnt through the thin fabric of my dress, almost frying the backs of my thighs in the sweltering heat. "And I wasn't lying when I said we've wasted enough time. I want it all with you, Faith." He dropped to his knee, but my head was spinning so quickly from his words that I didn't recognize the gesture as he crouched in front in me. "The thing is… that night when you hopped out of my truck, right before you did and I ran my hand through your hair, I knew, that at that moment, I had everything I'd ever wanted sitting in the cab of my run down pickup."

Tears welled in my own eyes as I saw an unknown expression in his. My hands trembled in his and my knees shook from nerves and fear at whatever he had to say next.

"We messed that up back then… or I did." His forehead dropped to my knee. He ran his head against my knee as one of my hands threaded through the hair on the back of his head. I could feel his nerves falling off him in rolling waves that only increased my pulse until it was all I could hear. "I'm screwing this up," he said as he leaned back and finally… finally… a small smile appeared.

"Screwing what up?"

He laughed once, shook his head, and then held onto my hands firmly in one of his. "It was just over five years that I pulled my truck into this town, parked it two blocks over, walked in Mickey's pub, and asked for the largest whiskey he'd give me. The bartender slid me a glass, leaned his elbows on the bar, and said, 'what the fuck did you just mess up?'" Ryker laughed again once, reliving the memory in distant eyes. "And do you know what I said?"

I shook my head, too terrified to speak, too uncertain as to what he was trying to tell me.

"I told him, 'the best thing that ever happened to me.'" He paused and took a long breath as one of his hands went to his front pocket. "What I'm trying to tell you, Faith, is that when we were younger, for years I couldn't get you out of my head… and that was even before we went out on a date. And as soon as we went on our first date, I knew… I knew then that there would never be anyone else for me. When I showed up here, I still knew there'd be no one else for me and there hasn't been. What I don't want to do is wait another day to give you the future I always wanted you to have."

I gasped as his hand lifted a black box out of his pocket. "What the …?"

Ryker smiled. Finally the grin I was used to seeing on him graced his lips as he exhaled heavily. "Marry me."

Tears fell from down my cheeks as he let go of my hands long enough to open the box and pull out a diamond. It was massive and sparkly, although it could have been the sun. I didn't care. It could have been a speck of coal, and I would have had the same reaction.

"Holy shit."

Ryker laughed as he slid the ring on my finger. "Is that a yes?"

I stared at the ring. I stared at him. My pulse beat in my ears as the quiet clapping of the strangers gathered around us, witnessing our moment, began cheering and celebrating us.

I shook my head, gathered my wits that had been spilled all over the scorching cement, and stared directly at Ryker.

"Yes," I laughed out the word as I launched myself from the bench—pulling a Brayden and tackle hugging the crap out of him.

"You said yes!" Meg cheered as soon as we arrived back at her house later that night. She began crying while she laughed and congratulated us the second she saw the ring on my finger.

I had been speechless.

Ryker's crewmate Pete walked around the corner, four champagne glasses in one hand and a bottle in the other.

"Was I that much of a foregone conclusion?" I asked, teasingly glancing at everyone in the room.

Ryker's hand on my hip tightened and he pulled me into him, pressing his lips against my temple.

"What can I say," Meg said, clapping her hands and helping

unload the glasses from Pete's hands. "Epic love like yours is simply meant to be."

Epic love. I smiled at the thought of Ryker and me always being destined for one another.

Before I knew it, we were spending the entire night finishing off two bottles of champagne, the four of us sitting in Meg's cozy living room long after Brayden went to bed.

It was when Pete excused himself for the restroom at one point that Ryker's expression grew serious.

A thick tension appeared in the room and his hand squeezed my thigh. He looked at Meg and nodded down the direction of the hall where Pete disappeared.

"He's not like that and you know it." Meg scolded him softly but firmly as soon as she recognized his look

"I know he's a man and you're beautiful." Ryker said it with a friendly smile, while his hand tightened on my thigh in reassurance. I wasn't worried. I had been around Ryker and Meg for days and fully trusted what Ryker told me about their relationship. It was that of family. Sure, I knew they considered the other attractive—how could you not? But there was never an inappropriate glance or jealous tinge in Meg's eyes when she saw us together.

And I couldn't have hated her even if there was. Meg was sweet and kind. She was genuine and full of love. She had strength that surpassed anything I felt like lived within me, and I knew she'd been through her own version of hell with losing her husband. Yet it hadn't hardened her in the least; it simply gave her strength to create the best life possible for Brayden.

Basically, I wanted to be Meg when I grew up.

Meg waved Ryker off, dismissing him and his concern. "It's fine, Ryker. We don't even see him much. He calls and checks in when he's in town and stops by occasionally to take Brayden to the park. I've known him my whole life."

"You'll let me know if you need help?"

By the way she rolled her eyes every time he did, I knew this weekend wasn't the only time she'd heard the question. I left them to their brother-sister argument, rested my head against Ryker's shoulder, and closed my eyes, listening to them bickering like siblings while the thick darkness pulled me under to sleep. I felt safer and more loved in that very moment than I could ever remember feeling before in my entire life.

When Ryker carried me to bed, only waking me to take off my clothes and pull me next to him in the bed we shared in Meg's guestroom, the glint of the outside light caught my ring.

"It wasn't a dream," I whispered, staring at my diamond ring. I rolled and turned to Ryker, propping my chin on his chest while he looked at me with amusement. "This is real."

I trailed my hand down the short stubble on his cheek and felt the vibrations from his laughter rumble under my chin and my hand.

In one swift move, Ryker had us positioned so he was over me, grinding his hips against mine. "This was my dream," he said huskily into my ear as he rocked into me, easily filling me with one swift push. "So I made it real. And I'll spend the rest of our lives making sure your dreams come true."

I pressed my fingers into the hard flesh in his lower back as he pulled out and then pushed back into me slowly, building my orgasm quickly.

"You already did," I whispered into his ear.

His rhythm faltered for a brief moment until he kissed me as if he was claiming me. As our bodies rocked together until we climaxed, hiding our groans of ecstatic pleasure, I knew that I'd spend a lifetime making sure Ryker knew how true that was.

EPILOGUE
Faith

I felt like throwing up. Twisting to look at myself in the three-way mirror for maybe the hundredth time in ten minutes, the woman in the white dress smiling at me and staring at my reflection made my stomach-flip and my skin grow tight.

What the hell did I have to be nervous about? It wasn't *my* wedding dress that I could see in the mirror's reflection.

Liv almost doubled over laughing at me... again. Had her wedding dress not been a corseted top essentially keeping her spine straighter than a metal rod, she probably would have.

"I can't wait to see you this summer at your own wedding," she said, tears threatening her eyes.

I rolled my eyes at her, trying to shrug it off. "I can't help it. It's a wedding and forever and all those people and oh my god I'm completely freaking out over nothing."

I waved my hands in front of my eyes, drying my tears. Liv dabbed underneath her eyes with a folding tissue in order to keep from ruining her make-up.

"If you ruin any of that make-up we just spent hours applying, we will cut you."

Staring at Cassie while she tried to hold a scolding expression for longer than five seconds only sent Liv and I into louder hysterics. We were wheezing and gasping for breath when Jules and Sophie entered the chapel room in the clubhouse. Sophie's flower girl dress was as white and flowy as Liv's. The lacy overlay on both dresses gave them a sophisticated but still casual appearance. Liv had insisted on it. Considering her and Daemon were getting married at the gun range on the Nordic Lords property, casual was required.

Granted, the gun range looked beautiful with the plants and flowers that had been brought in. The white wooden chairs that had been set up with an aisle in the center added a layer of sophistication to the clubhouse grounds that had all the men grumbling. The arched trellis that served as the altar where Liv and Daemon were being married was wrapped in ivy and speckled with bright white orchids. Everything was beautiful.

Cassie, Callie, and Cammie had styled our hair and done our make-up in two hours. Occasionally, Jules and I snuck outside to watch the big bad biker men gently unfolding white wooden chairs while Maria, Switch's old lady, bossed the men all around, pointing her finger and stomping her foot as she told them where to move the potted flowers.

I was thrilled we had had an easy winter and an early, warm spring. Now, in early June, trees were beginning to bud and the grass was a luscious dark green.

I had thought Liv was crazy for trying an outdoor wedding so early in the year, but she had insisted this club was her family and her home and there was nowhere else she'd rather be married. Daemon had simply shrugged his shoulders and did the typical man *whatever-she-wants* move.

Luckily, it had all come together nicely.

It still didn't explain why I was freaking out. Ryker and I weren't getting married for months yet. I still sometimes had an issue with people staring at me, my mind still wondering what their inner thoughts of me and my past really were as eyes stayed glued to me, and walking down the aisle, I knew everyone in the club would be watching me first.

I shook the nervous thoughts out of my head as a quick, hard knock rapped on the door to the chapel room Jules and Sophie had just entered.

Opening the door, Jules grinned and turned to me. "Someone's looking for you."

My lips stretched so wide I thought my face might split open. When I hit the doorway, I swayed on my feet and reached out to grasp for balance against the doorframe.

"Hi," I said breathlessly.

I couldn't help it.

Liv had convinced Daemon and Ryker to wear actual tuxedos for her wedding. I had never seen Ryker in anything other than cargo shorts and denim jeans.

He looked sexy in denim.

Ryker dressed in a black tuxedo, crisp white shirt, and dark maroon vest that matched my own bridesmaid dress? He was completely deadly. I swayed at the sight of him.

A light rumble fell from his chest as my eyes drifted down the length of his body. My eyes darted down the hall that led to his room at the clubhouse. In one swift move, Ryker's hand snaked to the back of my neck and he pulled me toward him until our chests pressed against each other.

"You want to go to my room?"

I swallowed slowly. Then I nodded. "No."

Ryker laughed and pressed his lips against my forehead. "You look amazing. I can't wait until it's our day."

"Uh-huh."

"You still thinking about eloping to Vegas?"

"Yup."

With his laughter brushing along my cheek and down to my throat, his lips trailed lazily down my skin. My entire body felt on fire.

I was certainly incapable of more than one word answers. My grip on the doorframe tightened as I leaned in closer to him.

Ryker's hands moved to my shoulders and he pressed me back until I was on solid footing. "I wanted to see you for a minute. And to tell you that we're ready for you guys."

My eyes were frozen on his chest. He looked absolutely edible in his damn tuxedo. "Okay."

One finger moved to my chin as he tilted my face to his. "I would kiss the hell out of you right now if it didn't mean ruining your make-up or your hair."

"Okay," I muttered again and leaned in.

Ryker laughed again, an easy smile filling his features as he shook his head. "None of that, now. Get Liv out to the yard. Daemon's being an impatient fuck today."

Right. The wedding. In my fantasies of stripping Ryker down to nothing and having him take me on the pool table in the clubhouse, I had forgotten about the wedding.

I nodded and took a step back, listening to the girlish laughter behind me. "We'll be right there," I told Ryker. His eyes grazed over my dress down to my toes, and when he looked back at me, his eyes were heated.

Probably much like mine.

Shaking himself out of his lust-filled stare, he spun on his heels. I barked out a laugh as I saw the Nordic Lords MC emblem on the back of his tuxedo coat.

With a look over his shoulder, he tossed me a wink. I stared at his ass until the door to the clubhouse closed behind him.

"You heard the man," I said to Liv when I had shut the door to the chapel room. "Your man is waiting for you."

Liv grinned and ran her slightly trembling fingers down the length of her wedding dress. "Best not to keep him waiting, then."

She took a step toward the door right as my phone began ringing. I ignored it, doing a final check on my hair and make-up as everyone else quickly cleaned up the room and our supplies.

When the phone rang for the third time in row, Jules turned to me with one eyebrow raised. "Are you going to get that?"

Liv faced me, looking equally concerned. "Who would be calling you today?"

I shrugged and reached for my phone, my nerves instantly prickling. I hadn't thought about it, but everyone I knew was sitting outside waiting for us.

My heartbeat calmed slightly when I saw Meg's name flashing on the phone.

"It's Meg," I explained as I answered the phone. "Hello?"

"Hey Faith," she said. Through the speaker I heard the rumbling of the road and knew she was calling from her phone. "I need a favor."

It was then I noticed that her voice was shaking and fearful as it came through the line. My hands clenched the phone tighter. In the last nine months, Meg and I had become close. She would often call just to talk, and even though I'd only seen her and Brayden at Christmas time when we visited New Orleans again, I knew she didn't sound like her normal, happy self.

"What's going on?" I asked. Looking around the room, I noticed everyone had paused and was staring at me.

"I need to get away from here."

Which didn't sound good. At all. Yet I had no idea what the problem was. "Is it Brayden? I can have Ryker call him back in a few hours, but we're getting ready for the wedding right now."

"Oh shit, that's right. I'm so sorry... I can call you back, but I was just calling to see if we could come stay with you guys for a while."

Stay with us? My legs shook on my heels. Except I wasn't wearing heels. I frowned into the phone. "Meg, do I need to get Ryker?"

"No," she snapped, and then I heard her exhale loudly. "I just...

we need a visit. I'll explain it when I'm there, but can you please not tell Ryker I'm coming?"

"Meg..."

"Please, Faith," she pleaded. I couldn't have told her no after hearing that. "I'll explain it when we get there... probably tomorrow or the next day."

I nodded and shrugged at the women in the room. "Okay, yeah, Meg. Definitely."

"Thank you," she sighed into the phone, and then I heard the distinct click of her disconnecting. Damn it.

"What was that about?" Liv asked, concerned etched between her eyes.

I glanced at my phone. "I have no idea." But I did know that whatever was making Meg rush halfway across the country on absolutely no notice with a fearful sound in her voice couldn't be good at all. Ryker was going to flip his shit.

Sophie was absolutely darling as she slowly made her way down the short wedding aisle. Classic wedding music played through speakers Liv had brought in, insisting she didn't need live music for the wedding. But she wanted the old-school wedding march entrance song.

Smiling along with everyone else, I watched Sophie carefully take a rose petal out of her wicker basket with every small step she took. She gently set it onto the grass and clumsily stepped around each petal so as not to crush a single one.

By the time she reached the makeshift altar, every man and woman in the club family were biting back their laughter.

She reached the end of the aisle and smiled at her mom next to me, who was trying to wave her forward to join us up front. But

Sophie, who I had learned over the last few months had a mind of her own, shook her head, dropped her basket, and then launched herself at Jaden, who was standing next to Ryker on the other side of the arched trellis.

As if he was expecting it, Jaden bent low and wrapped his arms around Sophie all while pressing his lips to her cheek with a soft smile. She wrapped her legs around his waist at the same time Jules reached out and grabbed my hand, squeezing tight.

I flashed a wink to Jules and blew Ryker a quick kiss.

Then everyone in the audience and at the altar turned to watch Liv walk down the aisle, finally getting her happily ever after.

ACKNOWLEDGEMENTS

This part of a book is almost becoming as difficult to write as the story itself. My list of people who help and encourage me seems to grow with each book and series, so if I forget anyone, please know it's not intentional! I am thankful for everyone who plays a part in getting my books into the hands of readers.

First, as always, thank you to my family. Thank you for your support and your encouragement, your understanding during all-day writing marathons to meet deadlines, and to being okay with cold dinners.

Special thanks to John Cook for all the photos and conversations you shared with me about what life is truly like on an oil rig. I know Ryker's story has changed a bit since we first spoke, but you were still a great help to me.

To my BadAss CP's—you ladies, as always, rock. I'm so thankful for all of you and absolutely adore the friendships we've made and the support system you all provide.

To RS Grey, Heather Carver, Samien Newcomb, Kristy Louise, and Natalie Gerber. Thank you for being such amazing beta readers. Your input and support has made Ryker's story stronger and I'm so thankful for all of you.

Thank you to my editor, Taylor K, and proofreader, Mary. Your polish and eyes on this story from beginning to end has made it the best it can possibly be. Thank you from the bottom of my grateful heart.

To my God and Savior, Jesus Christ. All Glory and Honor is Yours.

ABOUT THE AUTHOR

Stacey Lynn currently lives in Minnesota with her husband and four children. When she's not conquering mountains of laundry and fighting a war against dust bunnies and cracker crumbs, you can find her playing with her children, curled up on the couch with a good book, or on the boat with her family enjoying Minnesota's beautiful, yet too short, summer.

She lives off her daily pot of coffee, can only write with a bowlful of Skittles nearby, and has been in love with romance novels since before she could drive herself to the library.

If you would like to know more about Stacey Lynn, follow her here:

Facebook: www.facebook.com/staceylynnbooks
Twitter: @staceylynnbooks
Blog: http://staceylynnbooks.blogspot.com

**If you enjoyed this book, please leave
a review on the site where it was purchased.
And don't forget to check out Stacey's other books:**

Point of Return, The Nordic Lords #1
Just One Song
Just One Week
Remembering Us
Don't Lie To Me

Printed in Great Britain
by Amazon